# THE LOST MANUSCRIPT

# THE LOST MANUSCRIPT

## Rubem Fonseca

Translated by Clifford E. Landers

BLOOMSBURY

First published in 1988 by Companhia das Letras,
Brazil as *Vastas emoções e pensamentos imperfeitos*

This edition published 1997

Copyright © Rubem Fonseca 1988
Translation © Clifford E. Landers 1997

The moral right of the author and translator has been asserted

Bloomsbury Publishing Plc, 38 Soho Square, London W1V 5DF

A CIP catalogue record for this book
is available from the British Library

ISBN 07475 3013 0

10 9 8 7 6 5 4 3 2 1

Typeset by Hewer Text Composition Services, Edinburgh
Printed in Great Britain by Clays Ltd, St Ives plc

# THE LOST MANUSCRIPT

# ONE

## *The Lymph of the Labyrinth*

# 1

I awoke desperately trying to hold onto myself, everything whirling about as I fell, out of control, into an abyss. I managed to fix my vision on the band of morning light coming in through the curtains. The thin milky line fluttered rapidly. Moving my head in the direction of the window made my fall even more vertiginous. I remained motionless, my gaze focused on the line of light, waiting for the crisis to pass.

I was going to change apartments that day. After what had happened, I didn't want to live there anymore. I heard the bell: it must be the movers. If the attack didn't pass, I wouldn't be able to get out of bed. The men would leave without doing the moving.

Keeping my body immobile, I put out my hand and grabbed the medicine on the night table. I chewed the pill until it turned into a repugnant paste which I swallowed with difficulty, fearing I would vomit. Fortunately it didn't go beyond a violent nausea that racked my body, further increasing my torture. Sometimes the medicine took effect quickly, sometimes not. Two hours later, when I took the second pill, still feeling the same waves of nausea, the attack had passed. I was able to get up and open the door.

The men were sitting on the hall floor in the service area, waiting. We began the move.

The new apartment was on the fourth floor of a building without an elevator. No elevator; it didn't matter. I was working Ruth out of my memory, having got her out of my life.

The move was finished by eleven that night. I sent the men away. Furniture, books, objects and clothes lay scattered around the new apartment. From the midst of the confusion I separated Rouault's horse, the suitcase with the diary and Ruth's things; I went to the bed and lay down, Ruth's diary on my chest. I didn't have the courage to open it. I turned out the light. What would the dream be tonight? Would the vertigo come back? Liliana said I looked like a dead man when sleeping (and dreaming) with my eyes open. Ruth used to say the same thing. No, I don't want to talk about Ruth. Not yet.

Now, without a woman watching over me, I could look like a dead man without anyone nagging me.

I dream about a tall woman who has to bend down to kiss me. In fact I don't see a woman at all, for my dreams have no images. For a film director this is strange. I know the woman is in the dream, I know she's wearing a wide-brimmed hat – an old one with a veil entirely covering her face, which is completely white, luminous, phosphorescent – but I see nothing. I know her eyes are yellow; it's as if I saw the woman, but I don't see her, nor do I hear her words, but it's as if I heard them. I possess the information without the senses, the knowledge without visual perceptions. My dream is made of ideas.

I awoke with the doorbell ringing.

I got up and went to the intercom. 'Who is it?'

It was a child's voice. 'Help me, help me, they're after me!'

I pushed the button to activate the lock at the entrance. I opened the apartment door. From the little hall I looked down at the stairs below.

'Hello, anyone there?' I shouted.

'I'm coming.' The childlike voice, fainter now, came from the bottom of the stairs.

I heard the sound of footsteps climbing the stairs, slowly.

It was some time before she appeared on the third-floor landing. She climbed the last flight of stairs even more slowly. When she reached me, she smiled. She tried to speak but couldn't. Breathing with difficulty, she raised a small package wrapped in brown paper to her chest. I gestured for her to come in.

Once inside the living room, she threw herself into one of the armchairs. She looked at me as if asking me to be patient and allow her to catch her breath.

'Thank you very much,' she gasped finally. 'My name is Angélica.'

She stopped talking. I sat down beside her, also saying nothing. Little by little, her breathing returned to normal.

'Who was after you?'

'I can't say.' Her little girl's voice was no longer breathless.

'Why not?'

'They'll kill me.'

'I'm going to call the police.'

'No!' she shouted in her shrill voice. 'For God's sake!'

'Then I think you'd better leave.'

'Don't do this to me.'

'Get out,' I said.

Pursing her lips as if she were about to cry, she tried to get up from the chair and failed. I took her hand to help her. It was soft, warm, moist. She stood up, very close to me. I could see the scattered hairs on her chin, the beard of an adolescent boy. Angélica was a fat woman, vast; suddenly she seemed to become even larger – like a great plastic balloon that had been inflated while we had been together – and at the same time, having swollen, become fragile and unprotected. On an impulse, I said, 'All right, you can stay here till morning.'

Still grasping my hand, Angélica let out a small sob that shook her ample breast. Large tears fell from her eyes. 'Thank you, thank you!'

'You can sleep on that sofa,' I said drily, trying to prevent the dramatic scene from turning maudlin.

She stretched her immense body out on the sofa, completely filling it.

'I could never live in a fourth-floor walk-up. I'd die within a week,' she said.

'I moved here precisely because it has no elevator.'

'Who does that wheelchair belong to?'

'It's mine,' I said, sitting in the chair. I had brought the wheelchair. So? Did I really not want to forget?

'Are you unhappy?'

'Yes.' I wasn't ashamed to confess to that monstrous woman that I was unhappy.

'Usually men don't get sad. At least the ones I know. Why is your place so messy? It looks like a hurricane hit it.'

As soon as she said this, she went to sleep, without giving me time to answer. She snored, droning like a beetle.

I went to the bedroom, closed the door and lay down without removing my shoes. Ruth hated me going to bed in my shoes. I opened a book at random. I don't know how long I stared at the pages without reading.

Daylight came. I went to the living room to see Angélica. She was gone. I have no idea how she left so silently. The apartment door was slightly ajar. The brown-paper package was on the table with a note, written on a title page that she had ripped out of a book. It wasn't a book I especially cared about, but that predatory gesture irritated me.

'My friend,' Angélica's tiny writing was hard to read. 'Thank you very much for saving my life. In today's cruel and selfish world it is surprising to find a man as generous as you. Please take care of this package for me, hide it well, and one day I'll come back for it. Your friend Angélica.'

My friend Angélica. I looked at the package. What should I do with it? The best thing would be to throw it away. As I was taking it to the trash chute, I remembered the German producer who was supposed to meet me that afternoon. I needed to re-read the letter outlining his offer. I put the package back on the table and went to look for Dietrich's letter.

The meeting was not until the afternoon, but I went out in the morning, leaving the apartment in complete disarray. I liked wandering about the streets, seeing all the people. But that day I didn't look at anyone; I was thinking about Ruth, about Liliana, about the infamous work I was doing for my brother the television evangelist, about the difficulties I was having in arranging financing for a new film. Besides that, for the first time in my life I was experiencing a kind of distrust, even fear, of the people passing by – men hiding behind their beards, women camouflaged by cosmetics and wigs, children who looked like dwarfs, or vice versa. The automobiles, making irritating noises and giving off black smoke, seemed ready to run me down. Even the cloudless sky exhibited a false blue, a Fra Angelico badly restored. What the devil was happening to me?

Later, feeling hungry, I went into a restaurant. On the way in I bought a film magazine at the news-stand.

Only a few tables were occupied. Normally anyone, anyone

at all, can distract me, but that day, as soon as I sat down, I opened the magazine and began reading without looking at the people around me. I gave the waiter my order and continued to read, waiting for the meal to be served. But once, raising my eyes from the magazine, I sensed that a man was observing me surreptitiously. At that instant both he and I glanced away quickly, as if we were afraid of each other.

I went back to my reading. But the man kept on casting furtive glances at me. I stared at him defiantly. He stared back in the same way.

Then I noticed that the man looked like my father in his last days in the hospital bed, the bones standing out in his gray, dying face. Unexpectedly, I felt a pain so great that my eyes filled with tears. Seeing that the man at the next table was watching my suffering, I asked him brusquely: 'Is there something you want to say to me?'

We both froze and looked into each other's eyes in surprise. In that restaurant with its mirrored walls, there was no one at the next table: I was looking at myself, at my own reflection. It was I, that haggard person who looked like my father. My heart stopped. When my father died he was almost forty years older than I was now! Was that aged, ravaged face mine?

'You're not going to eat?' the waiter asked, pointing to the plate in front of me. I had spent a long time thinking, without touching the food.

I went back to walking the streets. What the devil was happening to me?

My father was a handsome man with many girlfriends, a man who played tennis, swam and was never ill, even with a cold – until his cerebral hemorrhage. He was always involved with 'hussies', as my mother called them, and in chronic business failures. He'd had a fur business, in a city where it was hot as blazes practically all year round. Naturally it went bankrupt, but his customers were never prettier, despite being so few. Earlier he'd had a hat shop and women had stopped wearing hats. At the end he had a small dry-goods shop – he'd always had stores that were frequented mainly by women – on Senhor dos Passos Street. My mother used to drop into the shop to see if some hussy was there. Sometimes they argued at dinner-time. In reality my mother did the arguing and he remained silent; if she wouldn't stop fighting he would get up from the table and go out. On such days my mother would go to the bedroom and cry. I would go to the window and spit on the heads of the people passing by and look at the luminous neon sign of the store across the street. That kind of light still attracts me even today and has yet to be captured by cinema or television. When my father returned, much later, my mother's desperation would have passed and I would see her go to the kitchen to make him a glass of warm milk. Once he told me it was too bad that men had to be judged like race horses, by their record. 'Your father's problem,' my mother once told me, 'is that he's very good-looking.' She didn't see him become paralyzed, nor did she have to clean up the feces and urine in his clothes, nor have to bear the immeasurable sadness in his look as he thought about the hussies. My father was still a good-looking man when my mother died.

The pitiless lucidity with which I now thought about my father filled me with horror – we can't with impunity see the people we love as they really are. In that mirror, for the first time I had seen his poignant face, his face that was mine. How could I be turning into my father, him, the sick man?

I arrived at the Copacabana Palace Hotel promptly at three o'clock. I called Dietrich's room and we agreed to meet at the poolside bar. I hadn't met him before. I tried to imagine what his face would be like.

He approached with his hand out, saying 'I'm Dietrich.' He was accompanied by a woman carrying a book.

'I know you're a very busy man, as am I, so let's get straight to the point,' he said after we had ordered drinks. We spoke in English. 'We saw your film *The Holy War*, which is going to the Latin American Film Festival in East Berlin, and we want you to take part in our project.'

Two years had gone by since I had finished *The Holy War*. The film's backers still hadn't managed to recoup their investment.

'You've seen my film?'

'Yes,' he said. 'I really liked it.'

Dietrich's assistant appeared indifferent to the conversation. Her interest was in the people in the pool.

'What did you think of our proposal?'

Their proposal, which I had received earlier by mail, was for me to film Isaac Babel's *Red Cavalry* in Germany.

'I still don't have an answer. I've been very busy.'

The woman pushed the book in front of her toward me. So she wasn't as distant as she appeared.

I looked at the book. *Collected Stories. Isaac Babel.* On the cover was a robust, almost fat man looking to one side, a fur cap on his head, wearing a uniform jacket trimmed with gold braid and with wide sleeves, also with gold trim. He looked like someone dressed for a Carnival dance in the 1920s. I had seen that face before. When I see a face, even in a photograph, I never forget it.

'That's Babel. This is practically everything he ever wrote.'

'I know. May I keep the book? I seem to have lost mine, or at least I don't know where it is.'

'We brought it for you. We'd like to have you go to Berlin to talk with our people. Are you planning to attend the festival?'

'I still haven't had confirmation from the organizers . . . I haven't received the program, still don't have the plane ticket . . .'

'We left a ticket for you at Lufthansa. Connecting in Frankfurt with Pan Am. Lufthansa doesn't go to Berlin. A carryover from the war.' He laughed. 'We'd like you to leave right away. For preliminary discussions. All expenses paid, of course.'

'I have some things to wrap up.'

'We can wait a few days.' He stood up as he said this. He handed me a card. 'Phone and advise us of your arrival date. I'll wait for you at the airport in Berlin.'

# 2

D ietrich struck me as a serious type. When I had received the letter from Germany I hadn't attached much importance to his project, even though I was anxious to get back to film-making. But after our interview the proposal had taken on new significance.

I shut myself up in my apartment, reading and re-reading Babel and making notes. At first I was motivated merely by the desire to get back to film-making after two years away from it directing commercials for TV. But as I re-read Babel's stories my interest grew.

I was working on the part of the script that describes the death of Dolguchov, to get an idea of the potential of Babel's text, when my brother José, the television evangelist, phoned. He wanted to talk about the film I was doing for his weekly TV program. He called daily with suggestions.

'I have to reach the hearts of the faithful. You do good work,' he said, 'but I think I ought to be more direct, like the Americans, say that I need money for the day-care centers, the nursing home . . .'

A hateful conversation. I agreed to go to his house in Ipanema at nine pm.

I went back to the death of Dolguchov. Babel doesn't

say how the Cossack Afonka applies the *coup de grâce* to
Dolguchov. The scene was described by Babel in this way:
'They spoke briefly. I did not hear a word. Dolguchov held
out his papers to the sergeant and Afonka secreted them in his
boot and shot Dolguchov in the mouth.' This was much better
than the scene I had written. The reader didn't need to know
exactly how Afonka shot Dolguchov in the mouth, needed
no details to see and feel, to imagine what was happening.
The reader wasn't told what Afonka's face looked like, or
Dolguchov's, at the moment the shot was fired, but he or
she knew everything that mattered at that instant. In the film
I could, for example, place the camera so that it framed Liutov
and the *coup de grâce* could be audible only, but that would take
away from the power of the narrative. Or I could show the
landscape, the sky or whatever, as the shot was heard. That
would be a cheap syntactical trick that would weaken the
scene even further and deprive the spectator of the tension
that Babel had built up. But did that matter? Who among
the millions of semi-illiterates produced by the educational
institutions, consumers of a comfortable art represented by
pop music, by the movies and television, would be familiar
with Babel? All they would know of Babel would be my film.
In other words, very little.

It was time to go and see my brother. In the taxi I thought:
Afonka puts a shot in Dolguchov's mouth. Fine. What kind
of shot? Babel doesn't say. I had Afonka using a revolver.
How would the scene play with a rifle?

It was after eleven when I got to José's mansion, one of
the last remaining in Ipanema.

Alone in the living room, he was watching the video I
had made. He wasn't wearing the girdle he normally used
so the faithful wouldn't see the size of his paunch. 'You're
late,' he said softly. He hated waiting, but he had learned
to control his irritation. He saved it for his preaching, when

he inveighed against sin and the devil. 'Gislaine has already gone to bed.' Gislaine was the woman he'd married back in the days when he still sold used cars.

He rewound the tape. 'I like the film, you know. The photography is beautiful, and I come out of it well. I liked your idea of putting in that young couple, the woman believing in what I say from the start and the man doubting, and then, when I finish my sermon, the man is convinced and nodding his head in agreement with what I'm saying.'

'You'll find that in the publicity films of any televangelist,' I said, knowing he didn't like to be called that. But José pretended to ignore my observation.

'Only here, in this short bit at the end, we could add what I spoke to you about.' José froze the image. 'Here I could make a frank and direct appeal to the members of the congregations, asking them to contribute to the spread of our Church and to the upkeep of its social work. No hypocrisy. As the prophet Malachi said, "Bring ye all the tithes into the storehouse, that there may be meat in my house, and prove me now herewith." A direct kind of message.'

His Church was the Evangelical Church of Jesus Savior of Souls. Over ten thousand people contributed part of their pay to the Church every month, voluntarily. The majority of them were domestics and laborers earning the minimum wage.

'Malachi . . .' I said.

'The name means Angel of the Lord. He's the last of the twelve minor prophets.'

José knew how to sell. He had dropped out of school, while still a boy, to sell things. He'd been a street peddler selling smuggled trinkets, then he'd sold encyclopedias door to door, then used cars, and now he was selling the salvation of souls.

We watched the film several times. When he was assured that I would add the parts he wanted, he offered me a whiskey.

Then he asked what I thought of his running for senator in the forthcoming elections. 'We evangelists need strong representation in Congress. But I have doubts about whether, at the moment, it might hurt my Church. We're growing fast; maybe this isn't the time for me to divide my efforts.'

He stopped talking and took a swig of whiskey. I said nothing. I could see a conspiratorial gleam in his eye. 'I'm going to surprise you,' he said, taking another swallow. I noticed he was hesitating; but he had already begun his revelation. 'Brother, the day isn't far off when this country will have a pastor as president.'

I left José's house depressed, as always happened when I visited him. He lacked the essential qualities – love, compassion, charity, tolerance. He had no love for his fellow man, which, contrary to popular belief, did not keep him from loving himself.

It was late, but there were still people in lower Leblon. I went to the Pizzeria Guanabara and ate a pizza standing up at the counter on Ataulfo de Paiva, along with taxi drivers, a couple of homosexuals and a prostitute. Then I crossed the street and headed toward home. I passed several young people, of both sexes, sitting on the steps of a bank, some of them high, some waiting for the dealer, others waiting for customers, waiting for Godot, waiting for the film (me, certainly), waiting for the night to end, for life to end. It was in the midst of these musings that I saw a girl get up from the steps of the bank and come in my direction. She was wearing tight jeans and had thick legs and thin arms. The make-up on her mouth and eyes, and her dark hair, gave her very white face a morbid fragility.

'Hi,' she said.

I turned away. She came after me and took my arm as we walked.

'I said hi and you didn't answer.'

I stopped. I looked at her. She couldn't be more than sixteen at most.

'What do you want me to say?'

'At least say hi.'

'Hi.'

'Wanna buy me some grub at the Guanabara?'

I kept quiet, thinking.

'Later I'll go home with you if you want.'

The girl had a decent and deserving face, even if perverted; she might be a student prostituting herself to buy drugs. Whatever it was, she promised release and tenderness.

'What's your name?'

'Dani.'

'Let's go,' I said. We crossed the street, back to the side where the Guanabara was.

'Can I order a steak and fries?'

'You can order anything you want.'

When her food arrived, Dani asked, 'Aren't you going to eat anything?'

'I'm not hungry.'

She ate voraciously. Between forkfuls she stopped and smiled gently. She chewed first on one side then on the other, a harmonious thing, healthy, bovine, perfect, to be envied.

'Well?' she said.

'Well what?'

'What now?'

'What now what?'

'Now.'

'Now what?'

'Now.'

We were standing on the sidewalk.

'Good night,' I said.

She held me by the arm. 'I have a rubber; you don't have to be afraid.'

'It's not that. I'm tired.'

When I got home I sat in an armchair and stared at the ceiling. Ruth's diary was still on the floor. The disorder of things seemed to have increased.

I went back to working on the script. I had to decide what to reply to Dietrich; he'd only given me a week.

I rewrote the scene, starting with the moment Dolguchov is found by Liutov and Grishchuck lying against a tree. His legs are spread and extended, his boots dirty and torn; his belly is ripped open and his guts are visible, as well as his beating heart. Dolguchov asks Liutov to kill him: 'The Poles are coming back to do their dirty work. Here are my papers. You'll write and tell my mother how it happened.' But Liutov doesn't have the courage to kill him and, spurring his horse, rides off. Dolguchov stretches out, after first examining the bluish palm of his hand. 'All right then, run away, you pig.' Then Afonka arrives and asks what's going on.

My text went like this: Afonka comes up to Dolguchov. He dismounts. The two men talk, the one on foot, covered with dust, radiating strength, and the dying man lying on the ground. Liutov, watching from a distance, can't hear what they're saying. Dolguchov gives Afonka his papers. Afonka puts them in his bag. He goes at once to his horse and withdraws the rifle from the saddlebow. Then, with slow but firm steps, he returns to Dolguchov, the light of the setting sun behind him. Dolguchov, supporting himself on his elbows, raises his head slightly and looks at Afonka. Afonka places the rifle barrel in Dolguchov's acquiescent mouth and shoots.

It was late when I turned out the light. To me, sleep was, was – what?

Dream. A woman with no face, beside me with her lips full of white foam, gives off a strong odor of wrapped presents, with dark fissures in the middle of her body. (In reality I don't see this, but it's what is happening.) 'Are you ashamed to be dancing in front of me,' I ask her – is Ruth the woman without a face? – 'ashamed of me with my callused hands and scarred prick who danced on the tiled pavement on Vieira Fazenda Street kissing on the mouth a girl with a dark false tooth?' Iron and fire in my head, hot coals in my retinas, saliva and sweat, shit and piss, bones, muscle. It's three o'clock; the neighborhood is sleeping in front of color television. A voice: 'Careful with the head wound!' The photo of my mother, in a frame edged in mother-of-pearl, fills all of the invisible screen.

# 3

The telephone woke me.

I recognized her voice at once: 'Are you the man who helped me that night when some thugs were after me? Are you the one who opened his door to me?'

'Angélica?'

'Oh, you remember my name? Look, I'm calling because of that little box I left there. Did you keep it nice and safe for me?'

'It's here somewhere.'

'Somewhere? My God, somewhere! Did you lose it?' She was shouting, panicked. 'They're things dear to me. See if you can find it, please.'

I asked her to wait and went to the living room. The brown-paper package was just where Angélica had left it.

'It's here, don't worry,' I said.

She gave a shrill cry of relief.

'Look, don't leave the box like that, all by itself. Your apartment is very messy. Not that there's anything of value in the box, just some trifles, but it'd be better if you kept it tucked away for me. Somebody can come and pick it up.' Her voice became cloying. 'Keep it for me, keep it . . . Promise . . .'

'I don't want to take responsibility for that, that – just what the devil is in the package anyway?'

'Little knick-knacks. Of sentimental value. One of these days I'll come round. But keep it for me. Put it in a drawer. Promise you'll put it in a drawer. Somewhere in that mess of yours there must be a drawer.'

To bring the subject to a close, I promised I'd put it in a drawer.

'You're an angel,' Angélica said, hanging up.

I spent the entire night reading Babel. But all the time I remembered Ruth. I had changed apartments to forget her, yet I'd brought the wheelchair with me. But I don't want to talk about that. Not now.

Next day I was startled by an item on the midday news.

I don't like television. I admit that my future, and that of all film directors, may lie in television. A somber scenario: television, having consolidated its position as the chief vehicle for leisure and information, becomes the sole medium of mass communication, maintained by cretins and/or sinister users who produce spurious and harmful pulp for a passive, apathetic public, easily manipulated by demagogues; every individual in all social classes (the rich using enormous screens of the size of those in old-time theaters, which no longer exist – they've become pharmacies and banks) watches television the greater part of the time, an average of twelve hours a day; many leave the television on even when they sleep.

I didn't like the scenario. It reinforced the existing prejudice against mass culture. Why speak ill of mass culture? It reflects and expresses the aesthetic and moral values of the majority of people, influencing in turn the ideas, feelings and behavior of these same people. Obviously the impresarios of mass culture think only of profit. But isn't that the best way to produce anything – potatoes, computers, beer, books? And who doesn't think about profit? What artist, thinker, scientist doesn't in some way think about profit as he carries out his profession? In today's world the production of cultural goods, because it is no longer an activity condemned to catharsis or dilettantism, has not necessarily become something to disdain. The artist is a professional like any other. But I shouldn't be wasting my time thinking about that. I had other scenarios to write.

The news item that worried me was about the mysterious killing of a woman named Angélica Maldonado. Angélica Maldonado, said the broadcast, had won recognition in luxury costume competitions at Carnival time. Her mutilated body had been found by her maid. The police believed she had been tortured before dying. A man by the name of Áureo de Negromonte – 'a famous Carnival figure and competition winner', according to the TV – stated that Angélica's death was an irreparable loss for Carnival in Brazil. The Carnival parade that year, according to Negromonte, was irretrievably damaged. There was a picture of Angélica in a dress with a long train, covered with stones and lots of plumes.

Seeing her, I became agitated. It was the fat woman who'd been in my apartment. 'They're after me,' Angélica had said that night. Whoever 'they' were, they had caught up with her.

I looked up the police in the phone book. I dialed 190. A female voice answered: 'Police station, good afternoon.'

I hesitated. What was I going to say? Certainly it wouldn't be her who would hear my story. She would pass me on to another person, who'd pass me on to another, then another. I imagined menacing men in leather jackets and wool caps on their heads, carrying sawn-off shotguns, breaking into my house and taking me away in the middle of the night to make a statement in some sinister precinct. Besides that, I knew nothing about the circumstances, not even what was in the brown-paper package that Angélica had asked me to keep.

'Sorry, my mistake,' I said.

I got the package from my shirt drawer, hearing a crystalline rattling sound that I hadn't noticed before. I found a knife and cut the string binding the package.

It was a cardboard box, on which was written *Casa Turuna – Fabrics – Items for Bed and Table – Notions – Articles for Carnival and Umbanda Rites.* I opened the box. Inside were innumerable blue, green and red stones of various sizes. The knick-knacks that Angélica had mentioned. I held one of them up to the light. By its brilliance it appeared to be a precious stone. For a moment I imagined they were valuable emeralds and rubies. When I picked up another stone from the box, I saw the words in blue ink *Articles for Carnival.* I deduced that these must be some of the common stones that Angélica used for her Carnival costumes, since all of them were colored. Even then I kept holding the stones up to the light, more and more fascinated by their brilliance. What if they were real? I remembered a friend, Maurício, who owned Florentino, one of the largest firms dealing in precious stones in Brazil.

It wasn't easy to get to Maurício's office: the security measures were tight. The store was downstairs, occupying the ground floor of the building. Several plainclothes security guards stood outside, scrutinizing all who entered. In the reception area I was given a badge after leaving my ID with the attendant. An armed guard went up with me in the elevator. In the elevator, as everywhere I passed on my way to Maurício's office, television cameras registered my steps.

I had to go through several doors, each opening only after the other closed, before reaching Maurício.

'What are emeralds like?' I asked.

'Emeralds?'

He laughed. He must have been surprised by my visit. 'It's for a film I'm making,' I added.

'Well . . . they're green . . .' he joked.

'That much I know. I want to know . . . I'm interested, really, in precious stones.'

'Do you want to know everything? There's a lot.'

'Everything possible for a layman.'

Maurício laughed. He'd always had a sense of humor that didn't sit well with me – I detest ironic people.

'I'm talking seriously; that's why I'm here taking up your time.'

'You want to know everything possible?' Another smile. 'Emeralds are part of the beryl group. On Mohs's hardness scale they have an index of 7.30 to 8; their relative density is 2.67 to 2.78; fracture: conchoidal, irregular, splintery; hexagonal crystalline structure, six-sided prism, elongated crystals; refraction index 1.576 to 1.582; birefringence 0.006; dispersion 0.014; definite pleochroism: green, greenish blue, even greenish yellow; absorption spectrum . . .'

'Enough,' I said.

'In simple language, emeralds have, naturally, a six-sided shape. All the crystals of a given mineral show the same type of symmetry.'

'What about diamonds? Don't talk about birefringence and all that shit.'

'Diamonds crystallize isometrically, forming a regular hexahedron, or with eight triangular sides in the form of a polyhedron.'

'And rubies?'

'They're corundum, red, very valuable. Hexagonal or trigonal crystalline system, six-faceted prisms, rhombohedrons.'

'Are they big, emeralds?'

'In the Leningrad Museum there's one that weighs over two kilos. In Peru there was one the size of an ostrich egg, which the Indians worshiped and called Mother of Emeralds.'

'Are there many emeralds in Brazil?'

'Yes. But the best come from the Muzo mine in Colombia. There are also good emeralds from other places: Zimbabwe, India . . .'

'Is an emerald the same as an aquamarine?'

'An aquamarine, an emerald, a morganite are all beryl, but the pleochroism, absorption spectrum, iridescence, opalescence, asterism and brilliance are different, establishing individual aesthetic characteristics for each. An emerald is an emerald, an aquamarine is an aquamarine. Understand? A rose is a rose is a rose.'

We remained silent for some time. Something in Maurício disturbed me, but I didn't know what.

'If the film is set in Brazil, it's best for the stones to be aquamarines. The most important deposits of this stone are in Brazil. If you're really interested I'll show you so you can get a better idea.'

'Are they expensive, emeralds? I'm asking because I think I have an emerald at home.'

'You have an emerald at home. So?'

'I think I have a diamond too. Tell me about diamonds. Don't tell me all that technical stuff. Just simple things like, for example, if they're colorless and very brilliant.'

'They are quite brilliant, but they're not always colorless. They can be yellow, green, blue, reddish and black. Nothing compares to them in hardness. Ten on Mohs's scale. The cleavage is perfect.'

'How do I know if the stones in my possession have any value or not? I think I also have a ruby.'

'You have no way of knowing.'

'Diamonds are more valuable because they're harder and more brilliant?'

'Yes, more or less.'

'Hardness and brilliance as parameters of value. Like people. Interesting,' I said. Fleming chose a good title, *Diamonds Are Forever*, I thought, but Guy Hamilton's film was mediocre.

'Do you really have gems, or are they imitations? Bring them here for me to take a look. Ordinary glass made of pure rock crystal, red lead and potassium carbonate can fool lots of suckers. The other day a client of ours bought a shipment of rubies that were actually aluminum oxide. You can make a synthetic ruby using the Czochralski method, developed by Bell Labs in the United States. The end result is almost identical to a Mogok.' Maurício's face had changed. Or rather, the way he looked at me was different; there was no sympathy there, as I had earlier supposed. It made me uncomfortable. 'I'd like to see those gems,' he said.

'I'll bring them, one of these days.'

'Do bring them.' A pause. 'Look, that business about Ruth. I was sorry, truly.'

'Yes. Thanks.' To get Maurício's opinion was it necessary to have Ruth brought into the conversation? 'I don't want to talk about it.'

'Forgive me,' Maurício said. We sank into an uncomfortable silence. He searched for something to say and finally found it: 'Do you know my firm is called Florentino?'

'No.'

'Do you remember one day when we were talking about dreams? You told me you dreamed in a strange way.'

Do I tell everybody about my dreams?

'And I told you I had an unusual dream too. Remember?' I didn't remember.

'It's always the same dream. About the Florentino diamond. I began to dream about it when I still worked at H. Stern.

There are diamonds more famous than the Florentino – the Cullinam, the largest of all, that graced the scepter of Edward VII and today is housed in the Tower of London; the Dresden; the Hope; the Koh-i-Noor, which means Mountain of Light, the name given it by the Shah of Persia in 1739; the Nassak, which was stolen from a temple of Shiva by the English in 1918. They all have a known history and whereabouts. But the Florentino is shrouded in mystery. In 1657 it was in the possession of the Medici family of Florence, where its name comes from. It may have first belonged to Cosimo, the art lover and patron of Donatello, Brunelleschi, Della Robia, or perhaps to his grandson Lorenzo, poet and murderer, maker of popes, a Maecenas and immoral tyrant who made Florence the most developed state of the Middle Ages. We don't know. What's certain is that the one who got rid of the stone can only have been Cosimo III – weak, vain, hypocritical – or else his son Giovan Gastone, a playboy, more dissipated than his father, submissive to the clergy and to foreign countries, and who finally ruined the house of Medici and his state. Between 1723, when Giovan Gastone assumed the throne, and 1737, the date of his death, the Florentino diamond ceased to figure among the possessions of the Medicis and became part of the Habsburg crown – more specifically the crown of Charles VI, made emperor of Austria in 1711. The Florentino remained with the Habsburgs for almost two hundred years, till the end of the First World War. Then President Wilson of the United States demanded that the rights of the peoples of what had been the Austro–Hungarian Empire be respected. Poland, Czechoslovakia and Yugoslavia came into existence as sovereign states. On November 11 1918, Emperor Charles I abdicated the throne and the Republic was proclaimed the following day. Then several things happened: the Habsburgs were banished in 1919, Charles I returned as Emperor of Hungary for a time and died in 1922. It was during this period that the Florentino disappeared. How could a priceless 137.27-carat diamond, generally regarded as perfect, simply disappear?'

'By being cut into smaller pieces?'

'No diamond cutter in the world would have the courage to commit such a savage, brutal, stupid act.' Maurício grimaced in horror. 'Now here's where my dream comes in. In it I know where the Florentino is. In a huge trunk full of trinkets, in the attic of a large old mansion.'

Maurício gripped me forcefully by the arm.

'In the dream I see everything, the façade of the house, above which, in a half-moon overhang between two repulsive gargoyles, is written 1831. I see the windows with their stained glass, the enormous wooden door. The house is in a valley surrounded by rocky mountains. The Florentino is in the attic of that house, inside the trunk, flawless, indestructible, eternal, gleaming indomitably.'

Maurício looked at me, smiling inscrutably.

# 4

On my return from Maurício's office, a man was standing on the corner looking at me strangely as the doorman opened the outside entrance. Although it was a hot day, the man was wearing a long raincoat, drawn shut.

In the apartment, looking out of the window, I saw him talking to another man as if giving him instructions.

I went to see if the box was where I had left it. It was, but the stones didn't appear to have any of the qualities that Maurício had mentioned. They had to be cheap imitations. In any case, when I had time I'd take them for Maurício to examine. I would say, 'I don't want to talk about Ruth, OK? Now take a look at these stones.'

The intercom sounded. The doorman told me in a worried tone that a detective wanted to talk to me.

'Did he show you any identification?'

'No.'

'Then how do you know he's from the police?'

'He said he was.'

'Only let him in if he shows his ID.'

Shortly afterward the policeman arrived. He was a fat man

who didn't look very healthy. He showed me his identification: Detective Sarraceno. He said he was investigating the murder of a woman named Angélica Maldonado.

'We found your address and telephone number in the dead woman's address book.'

'Oh?'

My brief reply seemed to disturb him.

'Do you live here?'

'Yes.'

'Do you know this woman?'

He showed me a photograph of Angélica.

Without hesitation I replied: 'No, I don't know who she is.' Anyway, the photo didn't resemble in the least the Angélica who had been in my apartment.

'But your address was in her address book.'

'That's a mystery that perhaps you can explain to me.'

He was no imbecile. He panned around the living room.

'The wheelchair?'

'It belonged to my wife.'

'She was a famous Carnival figure. The dead woman. You never heard of her?'

'What was the name again?'

'Angélica Maldonado.'

'Carnival figure. What was she, a color bearer?'

'No. The costume pageant.'

'Did you know her?'

'Me?' said Sarraceno in surprise.

'Yes, you.'

'I don't like Carnival. An exception to the rule,' he said with an unhappy smile. 'Cops usually like Carnival.'

'I don't like it either.'

His eyes rested on my face for a few seconds in an attempt at discovery or perhaps intimidation.

'Anything else?' I asked.
'No, no. Could you get me a glass of water?'

After he had gone I turned out the lights and went to the window. I saw him climbing into a police car parked at the curb. As soon as the car pulled off, the man in the raincoat came out of the shadows and looked very quickly toward my window. I had the impression that he had seen me and I drew back in fright. I ran to the door and checked that it was locked. I pressed my ear against the door, listening out for any suspicious sound. Nothing. No! What was that? The sound of footsteps, light footsteps on the stairs, stopping at my door!

The knock on the door frightened me. I held my breath. The doorman wouldn't have let anyone come up without notifying me on the intercom. What had happened? It was best to pretend no one was at home. But the man in the raincoat had seen me and knew I was there, behind the door. He could shoot through the wood and hit me, I thought, retreating and leaning against the wall.

The knocking began again. He knew. It was better to face him. I hate being afraid. There have been episodes of personal courage in my life that in reality resulted from my intolerance of being afraid. I prefer confronting the worst menace to feeling fear.

'Who is it?' I asked, noting with pleasure that my voice was firm.

'It's me, you idiot. Open up.'

It was Liliana. I opened the door.

She entered quickly.

'A guy with a sinister face was down there when I came in,' she said.

'A man in a raincoat?' I asked.

'Exactly. A man in a raincoat. He looked like a rapist.' She paused. 'Of course, most men look at me as if they

were rapists. Who is he, a friend of yours? You always did
have some pretty weird friends.'
   I went over to the window but saw no sign of the man.
   Why didn't I tell Liliana to leave?
   I noticed she was looking at Angélica's package on the
coffee table.
   'That package has a funny story behind it,' I said.
   I told her about Angélica's visit, without mentioning her
death or the stones.
   'A Sidney Greenstreet in skirts,' Liliana said when I had
finished. 'But the package is too small to hold a Maltese
falcon.'
   Liliana went to the window. 'I couldn't go to the cemetery.
I took a trip.'
   'I know.'
   'I did the right thing, didn't I – not going?' Her voice was
shaking. She looked as if she were about to cry, but Liliana
never cried.
   I changed the subject. 'I'm going to Germany to the Latin
American Film Festival and plan to stay a few months,' I said.
I told her about Dietrich. 'I think I'm going to accept his
offer.' If I couldn't kill her, why didn't I at least say goodbye
right away?
   Liliana laughed.
   'What offer are you going to accept? You haven't told me
what offer the German made. In objective terms: money.'
   'That comes later.'
   'The most important thing comes later?'
   'Money isn't the most important thing,' I said.
   'What's more important? Economists say that money is one
of the greatest instruments of freedom ever invented by man.'
   'I didn't talk money with him.'
   'You're going to make a film in Germany about a minor
war that took place in Europe over sixty years ago? Babel

was a weak, second-class, Frenchified writer. Make a film about the war that's going on here, in your own country, right now. This Hobbesian war of all against all . . .'

'Dietrich thinks I'm the right person to direct *Red Cavalry*,' I said. I showed her the book with Babel's picture. 'Does the photo remind you of anyone?'

'No.' Another laugh. 'Dietrich must be an idiot, or else real shrewd. He thinks you're going to make another *Holy War*. But you know why *The Holy War* worked out? First, because Euclides da Cunha wrote the story and the main character was Antônio Conselheiro; it wasn't some piece of shit by Babel. Conselheiro never read Maupassant. He didn't give a shit about Maupassant.'

'I wrote the script.'

'And the second reason for your film's success can be explained in the same way Orson Welles explained how he achieved the cinematic innovations in *Citizen Kane*: ignorance. You didn't know anything about cinema when you made that film. You were saved by your own ignorance.'

I had told Liliana the story about Orson Welles which she was now using against me without having the consolation of the rest of the answer Welles had given the journalist from *Cahiers*: 'If that word [ignorance] seems inadequate to you, replace it with innocence.' When I met Liliana she was a fifteen-year-old girl without a trace of erudition. Now, at twenty, she was giving me lessons.

'I don't want to see you for a while' I said.

'It is because of Ruth?' she asked captiously.

'It's because of me.'

'I know it's because of Ruth.'

'I don't want to see you again.'

'Never again? This scene is too contrived even for a mediocre director like you.'

*　*　*

I looked at the wheelchair, after Liliana had gone. Was this to be my life then?

I spoke to the doorman over the intercom: 'Don't let anyone come up without first letting me know.'

'But . . . I never let anybody . . . that girl . . . she said she was married to you and that she lived here.'

'She doesn't live here. And I'm not married to anyone.'

'You're new in the building and I thought . . .'

'I don't want anyone, any visitor of mine to enter the building without express authorization from me, understand?'

Before I went to sleep and dreamed, Liliana called me.

'The guy in the raincoat followed me home.'

'Did you tell the doorman you're my wife?'

'That doesn't matter. Listen: that sinister guy in the raincoat followed me home!'

'Is that true?'

'I swear it. I'm frightened.'

'You, frightened? You're not afraid of anything.'

'Could he have been following me for some time without my noticing? Or is he more interested in you?' Liliana asked.

'I think I'm his main interest. He was hanging around outside before you got here. Maybe he's from the police. They were here before you came.'

'No, he's not a policeman. He's not legitimate. He hides. What's this about the police being at your place?'

'It's a long story. I don't feel like telling it.'

'Tell me.'

'That woman who was here and left a box with colored stones. Remember that brown-paper package that you saw on the table?'

'Yes.'

'The woman who left it here was killed. I think the stones are emeralds, rubies and sapphires.'

'Emeralds, rubies, sapphires? Are you serious? How many stones are there? Did you count them?'

'About thirty, something like that.'

This was the dream. The same woman with yellow eyes, but now with a bony tail, not unlike a monkey's. I am being consumed by her, as if by a vampire. She says things in my ear: 'The weather bureau was wrong again with its predictions.' And: 'Did your other pretty women also treat you the same way?' As she says this last phrase her teeth are filled with blood, *my* blood. I tell her I'm afraid the house will collapse at any minute and I'll be buried in the debris. If it's a house, why don't I open the door and leave? The tip of her tongue is red, even when she's not sucking my blood. Her vagina is always damp. I'm nervous because I have to pack and unpack bags, make and unmake friendships, and also because I lost my life because I was unwilling to finish off the people I love.

As always, my dream has no images. When I was a child, and until adolescence, I didn't remember them when I woke up; it was as if I never dreamed. When I began to remember my peculiar dreams, I thought everyone dreamed as I did. Upon learning that my dreams were different, I became interested in the subject, for a time. I read countless books, saw doctors, all to no avail. The interpretation of oneiric phenomena, from Artemydorus in antiquity to Freud in modern times, has little to say about dreams like mine. Freud, though recognizing that, despite being predominantly visual, dreams may also possess auditive impressions and other types, stops there. He cites an author, J. Delboeuf, who dreamed about Latin nouns. But Delboeuf also *saw* things. It was then I memorized the definition of a dream that I found enlightening: 'an archaic world of vast emotions and imperfect thoughts'. I later discovered, in A. Maury's book *Analogies des Phénomènes du Rêve et de l'Aliénation Mentale*, a definition of the dream state that expressed what was happening with me: 'a vicious and irregular association of ideas'. They were moments when I suspected I was insane.

The next day I took three stones for Maurício to examine, one of each color.

Gaining entry to Maurício's office was again a complicated affair. After passing through several checkpoints on the jewelry store's ground floor, I was taken to a room with two doors where there was nothing but a table, a chair and a television camera with its small red light on. I tried the two doors. They were locked. After ten long minutes a very well-dressed and -coiffured woman came in.

'Pardon the delay. Normally we're quicker.'

'Was something wrong?'

'You tried to open the doors. I had to get Mr Maurício out of a meeting to let us know if you were a suitable person.'

'Am I a suitable person?'

She laughed. Perfect teeth, a requirement for the job. 'Yes. Unfortunately, Mr Maurício can't see you, but I'm at your disposal.'

I left the stones, wrapped in paper inside an envelope, with the woman. She did not give me a receipt. It was probably common practice in this business: they didn't trust you but you had to trust them.

The enormous building that housed the new installations of the Evangelical Church of Jesus Savior of Souls was in Copacabana.

José was waiting for me.

'How do you like it?' he asked after I had taken his *tour de propriétaire.*

'Why did you choose Copacabana? There's no place in the street to park a car.'

José laughed. 'First, you should have parked it in our garage.'

'I came by taxi.'

'Second, the members of our Church don't have cars.'

'You have three,' I said.

'Third, the psycho-social profile of the Copacabana resident is very similar to that of the resident of the North Zone. Copacabana is a good starting point for those of us who come from the outlying districts. A fancy address like Delfim Moreira Avenue can come later.'

'Ah, so you've done a market study.'

'Anything wrong with that? My brother, my brother, you have only hatred and despair in your heart. You should join us.'

'What for?'

José looked me in the eyes. 'To bring about a religious and ethical revolution through the teachings of Jesus. Moral rectitude and love as the source of salvation. The old Catholic Church doesn't want to hear about Jesus – it wants, and always has wanted, power; the primitive African-based beliefs have no ethical foundation and are hedonistic. Neither one nor the other has the answer. Do you like this cruel and corrupt world in which we live?' He said this with his clear and convincing eyes fixed on mine. Could it be that he had changed? Or did José merely believe his own flim-flam, like every good confidence man? Or again, was there really nothing but hate in my heart? Hate for him? Yes, I had despised him since I was small, from the time when he used to catch flies and tear off their wings and then put them on the floor and say, 'I'd like to see you fly now, Mr Fly.' But I didn't hate him for ripping the wings off flies; I hated him for his fantastic ability to catch the flies. José could see a fly light on a surface – it could be either vertical or horizontal – and in rapid motion catch the insect before it flew away. 'It's in the bag,' he'd say, showing me his closed hand. Then he would put his hand under the faucet to wet the fly's wings and thus prevent it from flying away when he began his act of mutilation. I never succeeded in catching flies in my hand and envied him his ability. That was it: I was envious. I must have known that someone with such inventiveness and impiety had a brilliant future, and I was dying of envy.

'This week I'll make those changes to the film,' I said.

'After Carnival we begin our new campaign. I'd appreciate it if the film were ready.'

I spent the night reading and re-reading Babel. Each story was a masterpiece. I don't know what impressed me most: the tension, the balance between irony and lyricism, the elegance of phrase, the precision, the conciseness. I dislike re-reading a literary text, whatever it is, unless I'm adapting it for film. I read *Rebellion in the Backlands*, that masterpiece by Euclides da Cunha, countless times and by the fifth time no longer felt the slightest pleasure in it. And Euclides's life, for all its drama, had never interested me. For that matter, no one's life interested me. It didn't matter to me, for example, that Gauguin was a pedophile; my concern was to find out how he managed the light and color of his canvases. But, inexplicably, I felt like finding out things about Babel's life.

At the end of the book was a small biographical note saying that Isaac Babel had been born in Odessa in 1894 and had grown up in a middle-class Jewish family. During the Revolution and the civil war he fought in the Cavalry; later he opened a print shop in Odessa. He returned to literature in 1923, publishing some stories in magazines. He published

*Red Cavalry* and *Odessa Tales*. He was arrested in the purges at the end of the 1930s and died in a concentration camp in 1939 or 1940, either from typhus or a bullet wound.

The following morning I went to work on the film for my brother José. As I re-edited it, I thought about the extent to which I was reinforcing the power and furthering the ambition of evangelists. To me, all evangelists were crafty opportunists like my brother, as false as the priests of all existing religions. Religion was big business run by swindlers. Modern man didn't need God, he needed an ethic, one of love, of tolerance . . . What shit, there I was inventing a new religion, reinventing the wheel. Fuck 'em.

I don't know what impulse made me do it, but I picked up the phone book and looked up the name Negromonte. There were five Negromontes listed. Áureo was one of them.

'Yes, I'm Áureo de Negromonte.' Cold and suspicious.

'Are you the gentleman who takes part in costume pageants?'

'Who is this?'

I explained that I was a film director who was interested in costume pageants.

His attitude changed: 'It's about time they made a film about us.'

'Right. That's why I wanted to talk to you.'

'When?'

'As soon as possible.'

'I'm running around like crazy, there's just three days before the pageant and my costume still isn't ready. It's a horrid situation.'

'It wouldn't take much time. I want a preliminary talk first, which will take only a little of your time. May I come to see you?'

'It's chaos around here, everything's messy. I don't want you to see my house in this state.'

'I'm used to messy houses. My own, for example.'

'You swear?'

'I do. I won't even notice the mess at your place.'

Negromonte gave me the address. An apartment in Tijuca. We made an appointment for that evening.

Negromonte lived in a small apartment. He was a man whose age was difficult to determine, perhaps because of the make-up he wore.

'Didn't I tell you?' Negromonte said after he had opened the door. On tables and chairs around the living room was spread a profusion of pieces of cloth embroidered with paillettes, brightly colored glass ornaments, small cylindrical pieces of decorative glass, and encrusted with shiny colored stones. Two women were embroidering the fabrics.

'Oh, good heavens, only three days left and I'm so desperate that sometimes I feel like killing myself!'

'It'll be ready, Mr Áureo. It's like this every year, you should be used to it by now,' said one of the women, a fat mulatto.

'You know I'm not joking, Mildred. If the costume isn't ready I'll kill myself! And you . . . you two will be to blame. I'm going to leave that in the note to the police.' Changing tone suddenly, he now addressed himself to me: 'Everything in gold and black. I always use gold and black in my costumes. Áureo in Latin means gold, did you know that? Of course. You're a film director, you must know. It was my mother who gave me that name, my dear sweet mother that God took last year – I suffered so, I was so alone. She knew that the name would be like a glove for me. Just imagine if I were called Mildred.'

'Mildred was a queen,' Mildred said.

'Queen of what?' Negromonte asked ironically. 'Not of Angola. That's a white name. Bring us some coffee, Marijó, while this gentleman tells me about the film he wants to make about me.'

'The person who was going to help me with this project was Angélica Maldonado. Did you know her?'

'Fat Angélica? Certainly. She was a good person, but very distrusting. She wouldn't let anyone see her costume; she wasn't like me who shows it to everybody. I even tell people the name – the name of the costume is a secret you should guard with care, otherwise they'll use it all over Brazil. I show everything. Know what the name of my costume is? The Treasure of King Solomon's Mines. Do you like it?'

'Yes. Tell me more about Angélica. Did she have relatives? Was she married? I didn't know her well at all.'

'No, she was single – who'd want to marry a woman of that size? – and she had no relatives. Her story is a curious one. She was raised in an orphanage and was very poor; she got ahead in life through great sacrifice. She was very hard working; she made her own costume. She used to say it was so no one would copy her styles. But no one would have wanted to copy Angélica's styles; her costumes were nothing special. However, since Angélica was Diderot's protégée, she appeared at the Glória, the Monte Libano, the Scala, in the Português in Recife – everywhere, even abroad.'

'Who's Diderot?'

'You don't mean to tell me you don't know who Diderot is?'

'No, I don't.'

'You don't know who Diderot Assunção is?'

'No, I don't.'

'The biggest promoter in the field. A great promoter. His clients travel to Europe, the United States to show their costumes in large hotels, clubs, making a lot of dough.'

'Are you one of his clients?'

'Not yet. But when he sees the Treasure of King Solomon's Mines he'll put me under contract, I'm sure of it. Look at this cabochon here,' he said, showing me an enormous round stone. 'Did you ever see anything lovelier? It looks like it was made by Mother Nature. All my stones are like that; my strasse is French, as well as the paillettes – everything imported, the finest. This year will be the Year of Reparation, the year the injustices committed against me are avenged. I deserved to win last year, with My Kingdom for Love, and I came in second. The year before that it was even worse. Nebuchadnezzar II and the Hanging Gardens of Babylon came in third – a masterpiece, a grand and dazzling thing came in third. I put so much into that costume! . . . I do research, you know, in books, encyclopedias, I talk with specialists, with learned men, something nobody does, I track down all the information about the theme before I create my costume . . . Isn't that right, Mildred? I felt like killing myself when I came in third. You're going to watch me compete this year, aren't you? The best one is at the Glória, you know; there's no dance, just the pageant. It's not easy to get in; the pageant is geared toward television and the only ones allowed in are people staying at the hotel and a handful of guests. But I'll arrange an invitation for you. Where's that coffee, Marijó?'

# 5

M aurício came to my apartment.
'I came to talk about the gems you left at my office.'

He reached into his pocket and took out a small package wrapped in silk paper. He opened it. 'Just where was it you said you got these stones?'

'I didn't get them anywhere. I've always had them. They belonged to my mother.' I used my mother, as Negromonte had done.

'The stones are very valuable,' Maurício said. 'They're worth a small fortune. Do you want to sell them?'

'I don't know.' I tried to hide my surprise. Valuable! What was a small fortune? If three stones were worth a small fortune, how much would thirty be worth? I thought about millions of dollars. With two million dollars – which isn't that much money in cinema – I could make a film even better than *The Holy War*. Were the stones worth that much? I felt like asking Maurício, but I was afraid he might suspect something. I had to be careful.

'Do you have any more? If you want to sell, we'll buy.'

'I may have, but I'll need to look for them.'

'Look for them, man; if you have a lot of them, it'll be

enough to finance the film.' The wretch seemed to read my mind! 'But look, if there's a lot of them, I need to know their origin.'

Again that discomfort I had felt at his office. I had known Maurício for many years – we had grown up together – and never before had he made me feel like that. Could he suspect that I had come by the stones illegally?

'I'll look; if I find others I'll let you know,' I said, seeing him to the door, wanting to get rid of him before he discovered something.

'I'm going to spend Carnival out of town but I'll be back Thursday. Call me.' He paused. 'You can trust me . . .'

When Maurício had gone, I returned to my reading of Babel. In the small book were all the stories Babel published in his lifetime: the Odessa stories, those that told of his experience with the First Cavalry, commanded by General Budenny during the campaign against the Whites in the Ukraine and eastern Poland; and, finally, the stories of his childhood. I had always liked reading stories, ever since I was a child. The literature that I devoured at the age of ten had titles like *Best Russian Stories, Best American Stories, Best French Stories, Best Italian Stories.* At fourteen I thought I had read every story in the world ever written. (I don't know now how I became a film director and not a short-story writer.) There was a period when I thought my favorite short-story writer was Maupassant; on other occasions, Poe. As might be expected, I had my Chekhov phase. Now it was my Babel period. I remember there was an effort to call attention to Babel because of his having been a victim of Stalin's purges. They made a martyr out of him. Martyrs are such a bore.

Why did Babel's life interest me so? Did it matter that he began writing in French, imitating Maupassant and ending up writing better than his model? Was there any importance to the story that one day he saw his father kneeling at the feet of a Cossack officer, kissing his boots? (Could that be why he later enlisted in the Cavalry, to become a Cossack himself?) Why did I spend so much time looking at the picture of him dressed in the military jacket with gold trim? Only a Jew could have a face so expressively recalcitrant, a look in which irony and skepticism blended with compassion. Who was that man? Actually, I did want to know more about Babel. I wanted to know everything.

I spent two days in the editing room making the changes my brother had requested in the film for the Evangelical Church of Jesus Savior of Souls. To tell the truth, his suggestions were very good, like all the others he had offered before, and they made the pathetic little film more persuasive. A few thousand more poor wretches would give ten percent of their pay to the Church, and I was an accomplice in the exploitation of them.

On the Friday before Carnival the videotape was ready. I called José's house. Gislaine answered.

'José went to Brasília for an interview with the President.' Gislaine seemed to be saying: Would the President receive you, you poor envious devil?

'I didn't think anyone stayed in Brasília on a Friday, especially during Carnival . . .'

Gislaine hesitated, not knowing what to say. 'He'll be back tomorrow . . .'

'I'm going to leave the film at the lab for them to make the copies. José knows where it is.'

From the lab I went to visit my friend Boris Gurian, a wise old Jew. Gurian was born in Russia and his family emigrated to Austria, fleeing the communists, when he was still a boy. Twenty years later he was a professor of Russian literature at the University of Vienna, and they had to flee again, this time from the Nazis. He went to Holland, and from Holland to France, with the Nazis on his heels. Finally he ended up in Brazil, accompanied by his sister Sarah. His mother, his father and a brother did not manage to escape the Holocaust. But Gurian disliked talking about the past, and other than this I knew very little about his life.

It was four pm. Gurian was still slightly drunk. Alcohol had no visible effect on him, except for an almost imperceptible tic of running the tip of his tongue over his lips. Walking with difficulty – not because of drinking; he had broken a leg and never fully recovered – Gurian took me to his office, a room whose walls were lined with dusty books placed chaotically in bookcases. There were also books on the floor.

We sat in two broken and faded armchairs.

'Do you want some whiskey?' he asked, pointing to a bottle, glasses and a bucket of ice on the desk. 'I usually drink Brazilian whiskey, but since you were coming I got a bottle of Scotch.'

'What do you know about Babel?' I asked when our drinks were ready, mine with ice, his straight up.

'Everything,' Gurian replied. 'You think I wouldn't know about the greatest Jewish writer of the twentieth century? Where do you want me to begin?'

He began by saying that at home Babel's parents spoke Yiddish between themselves and Russian with the children. They were from Odessa. Isaac was sent to a Jewish religious school at the age of six. Key to his formation was the training he received in French literature and culture in the Nicholas I Commercial School. At fifteen he was writing stories in French. He could have chosen to write his later works in French, but he soon gave up that language.

'He also didn't want to write in Yiddish, like Singer, for

45

example, or in Hebrew, like Kanyuk.' There was a meditative pause. I noticed that Gurian was paler and frailer than the last time I had seen him. 'One critic said that, to Babel, Hebrew and Yiddish were the ghetto from which he wished to flee. He preferred writing in the language of the goyim: Russian.'

At sixteen Babel went to Kiev to study at the Institute of Finance and Administration. Because he was a Jew he was barred from entering the University of Odessa.

In Kiev he met Eugenia Gronfein, daughter of a friend of his father, whom he would marry in 1919. In that city he published, in a magazine, his first story, written in Russian. As soon as he graduated, in 1915, he moved, illegally, to Petersburg, the literary capital of the country.

'He would walk through the streets of Petersburg,' Gurian continued, 'with false documents in his pocket (as a Jew he was unable to get permission to live in the city) and without an overcoat, in the winter. He himself speaks of the fact that he owned an overcoat but wouldn't wear it on principle. In Petersburg he met Gorky, who published two of his stories in the newspaper *Letopis.* He became part of a group of intellectuals who revolved around Gorky – the futurists Brik, Shklovski, Mayakovski. Babel says that Gorky told him to "learn among the people". Well, the war came soon and Babel enlisted. In October 1917 he was sent to the Romanian front. Do you know what happened?'

'He was decorated for bravery,' I replied.

'Babel's life has no great events. He contracted malaria and was sent home.'

At that moment Gurian had a coughing attack that lasted what seemed a long time but was probably less than a minute. When he had stopped coughing, he tried to speak, unsuccessfully.

'Wait a bit,' I said.

We drank in silence; Gurian breathed heavily in a way that worried me.

'I don't have much time,' he said finally.

'I can come back tomorrow.'

Gurian laughed, amused at my misunderstanding.

'I can hold out a few months . . .' He laughed again: 'Maybe.' His voice was very weak. He ran his trembling hand, discolored and lined with blue veins, and dotted with freckles, over his face. Before I could catch him, his body lunged forward and he fell to the floor.

He had fainted, but he was breathing normally. I lifted him up and put him in the chair. His position struck me as an uncomfortable one, even for an unconscious man. I took him in my arms and carried him to the bedroom. He weighed very little.

In the bedroom there were also books on the floor and scattered over the bed. I found a space and put Gurian's fragile body down. I ran back to the living room and called one of those hospitals with emergency ambulance service, the first I found in the phone book.

While waiting for the doctor, I looked in Gurian's library for a book on Babel. A methodical search was impossible in those bookcases with books piled on top of one another without order or logic. Then I remembered his sister Sarah. On one of the tables was an address book with her phone number. No one answered.

The doctor arrived, accompanied by an orderly. He examined Gurian.

'Are you a relative?'

'A friend.'

'We're going to have to take him with us. Will you take responsibility?'

I went with them in the ambulance.

When we arrived, the doctor asked me to go to the clinic's

reception area, where they demanded a deposit, in the form of a check, as a guarantee of payment of costs arising from Gurian's treatment.

I called Sarah again. This time she answered.

'This is a friend of Gurian's.'

'Ah, a friend of Gurian's . . . Boris has lots of friends . . . but none of them help Boris . . . and Boris helps everybody . . . I'm very busy, my good man.'

'Dona Sarah, Gurian is in the hospital.'

'Boris in the hospital? It was from drinking, wasn't it? Always I say to him, Boris, you're too old to drink, but will he listen?'

Time passes very slowly in hospital waiting rooms.

Sarah took quite a while to arrive. She had shrunk with age. She was much frailer than Gurian, but her look was one of great intelligence.

'Boris doesn't have the money to stay in a hospital like this,' she said.

'Don't worry about it.'

'He spends all his money on books and drink,' Sarah said. 'But I have my savings. Tell the hospital to send the bill to me.'

'That's already taken care of.'

'Listen, I'm telling you to have them send the bill to me. You think maybe I don't have money?'

Before departing, Sarah tried, unsuccessfully, to see her brother in the ICU. Finally we left the hospital together.

Liliana was waiting for me at the door of the building where I lived. We exchanged greetings.

'Aren't you going to ask me in?'

When we were in the apartment, Liliana asked, 'Is the bedroom like this too, crazy?'

Without waiting to be asked, she went into the bedroom.
'It's a little better here,' she said, sitting on the bed.

I sat in a chair.

'Sit here next to me,' she said.

'I'm fine here.'

'You don't want to . . . fool around with me?'

'No.'

'You don't feel like it?' Liliana asked this without a trace
of any sensual charm; she knew that, when they attempt it,
women come across as cheap imitations of Marilyn Monroe.
She asked the question looking me straight in the eye. She
wanted a truthful answer.

'Going to bed with you is good at the time. Afterwards it's
horrible.'

'I feel sorry for you.'

I said nothing.

'If I didn't know you, I'd think you were like most men.
Men don't like women who like them. That's a fact.' She
paused. 'Have you found a new girlfriend?'

'No.'

'You're very strange, you know that? When you were
married to Ruth you used to meet me . . . Since then . . .'

'I don't want to talk about that.'

I left the room. She came after me.

'Have I committed some crime?'

'Go away,' I said.

'I'm going to end up hating you,' she said from the door.
'You need to see an analyst. I think you're sick.'

After Liliana had left I picked up Babel's book and looked
at his picture, trying to remember where I had seen him
before. In a film? He looked like Alexander Knox in *Man in
the Middle*, but it wasn't in a film that I had seen his face. It
was in a book or a magazine. Then I remembered: a painter,

that was it, a painter! I opened the packing crates containing my books and started to hunt. I was about to give up when I saw a book with paintings of Goya. There was the person who resembled Babel-Goya himself, in a self-portrait of 1787 which is in the Fine Arts Museum in Castres.

I placed the painter and the writer side by side. Both are looking askance at the world, wearing steel-rimmed glasses. Goya, perhaps a bit fatter, allows pessimism to show in his gaze, the resigned despair of one willing to do anything to achieve a perfect work – collaborate with the French invader, outwit through craftiness and compromises the threats of the Inquisition and the distrust of the aristocracy whom he served – but whose ugliness and vulgarity he portrayed pitilessly. Babel's look is more ironic; he was not yet overcome by the despair that will dominate him when he perceives his inability to serve the Revolution, to belong to a new order. Like the Spanish painter, the Russian writer will only be able to dedicate himself to one thing – the creation of a masterpiece. Two artists who faced the choice of perfecting their lives or perfecting their work, as Yeats put it. Babel and Goya chose their work. *Red Cavalry* by Babel and *The Disasters of War* by Goya both captured with the same rawness the horrors of war and its brutal effects. *Odessa Tales*, on the other hand, corresponded to the painter's *Caprichos*. This coincidence excited me. I decided I would make the film using the same light as Goya, the same black colors, the browns, the dark reds of his paintings of war. I wouldn't accept the impositions of any producer. I would choose a cameraman who would help me capture those colors, that light, that shadow.

I dream I'm on a street corner, with a letter in my hand, and I feel an ardent desire, unidentified. The sound and flash of thunder and lightning (which I neither see nor hear). I know that a bluish light illuminates a large drain through which things disappear, like dirty water. I have a cyst on my nose and I'm suddenly transported to a train in motion. In the window, the hands of people hanging onto the outside, their fingers broken, and a picture of me dressed as a legionnaire reflected in the glass. Disappearing down the drain. There is also the awareness of a girl's breasts smelling of apple blossom and a large glass of blue paint. Disappearing down the drain. Until she (who? who?) places her foot over the drain and says in the dark screen: 'Kill me, strangle me, shoot me in the head, here in this bar, there on that corner, then go to my funeral, nothing will make me as happy. Wait, wait a bit, let's go home, these people here could hurt you; let's go home, certain things can only be done at home.' She removes her foot from the drain.

José had a two-hour television program every Sunday morning. I hated the program but, for some reason that I couldn't identify, I always turned on the TV, watched a little, and then turned it off, saying I'd never do that again.

The program was being broadcast direct from the new church in Copacabana, which was packed despite it being Carnival weekend. José was the only televangelist on the air that sinful Sunday.

'Thus, the Lord knoweth how to deliver the godly out of temptation and to reserve the unjust unto the Day of Judgment,' José was saying. He paused. The studio director went to a close-up of José and then cut to one of the faithful, a woman who looked terrified. Another close-up of José, expressive: 'The Lord reserves the unjust unto the Day of Judgment TO BE PUNISHED!'

José had learned all the possible nuances of biblical oratory. I had seen him console the afflicted, encourage the downhearted, give comfort to the sick, courage to the weak, hope to the defeated, faith to the uncertain. But this was a Carnival Sunday, a perfect day to denounce the temptations of mankind. And this José did with all the eloquence of Burt Lancaster in *Elmer Gantry*.

'But He will punish above all those who walk after the flesh in the lust of uncleanness; heedless and willful, they fear not to blaspheme, whereas angels, which are greater in power and might, utter not blasphemy before the Lord.'

I had caught the program in the middle, and since I knew very little about the Bible I had no idea which of the Apostles my brother was quoting that day. One thing was certain: it wouldn't be the exact words of the Apostle, for my brother had the habit of adapting biblical texts to his melodramatic ends.

'But these sinners of Sodom and Gomorrah, like natural brute beasts that blindly follow nature, made to be taken and destroyed, blaspheming that which they understand not, shall utterly perish in their own corruption. Spots they are, and blemishes, delighting in the error of their ways, having eyes full of adultery; and they cannot cease from sin, and their hearts they have exercised with corruptions of the flesh, cursed children, they have forsaken the right way, following the way of Balaam, son of Bosor; they are wells without water, clouds that are carried with a tempest, to whom the mist of darkness is reserved for ever.'

José had descended from the pulpit and was walking down the aisle. The faithful turned their heads to follow him with their eyes.

'However,' José raised his arms menacingly, 'if after they have escaped the pollutions of the world through knowledge of the Lord and Savior Jesus Christ, they are again entangled therein, and overcome, the latter end is worse with them than the beginning. For it had been better for them not to have known the way of righteousness than, after they have known it, to turn from the holy commandment delivered unto them.' After a traveling shot of the auditorium: 'But it is happened unto them according to the true proverb: the dog is turned to his own vomit again and the sow that was washed to her wallowing in the mire.'

When the sermon was over, a woman interviewed the faithful in the church. The interviewees had been carefully chosen.

'The pastor is right,' said a large man with an honest face. 'Those who sleep at this time of day like pigs, after spending the night wallowing . . . wallowing . . .'

'In lust,' prompted the interviewer. She was an intelligent woman.

'. . . in lust, satiating the most ignominious sins . . .'

Another one, this time a woman: 'Here are some of the few among the many who have not delivered themselves to sin and decay. Those who know that their immortal soul cannot be sullied, who know they must help Jesus to save the world, by helping our pastor José, who represents Jesus on earth.'

Another: 'By helping Jesus prevail over the lack of charity, we are saving our souls for all eternity and we are also creating for ourselves here on earth a life of peace and love.'

The final one: 'All of us – and we are not only those here today, but there are many of us spread throughout the country – all of us together are contributing with faith, with love, with our tithe, to the glory of Jesus. Jesus is our salvation.'

On the screen appeared the address and phone number of the Church of Jesus Savior of Souls. An appealing voice was saying, 'Don't wait till tomorrow; Jesus needs you.'

I turned off the TV, feeling sorry for the people who were listening to my brother. I'll never do that again, I thought.

*     *     *

I telephoned the hospital. Gurian was out of the ICU. I went to visit him. He was in his room, wearing a night shirt and appearing even more feeble.

'Are you feeling better?' I asked. I told him about my meeting with his sister.

'Ever since my mother died Sarah has taken her place.' He paused. 'Where did we leave off in that conversation about Babel?' He seemed eager to tell me what he knew.

'Babel contracted malaria and was sent home.'

'Ah yes . . . In March 1918 he was in Petersburg, working for Gorky's newspaper *Letopis.* The following year he returned to Odessa to marry Eugenia Gronfein. In 1920 he was working for a government news service. Under the name Liutov he wrote for a newspaper published by the First Cavalry called the *Red Cavalryman.*'

'Why did he use the pseudonym?'

'To hide the fact that he was Jewish.'

'Why did Babel want to join Budenny's regiment? To become a Cossack and nullify the scene of his father kissing the Cossack's boots?'

'I don't know if it's true, that business of his father kissing the Cossack's boots. Jews were in fact often humiliated and it wouldn't be impossible for it to happen. But I think Babel was looking for material to write about. Writers do that, go out into the world looking for subjects for their books. The ironic part of the situation, if my hypothesis is correct, is that according to his diary the stories Babel wrote during the war, and which he carried with him into combat, were lost.'

'I'd like to know what Eugenia Gronfein was like. Women interest me.'

'I don't know. If Babel, who was married to her, didn't know, how could I know?'

Gurian looked away and asked a surprising question:

'You don't by any chance have in your pocket a flask with something to drink?'

'A flask in my pocket?'

'When I was a child all the adults used to have one . . . I guess they went out of style.'

'Are you allowed to drink?'

'No. I mean, that's what the doctors say, if you ask.'

'You want me to go and buy one for you?'

He did. There was no need to answer.

Near the hospital there was a small market, where I bought a bottle of Scotch.

I poured two fingers of whiskey into a glass that was on the table by the bed.

'Aren't you going to drink?' Gurian asked.

We toasted Babel.

'He lost the stories and fell ill,' Gurian continued, now more animated. 'His health wasn't all that good. He lived for a time in the Caucasus because of that. When he returned to Odessa, after the military campaign, he was a famous man; after all, he had served with Budenny and become a friend of Gorky. Later his situation became more complicated. At the 1934 Writers' Congress, three years before he was arrested, Babel made a speech apologizing for writing so little. "If we are speaking of silence," he said, "I mustn't be left out, for I am the great master of the genre." He wasn't speaking seriously. Babel affirmed at that Congress his dedication to the Revolution, which was true, but he also praised the literary canons of the period, which could only be irony. Just as sarcastic was his claim to the right "that has been taken away from us to write badly". Any idiot could see from his texts that he was a perfectionist. In reality, Babel, "the great master of silence", wished to claim the right of the writer *not to write*, which was considered heresy by the Soviet writers' organizations. Or rather, he preferred not to write unless he had full freedom to do so.'

Gurian asked me to pour some more whiskey into his glass. He continued to drink, wrinkling his brow and looking sideways as if trying to remember something.

'More,' he said, extending the glass. I poured a small amount of liquor.

'In Odessa he became friends with the fellow who would become his biographer, Konstantin Paustovsky. I have Paustovsky's book at home, *Story of a Life*. Do you read Russian?'

'No. I read Babel in English and Portuguese,' I replied.

'The Russian words in your script should probably be written following the system of Thomas Shaw, *The Transliteration of Modern Russian for English Language Publications*,' Gurian said. 'I hope you'll enroll in a Russian course immediately. Getting back to Paustovsky, he was the one who called Babel the first great *Soviet* writer. But Babel is more than that. He owes nothing to the great Russian writers who preceded him – Dostoevsky, Tolstoy, Chekhov, Pushkin, Turgenev, Gogol, or his contemporary Gorky. It's a shame you don't read Russian. Young people today are very ignorant. Russian is a beautiful language. A language as lovely as Portuguese.'

'Is Babel greater than Chekhov?'

'There was a period in which Russian-language writers were divided into two categories: Russian writers and Soviet writers. Babel would be the first, and greatest, of the Soviet writers. But that classification is artificial.'

'You didn't answer my question. Is Babel greater than Chekhov?'

'To answer that I need another drink of that nectar,' Gurian said, with a knowing smile. 'The *nastroenie*, the atmosphere, of Babel doesn't allow comparison with Chekhov. You're very clever. If you asked me if Babel was greater than Dostoevsky the answer would be easier.'

I served Gurian another dose. The tip of his dark tongue began to appear between his lips.

'Babel sought patterns of excellence impossible of attainment by any artist. That's why he wrote so little, with such resplendent exactitude. In this respect he's better than Chekhov, that other demon of perfectionism.'

'I've spent the last few days working on Dolguchov's death. I'm looking into the possibility of filming *Red Cavalry*.'

'Cinema is a funny thing . . . How will you achieve the same concision as Babel; that is, the immediate closing of the narrative when what must be said has been said?'

'I don't know; I still don't know how to solve that.'

'Pushkin said that precision and brevity are the principal qualities of prose. Babel knew that . . . Dostoevsky didn't . . . If you give me another drink I'll tell you something important.'

We drank another toast to Babel.

'Film doesn't have the same metaphorical and multi-layered resources as literature. Film is reductionist, simplifying, shallow. Film is nothing.'

'Film is nothing?'

'If I sit in the corridor of a hospital I see a film – people moving about, talking, crying, carrying things, waiting. That's all film is.'

'You can also see a book, looking at the corridor. That's all literature is too.'

'That calls for another drink. Profound thoughts always deserve a toast,' Gurian said.

'I'm going to let you rest a bit. I'll be back tomorrow.'

'Leave the bottle.'

I took the bottle with me.

# 6

When I got home the doorman handed me an envelope. It was a ticket to the pageant, with a note from Negromonte: 'Be sure to come, to lend me support.'

'That lady was here.'

'What lady?'

'That one.' The doorman must have been referring to Liliana.

I went up to the apartment. Whiling away the time before the costume pageant at seven pm, I looked at Ruth's wheelchair, and at the photo of Babel. There were books, clothes, cassettes, an enormous number of various objects on the floor and on all the chairs and furniture, but Ruth's chair was free. I felt like looking at Ruth's picture. I opened the suitcase containing her things that I had brought in the move.

I took the items out of the suitcase. A book, *Modern Dance*. Half a bottle of perfume. A glass-bead necklace. A silk handkerchief. A packet of sanitary napkins. Seeing this gave me an acute memory of Ruth unlike any I'd ever had before: for the first time I saw Ruth as a living, fragile being who now revealed herself to me in all her beauty through a menstrual pad. Why had I not seen before the way in which that item linked to the vitality of my loved one? Why had I always remained so distant from Ruth, why hadn't I ever known her as she really was?

I held that article made of paper and cloth, feeling pain, remembering. But I didn't want to remember.

I put the pad in the suitcase. I left at once for the costume pageant.

At a long table in the pageant room sat the formally dressed men and women who would judge the costumes: personalities from the social and artistic world whose names were read out by an announcer. The pageant was to be staged for television. A few spectators stood in front of the judges' table.

Through a side door were other rooms where the contestants – close to fifty of them, previously selected – were applying their make-up and putting on their costumes.

It wasn't hard to find Áureo de Negromonte, in the largest, pillar-filled room, accompanied by Mildred and Marijó. He was already made up, but not like the last time I had seen him; the make-up on his lips, face and eyes was quite a bit heavier. He hadn't put on his costume yet.

First to compete would be the contestants for the originality prize, male and female, followed by the luxury category, female and male, in that order. Obviously The Treasure of King Solomon's Mines was included in the latter category.

'I'm so nervous . . .' said Negromonte. 'My heavens! I'm an old-timer at this, but when the pageant begins . . . Look at my hands!' They were cold, covered with sweat.

With a small linen handkerchief, Mildred constantly wiped the sweat forming on Negromonte's brow and above his upper lip.

'Is Diderot Assunção here?' I asked.

'Diderot Assunção? Why do you want to meet Diderot Assunção?'

'For the film. Didn't I tell you about the film?'

'But isn't the film going to be about me? Why Diderot? He's an old faggot, and ugly.'

'I just want to talk to him.'

'If I told you certain terrible things I know about Diderot, I doubt you'd want to ask his advice about anything.'

'I'm not going to ask his advice. I just want to talk.'

'Talk about what?'

'About the pageants. For example, how much a hotel pays to host the pageant. That sort of thing.'

'You're not going to ask Diderot to suggest some other person to make the film about, are you?'

'No.'

'Really?'

'You can trust me.'

Áureo took me by the arm and led me through the fantastic hubbub of the rooms where the contestants were dressing. Finally we came to a man with a goatee and red dyed hair. He had delicate, flaccid arms and was wearing a black T-shirt covered with sequins. It was Diderot.

Negromonte explained that I wanted to make a film about the pageants.

Diderot appraised me.

'Yes?' he said finally.

'I wanted to talk to you.'

'So talk,' he said, indifferently. 'You may go,' he added, to Negromonte.

Biting his lips, Negromonte withdrew. I saw that he stayed at a distance, behind one of the pillars in the room, looking in our direction.

'I was going to make a film with Angélica Maldonado, but that thing happened.'

'They told me you're simply to die for, Lulu,' Diderot said to a passing contestant, still not in costume, 'I can't wait to see.' The two kissed. Then Diderot looked at me as if surprised I was still there, and said offhandedly, 'Yes?'

'It's about the film.'

'What film?' he pretended.

'The film I was going to make with Angélica Maldonado.'

'Ah, I know . . . The poor thing died, didn't she? You'll have to make it with someone else. Do it with Áureo. Isn't he a really good friend of yours?'

'Yes, but Áureo doesn't travel. I want to make the film with someone who travels. I also want to film the person competing abroad, understand? I know you're the one who arranges the trips.'

For the first time, Diderot looked me straight in the eyes. A quick, significant glance. He, however, didn't see how much he had revealed to me.

'Cláudio, you'll be a smash,' said Diderot, grabbing the arm of a tall black-haired man.

'You think so? I'm scared to death. I feel everything whirling around inside. I think I'll die!'

While Cláudio and Diderot talked, I sensed someone observing me. It was a very pale man, leaning against one of the pillars in the ballroom. He clashed visibly with the setting. His pallor was such that he seemed to have covered his face with clown-white, like Japanese actresses in samurai films. His eyes were dark and febrile.

'Well?' I asked Diderot.

'I'll think about it,' he said. 'Do you have a phone?'

I gave him my phone number and address.

Diderot walked away and was lost at once amid colored feathers and glittering capes and trains. The pale guy had also disappeared. I was making my way back through the rooms when Negromonte suddenly appeared.

'He's a viper,' Negromonte said.

'Who?'

61

'Diderot. After the contest I want to talk to you. Will you wait?'

'Yes.'

I saw the entire pageant. In each category there were three prizes. Áureo didn't win any of them.

After the contest, the rooms slowly emptied. At the end, sitting on a bench in the great pillared ballroom, there remained only Negromonte, still in his immense, glittering costume, Mildred, Marijó – and me.

'I'm going to kill myself today, isn't that right, Mildred?'

Mildred turned to me: 'He's going to kill himself all right.'

'Six thousand peacock feathers,' said Negromonte, 'two thousand ostrich feathers, millions and millions of glass decorations and spangles and strasses, a whole year's work, isn't it, Mildred?'

'Three thousand ostrich feathers,' Mildred corrected sadly.

Marijó began to cry.

'I did research, spent days and days at the National Library ... The books were never there ... I went back again ... I read all the books that mentioned King Solomon's mines ...' He gave a deep sigh. 'Each and every one of these cabochons symbolizes a different thing, has its own meaning ... All for nothing ...'

'Next year you'll have another chance. Who knows ...' I said.

'Next year I'll be in that great pageant in the sky. I know there must be more justice in that place!'

'God willing!' Mildred said. 'You deserve it, after all that sacrifice.'

'Here on earth I'm a failure ...'

'Don't do anything foolish, Negromonte,' I said.

'Negromonte, Negromonte ... That's not my real name. Tell him my name, Mildred.'

Mildred said nothing.

'Tell him my disgusting name!' Negromonte screamed. His voice echoed through the ballroom.

A man in a security guard's uniform came up and said it was time to close.

'Tell him my disgusting name, Mildred!'

'Benedito,' Mildred said.

'Ha! Ha!' shouted Negromonte, getting up from the bench, still carrying on his back the construction of wire, wood, plastic, cardboard, fabric, stones, feathers and various decorations, some sixteen feet high, causing the security guard to draw back in alarm. Negromonte then spun around awkwardly with his arms open and fell to the floor, where he lay crying.

Mildred, Marijó and I, aided by the guard, picked up Negromonte. We removed his costume. Then we took the unhappy artist and his clothes home, in two taxis. I thought I might then be able to ask Negromonte about the terrible things he knew about Diderot.

Unfortunately, that wasn't possible. As soon as I mentioned Diderot, he began to sob and speak incoherently of the injustices he had suffered over the years.

When I left, Mildred and Marijó were lying in the bed with Negromonte; he asleep under the covers; they dressed and as vigilant as a pair of watchdogs.

There were two police cars parked at the door of my building and a small crowd of people had gathered.

A policeman blocked my way.

'I live here.'

'The doorman was killed,' said the policeman.

'How?'

'They were robbing an apartment and the doorman heard them and tried to intervene.'

'I'm going to sleep,' I said to the policeman. I already had enough problems without looking for any more.

As I was going up the stairs, two men rushed past me: a policeman and a guy with a camera. I'm not interested, police matters don't interest me, I thought, I'm going to sleep.

The door of my apartment was open and several people were inside. When I entered they stopped what they were doing and looked at me.

'Do you live here?' one of them asked.

'Yes.'

'We'd like you to tell us if anything is missing,' said a man, who must have been from the police, looking appraisingly at the disorder in the living room. 'Thieves broke into your apartment and killed the doorman.'

'They killed the doorman here?'

'Right here. At the entrance. He fell in the corridor.'

I looked, embarrassed, at the confusion in the living room. But the police thought it had been done by the thieves.

Accompanied by the policeman, I inspected the various rooms in the apartment.

'I don't think anything is missing,' I said.

'Everything indicates that they had finished turning the apartment upside down when the doorman got here. They shot him and ran away. The doorman of the building next door saw two men run out and get in a car. He didn't get the license number.'

'What time was that?' I asked.

'Around eight o'clock. The doorman was watching the news with his wife when he heard the noise and went to check.'

'I was at a costume contest,' I explained.

'Your apartment is cleared. The inspection of the break-in is finished. You may be asked to make a statement later at the precinct.'

'Do you think the thieves could come back?' I asked.

'Could they come back? I doubt it. Do you want me to post a man here tonight?'

'No, that's not necessary. I'll block the entrance with a piece of furniture. Tomorrow I'll have the lock fixed.'

I went to the doorman's apartment. A woman, her face swollen from crying, opened the door. She was dark-skinned, but in the weak light from a bulb hanging from the ceiling she looked gray.

'I live in apartment 401,' I said. 'Are you . . . were you . . . the wife of . . . of . . .'

'Edmílson,' she said.

I looked over her shoulder: a small room occupied by three beds covered with cheap spreads, an old armoire in a niche in the wall, a small stove with two burners; sitting on one of the chairs, two frightened children gazed in my direction.

'If you need anything, just let me know,' I said.

The woman's sobbing increased.

'Don't open the door for anyone,' I said.

I returned to the apartment as soon as the police had left and began to make a barricade against the door. I stacked in several successive piles all the pieces of furniture I could drag, except the wheelchair. The rear door had a lock that would make a lot of noise if it were forced. Then I went to see if the box with Angélica's stones was still in the drawer. There was no doubt that the thieves had broken into the apartment in search of them.

The stones were there. I examined them one by one.

I lay down on a mattress on top of the barricade, fully dressed with my shoes on and the box of stones in my pocket. I remembered Mildred and Marijó, lying on Negromonte's bed, keeping watch.

I fell asleep. This was the dream: a woman watches television

65

non-stop for almost half a century, dubbed films, newscasts, soap operas, advertising, interviews with idiots, all stuffed into her skull. Hundreds of times she changes her clothes, her face and her voice, her way of speaking, her detergent, her deodorant, her brand of cigarette, her margarine. She says: 'I don't rush during the breaks anymore to make popcorn or rummage through the refrigerator.' She no longer even gets up. She extends her hand, gets the cheap whiskey, ice from the styrofoam bucket. Soft are the colors of indifference: no one any longer tells her what to do.

I was awakened by Dietrich's phone call.

'Hello,' I said, startled.

'Is it very late there?'

'No, no.'

'The Latin American Film Festival has been postponed.'

'Nobody told me here in Brazil.'

'Dr Plessner, who's going to finance the film, has asked you to come right away. Pick up your ticket at Lufthansa. Dr Plessner has lots of ideas. He's anxiously awaiting you.'

There's nothing in the world worse than an anxious producer with lots of ideas.

'He's going to suggest that you make General Budenny the villain of the film.'

'I thought you were the producer.'

'I'm the executive producer. Who was it that said, "This is the great rule of cinema: the more perfect the villain, the more perfect the film"?' Dietrich asked.

'You know very well it was Hitchcock. But that's only true for crime films. *Cavalry* isn't a crime film.'

Budenny would be a perfect villain, I had to admit, if the film's protagonist were Babel-Babel and not Babel-Liutov. Certainly Budenny had helped destroy Babel-Babel. But Budenny hadn't known Babel in the guise of Liutov, in the

Cavalry. Budenny's hatred came later, when he read what Babel had written, something less than the glorification of military men that he had expected. Budenny believed the writer's role should be that of propagandist. To complicate matters, the protagonist of the film was Liutov, and Liutov was Babel; I had to take all that into consideration.

'Look,' I said, 'things here are a bit difficult. I'll call you soon . . .'

'Dr Plessner . . .' Dietrich interrupted.

I hung up.

# 7

I couldn't find anyone to fix the lock on a Carnival Monday. No one even answered the phone.

I left the barricade untouched in front of the door – actually, I placed another small table on top of it – and went out by the rear door, the box of precious stones in my pocket.

I bought pears, mangoes, peaches, sweetsops, papaya and a large slice of watermelon.

When I entered Gurian's hospital room, he looked at the voluminous bag that I was carrying and said, disappointed, 'Don't tell me that's fruit.'

'It is,' I said, disappointed too. 'You don't like it?'

'Do you have a bottle hidden there somewhere?'

'It's too early to drink,' I said.

'This business of only drinking after a certain hour is nothing but an English convention, idiotic like all English conventions. Russians drink at any time of day. Don't you want to talk about Russians?'

I went out and bought another bottle of Scotch.

'Isn't it bad for you?' I asked as I poured the liquor into his glass.

'In the shape I'm in, everything is bad for me. Even chicken soup,' Gurian said.

We drank.

'After you left, I thought about what you said about Dolguchov's death. It's better to die like Dolguchov, leaning against a tree with your intestines exposed, than in the way that awaits me.'

What could I say to that? I said nothing.

'It's so boring being in a hospital bed that you end up thinking "Dying can't be worse than this" and so you kick the bucket to escape the boredom.' He looked at me. 'You think that's just an old man talking tough, don't you?'

'I don't know.'

'You want me to talk about Babel, don't you?'

'If you feel like it.'

'Do you remember the stories "Salt" and "A Letter"?'

'Yes.'

'What do you think of them?'

'They're not my favorites. But I plan to use them in the film. Balmachev throwing the peasant woman from the moving train and then shooting her – it makes for a scene of great drama. Simeon Kurdiukov killing his own father in front of the regiment, to avenge the death of his brother, is also very interesting.'

'I don't think interesting is the correct word to describe that tragic narrative. What makes the story fascinating is not its brutality. It's the way it's told by Vassili Kurdiukov, the youngest brother spared from the tragedy, in a letter to his mother. Take that into consideration when you make your film. You can read about such things in the newspapers – fathers killing sons and vice versa – but it's nothing more than a sordid news item to be forgotten. As Babel described it, the Kurdiukovs killing each other is not an item in the newspaper. A little more,' Gurian said, showing me his glass.

'These two stories and "The Death of Dolguchov" were Babel's favorites.' His voice was now a murmur. 'Babel said that only in 1923 did he succeed in learning how to express his thoughts. "My literary career started at the beginning of 1924," he said. It was in 1924 that he published these three stories in Mayakovsky's magazine, *Lef.*'

Gurian, who had been sitting up in bed, lay back, murmuring something and clutching the glass.

'What?' I asked, bending over him.

'Art makes people see things better,' he repeated. His voice was very weak. I brought my chair closer to the bed.

He closed his eyes. His thin and pallid face was filled with sadness. His eyes still shut, he said, 'I have a theory, which I'll leave for some future discussion, since I'm very tired today. I'll just mention it.'

He stopped talking. I thought he was sleeping and rose carefully from the chair.

'I believe,' Gurian said, opening his eyes, 'that if Babel hadn't been killed, he would have committed suicide, like Mayakovsky.'

He closed his eyes again.

'I'll come back tomorrow.'

'Can you leave the bottle?'

I took the bottle with me.

The traffic was jammed, thanks to Carnival, and it took me a long time to get to Negromonte's house.

For the first time I saw him without make-up. His face was pale and wrinkled. He seemed to have overcome the suffering of the night before.

'For me?' he said, taking the bottle from my hand. 'Scotch! Thank you, dear. Oh, merciful heavens! It's so good when you meet an intelligent and sensitive person!'

'Are you all right?'

'I didn't let it get to me. You have to be strong, not let things get you down, not get yourself worked up over the same old worries. Life really is to be lived. I'm not going to let those bastards defeat me. Would you like something to drink? There's whiskey, vodka, some nice cold beer. I can't drink very much because tonight I'm going to the Gay Gala dance. Want to see my costume? No, I won't show it to you, I'm embarrassed. I'll get the drinkies, just a moment.'

Negromonte left the room. There was a color television set showing scenes of a samba school parading, without sound.

'I brought vodka. I feel like trying that Scotch you brought. Just the tiniest bit; I can't drink much because of the dance.'

He drank quickly.

'What about Diderot?'

'Don't mention that scum to me. It's enough to make me lose my hard-on.'

'You said you had something terrible to tell.'

'I don't want to talk about that piece of shit. I want to show you my costume.' Negromonte's speech was becoming imprecise. He was rapidly getting drunk.

'First tell me that terrible thing about Diderot, then show me your costume.'

'I'm embarrassed to show you my costume. You're so straight . . .'

'But I want to see your costume.'

'Really and truly?'

'Really and truly. But first tell me the terrible thing about Diderot.'

'And then you'll take a look at my costume?'

'Yes, afterwards.'

'You'll show me wearing it in the film?'

'Yes.'

Before starting to talk about Diderot, he had two more large drinks.

'He's a killer.'

'Is that all?' I felt Negromonte had other things to tell.

'Is that all? You don't think that's enough?'

'You want to tell me other things. Go ahead, tell.'

'How do you know?'

'I know. Go ahead.'

'Then you'll look at my costume?'

'Yes.'

'Diderot works for a smuggler of precious stones, a pale and mysterious man named Alcobaça. They say he's extremely rich. But what thief doesn't get rich in this country? Know what they do to smuggle the stones?'

So that pale man was the leader of the gang. Alcobaça . . . A strange name . . .

'In the costumes,' continued Negromonte in a thick voice. 'The precious stones are encrusted in the costumes along with the worthless glass jewels. Angélica did the smuggling for Alcobaça and told me. She was a very close friend of mine.'

'Do you think they killed Angélica?'

'I don't want to talk about this anymore. Look, don't tell anyone what I've said to you.'

'Don't worry. Do you know if Alcobaça is his real name?'

'No one does. I don't think even Diderot knows.'

'Was he at the pageant? Alcobaça?'

'I don't know. Now sit there nice and quiet and I'll show you my costume.'

He staggered off.

While Negromonte was out of the room I thought about Kurdiukov whipping his own father, who asks for no clemency, in full view of the Cossacks of the regiment standing at attention as was military custom. It would make a good scene.

Finally Negromonte returned. Through the veil covering his face I could see he was carefully made up. He wore a

diadem on his head, an embroidered lamé jacket, transparent
bouffant pants and sequined panties.

'The Favorite Odalisque in the Sultan's Harem! Do you
like it?'

'It's very pretty.'

'Are you leaving already?'

'I have an appointment,' I said, already at the door, looking
at my watch.

'Are you angry with me?'

'No, of course not. I'll go to your pageant next year, and
I hope you win first prize.'

'Next year? What about the film?'

'I'll phone you later about the film.'

He held me by the arm. 'You're my friend, aren't you?
My god, I need a friend so badly!'

'Mildred is your friend. I have to go, Negromonte, I
really do.'

I left, unhappy at having been so duplicitous with someone
as vulnerable as Negromonte. I called Liliana from the first
public phone I saw.

'Can I come round?'

I hailed a cab. When we got to Barata Ribeiro Street, the
traffic slowed to a crawl.

'It's those Carnival groups,' the driver said ill-humouredly.
'The sons of bitches like to parade down the busy streets . . .
Everybody else, the ones who're workin', fuck 'em . . . This
country is shit . . . There's no order anymore, it's chaos . . .
All anybody thinks about is sex . . . Did you see the Carnival
dances on television yesterday? You see the guy eatin' a
woman? On television! Can you imagine somethin' like
that? What about the families, at home? Television comes
into people's homes.'

'Television shows worse things,' I said.

'Worse than some guy eatin' a pussy?' he shouted angrily. 'And what about all them faggots sayin' dirty words?' He looked at me in the rear-view mirror. 'You got a family?'

'No.'

'So that's why you don't give a shit. I'd like to see how you'd feel if you had daughters, like I do.'

The rest of the trip passed in silence. From time to time the driver looked at me in the mirror and hit the dashboard and steering wheel with his fist.

Liliana opened the door and said, 'You're about to see something no man has ever seen before.'

I surveyed the living room.

'Look at me,' Liliana said, closing the door, 'at me.'

'I'm looking.' I saw a twenty-year-old girl, pretty, wearing linen shorts that displayed legs so lovely that I was moved despite everything that had happened, a thin cotton blouse that emphasized her pointed breasts – I suddenly thought of the phrase in Godard's film *Détective*, '*Ah! Les poitrines des jeunes filles*' – and a scarf on her head. 'I don't see anything,' I said.

'You will now,' she said, removing the scarf.

I still didn't see anything, except her red hair curled up in a plethora of rollers.

'The rollers! The rollers!' she said.

'I was just with a pathetic type who made me realize I don't have any friends.'

'What about your brother?'

'He's not my friend.'

'And the guys who worked with you?'

'They weren't anything.'

'Ruth?'

'I don't want to talk about Ruth.'

'What about me? Am I your friend?'

'I don't know. There's something between us. But we're not friends. I hate you.'

'I know why you think you hate me,' Liliana said.

'I didn't come here to talk about that.'

'I don't want to talk about it either. At least not now,' Liliana said. 'Let's talk about friendship . . . between men. Tell me about your pathetic friend.'

'He's not my friend. He's a person who desperately needs friends.'

'Come and tell me the story while I take out my rollers,' she said, as I followed her to the bedroom. 'There's not a hairdresser's open today and I'm going to the dance at the Scala.'

Liliana sat down at the vanity unit in the bedroom and slowly began to remove the rollers while looking ecstatically at her face reflected in the mirror. Nothing existed for her at that moment beyond her own image.

Ruth had black hair; Liliana, red. Ruth was shy, reserved, sensitive. Liliana was aggressive, indecent, hard. Ruth had strong legs and breasts that were perhaps on the large side for a dancer. Liliana had long legs and small breasts. Ruth used to say that Liliana looked like 'a young boy'.

'What about the pleasures of sex?' Liliana asked as she took the rollers out.

'I'm not interested.'

'Oh really?' Liliana said, taking off her clothes. Her breasts had red nipples. 'What are you doing – exercises in asceticism? Masturbating? Or did you find yourself one of those would-be actresses who'll put out for any director to act in any film? Come on, lie down here with me.'

She turned out the light: Liliana always turned out the lights to make love. I could see her in the darkness, there on the bed beside me, glowing like incandescent iron.

'I want you to turn on the light; if you don't, I'm going. I want to see your red pussy.'

'You're crazy!'

I got out of bed. 'I'm serious.'

Liliana turned on the light.

'You're not right in the head; you never talked that way to me before,' she said. 'I don't know why I do what you tell me to.'

I opened Liliana's legs and looked. Her scarlet pussy was damp and glittering, as if it were bleeding, not blood but nail polish.

'Now turn over.'

Delicately I opened the two firm gluteus hemispheres of Liliana's muscular ass – her buttocks were separate, like a dancer's – and contemplated the small pink orifice, which seemed to contract before my gaze.

'This is giving me a funny sensation,' she said. 'I think I'm getting hot.'

Afterward Liliana asked whether I wanted to go with her to the dance at the Scala. No.

'Will you wait for me to return? Wasn't it good?'

'I have things to do,' I said, beginning to get dressed.

'At night? Are you going to work on that script? I don't know how I can be so hot for a man like you.'

I felt unhappy, sorry I had gone to bed with her.

'Speaking of scripts,' Liliana continued, 'the other day I saw that guy in the raincoat again. The one who was watching your house, remember, and made you paranoid?'

'Was he following you?'

'I don't know. I don't think so. He was standing at the window of a bookstore. A guy who stands looking at a window filled with books can't be all that bad, can he?'

'Where was it?'

'At that bookstore near here.'

'I don't like this.'

Liliana's costume was discreet and pretty. The Scala ball

would be full of nude women. Liliana knew that modesty would attract more attention than nudity.

I went with her to the door of the Scala. There was a crowd of nincompoops watching the merrymakers as they went into the dance.

'This mulatto rabble irritates me,' Liliana said, making her way through the onlookers. We finally arrived at the place where a triage was made of invited guests. After showing her invitation, Liliana went up a set of stairs to a ramp that led to the ballrooms.

Liliana crossed the bridge built especially for Carnival, her red hair shining under the strong light of the reflectors.

I walked toward Ataulfo de Paiva. The street had become dark and deserted. Then I remembered the box of stones in my pocket. I felt like being somewhere safe, reading Babel.

I took a taxi to the hospital and I walked confidently past the man at the desk. 'Good evening,' I said, as if I had the right to enter at that hour. 'Good evening,' he replied. I went up to Gurian's floor. The corridors were in half-shadow. I entered his room cautiously, not wanting to wake him.

Gurian was sitting up in bed watching television.

'Sarah brought me the television,' he said. 'I was watching the samba school parades. It's an exciting thing – for an hour. After that it's boring. It reminds me of a large fire. I love fires. At the start a big fire fascinates me, amazes me, but after a time – fires and samba school parades take a long time to end – all I feel is boredom. The fires that had the greatest effect on me were the Andraus and the Joelma – did you know I caught a plane and went to São Paulo to see the cinders of both?' He laughed. 'They don't make fires like they used to. Would you please turn off the television?'

I turned it off.

'Don't you want to sleep?' I asked.

'I slept a lot today.'

'I have here in my pocket a box full of precious stones which belonged to a woman who was murdered. My apartment was broken into and they killed the doorman; a sinister man in a raincoat is following me, but none of that is what I'm thinking about.'

'What are you thinking about?'

'About a writer considering himself a master of silence.'

'Do you want to talk about him?'

'Yes.'

Gurian closed his eyes, remembering. His eyelids were turning black.

'Someone named Konstanin Fedin wrote Gorky a letter in 1924 saying, "Everyone here in Moscow is ecstatic over this fellow called Babel." Moscow had become the center of Soviet literary life. The rivalries and struggles among the various groups were tremendous. Babel's stories were the subject of controversy and debate. General Budenny had stated that he considered injurious the portrait that Babel had made of "his men". There's a letter from Babel, written when he was on the Polish campaign, in which he speaks of the despair he felt because of "the cruel ferocity that never stops for a single minute . . . I wasn't made for this task of destruction." Babel says further in this letter that it was difficult for him to forget the past, which might be bad but it had the aroma of poetry as the hive had the aroma of honey. "Some will make the Revolution, and so what? I, I will do the marginal things, that which goes deeper." This and other statements – "I am the master of silence" – and his way of looking at the Revolution were discussed in the meetings. In a letter to his sister Babel said, "Like all in my profession, I feel oppressed by the conditions of our work in Moscow." And he added a phrase unforgivable in those times: "We are being cooked over a slow flame in an atmosphere without art and without creative freedom." In November 1925 Babel got a visa for France. He wanted to free himself, in what order of priority I don't know, from family, his country, the bureaucrats, the cold (he was asthmatic), the publishers. He should have stayed in Paris. An American once said that a true artist hates the country in which he was born. Imagine him living under the dominion of Stalin.'

Gurian paused and looked at me with his small, gray, moist eyes. 'You must be thinking that I'm a reactionary old man trying to denigrate one of the greatest revolutions ever achieved by humanity, right?'

'I know your history,' I said. 'You can be accused of everything, but not of being a reactionary.'

'It's a catastrophic error to suppose that to consolidate a revolution it's necessary to take away the freedom of artists. The Soviets committed that error and paid dearly, very dearly, for it.'

'How did Babel live? Did he have any money?'

'No, he didn't. That's why he decided to write film scripts. The first he wrote was *Benya Krik* based on his Odessa stories.'

Faulkner wrote the scripts for *The Road to Glory, To Have and Have Not, The Big Sleep* and *Land of the Pharaohs* to make money. All these scripts were bad. Fitzgerald was a failure as a scriptwriter. Were good authors always bad scriptwriters? Chandler wrote two good scripts, *Double Indemnity* and *Strangers on a Train,* but there are some doubts as to whether he was a great writer like Faulkner. Kennedy's scripts – *Cotton Club* and *Ironweed* – added little to his work. I would have to take another look at *Hiroshima Mon Amour* and *Moderato Cantabile* to know where to put Duras. I'd also have to re-evaluate *L'Année Dernière à Marienbad* and the application to cinema of Robbe-Grillet's *choisme* thesis. What about Peter Handke? So much to reassess.

'Maybe great fiction writers can't make it as good script-writers,' I said after these thoughts.

'I don't think they actually filmed that script in which the Jewish bandit Benya Krik is the main character,' Gurian said. 'If they did film it, it couldn't have been all that great.'

Gurian then began a long, digressive dissertation on the inferiority of film compared to literature, to which I listened patiently.

At the first opportunity – a coughing fit of Gurian's – I said, 'Conrad states in the preface to *The Nigger of the Narcissus,* "My task is to make you hear, to make you feel and above all to make you see; that is all, and is everything." Don't you think that with this phrase the writer is confessing to the limitations of literature? Conrad would like to make the reader *see,* but the one who does that is the film director.'

'Don't be so simplistic,' Gurian said. 'Conrad's problem was wanting to explain his work in long and boring prefaces like the one you cited. The artist doesn't have to explain his work. Conrad should have ended like this: ". . . and above all to make you think". That's what is *everything,* really. The evil of our world is that people think less and less. In any case, Conrad when he speaks of "seeing" isn't referring to the perception of light and movement picked up by the eye; he doesn't wish to transform the reader into a mere spectator.'

Gurian intercut this speech with furious coughing bouts.

Day was beginning to break; a changing light illuminated the lividness of Gurian's face.

'Are you feeling all right?'

'You're always asking me that. If I were feeling all right I wouldn't be here. There are times when I question your intelligence.' Gurian paused. 'No, no, you're very intelligent. What irritates me about you – rarely, but then again we see each other very little – is your ignorance.'

The second person to call me ignorant in less than twenty-four hours.

'When I'm your age I'll be as wise as you.'

'I doubt it. You waste a lot of time on trifles.'

'Like what, for example?'

'Women. You're always involved with two or three women. Even one is bad enough for a man seeking wisdom, knowledge. Just imagine three. Tell me about the stones.'

'Stones?'

'You said you had a small box of precious stones in your pocket. We Jews are crazy about precious stones. Show them to me.'

I handed the box to Gurian. He opened it and took out a stone, which he held against the morning light to examine.

'This undulating band ... Chatoyance ... The French invented the word, but it was surely a Jew who first applied it to a precious stone ... A woman was killed because of these stones ... What woman? One of yours?'

'No.'

'Is your life in danger?'

'I don't know. Maybe. I can run away, go to Germany. I was invited to make a film in Germany.'

'But if you run away you'll lose all that emotion you're feeling, won't you? Living dangerously is fascinating.'

'I need to hide these stones. At my place it's impossible. I thought of a bank safe-deposit box, but with Carnival everything's closed. There are only three people who can keep them for me – you, my brother and a woman friend. I would prefer it to be you. At your apartment. It's just for a few days.'

# 8

A car was following my taxi on the way to Gurian's apartment. I had driven past my apartment first, where I planned to pick up a checkbook because I was running out of cash, and had seen a suspicious-looking car outside. I had told the driver to keep going.

Now I saw that the car, with only one occupant, was following me. Could it be the man in the raincoat?

'Head toward the bus station,' I told the driver.

I had seen too many detective films in my life not to know how to get away from someone following me. At the station I'd shake off whoever was on my tail.

When I stopped the cab, the pursuing car went past. It was the man in the raincoat. He looked at me pointedly, but phlegmatically. I felt he was a dangerous man, cruel, a cold hunter. He went toward the parking area.

I quickly caught another taxi and headed away from the station.

In any case, I went past the door of Gurian's building twice, to make sure I wasn't being followed. When I entered his apartment I imagined the following pessimistic scenario: the man in the raincoat might have found the driver who took me to the bus station and gleaned the information that

I had been to the hospital. Question: by going to the hospital could the man in the raincoat find out I had been there to visit Gurian? Answer: impossible; no one had seen me enter or leave the old professor's room.

I stood in the middle of the living room with its book-lined walls. Those disordered, dusty bookcases were the best place to hide the stones. I looked for a book, among the thousands, whose title was easy to remember. I chose the *Mahabharata*. After all, India was a country where there were many precious stones.

After paying the taxi driver I didn't even have enough money for a bus. José could lend me some. Gurian's apartment was in the Flamengo district and José's house was in Ipanema, a long walk.

Before leaving I called José.

Gislaine answered. 'He's with the people from the Congregation of Evangelical Churches, a very important meeting. He can't talk at the moment.'

'On Carnival Tuesday?'

'A very appropriate day for deep reflection,' Gislaine said in an evangelical tone.

'Tell him I'm coming round and to wait for me.'

When I left I noticed the box was still in my pocket. I must have been really confused to act in such a manner, since I had gone to Gurian's place specifically to hide it.

It took me nearly three hours to walk those six miles between Gurian's apartment and José's house. There were many streets heavy with traffic and a tunnel to cross. Of course I could have asked a passer-by for money 'to complete the fare' – people making such requests were common enough but I didn't have the courage.

The door was opened by a uniformed servant. Gislaine designed the uniforms of all of them – chambermaids, butlers, gardeners, chauffeurs. She had also done the decorating of the house, after taking a six-week course in interior design.

I was led by the butler to the library. There was a great difference between José's library and Gurian's, which I had just left. José's was meticulously arranged and catalogued by a librarian who was a member of the Evangelical Church of Jesus Savior of Souls. One of the bookcases held wooden drawers full of catalog cards. I opened one of the drawers, but before I could read the first card Gislaine came in, followed by a servant carrying a tray with cups of coffee.

'José asked you to wait. You take your coffee with sugar, don't you? I don't know why you don't put on weight,' she said, pouring sugar into my cup and artificial sweetener into hers, while the prim and reverent maid held the tray. Gislaine probably gave the servants rigorous etiquette lessons. I vaguely recalled her saying that she had taken a course in etiquette, probably at the same school where she'd studied interior design.

I never knew what to talk about with Gislaine. It was torture to be alone with her.

'Your servant looks like a real English maid,' I said.

'You should see what they look like when they come here,' Gislaine replied with a sigh, 'untrained and tacky, not knowing a thing; it's a horrendous job to bring them up to scratch. One even asked me, "Why so many different glasses, ma'am?"' Another sigh. 'It's agony ...' Pause. 'Don't you want to have a seat? José may be a while.'

I sat down, hoping she would leave. But she sat down in an armchair beside me, her legs crossed, hands in her lap. The Gislaine who had been a waitress in a luncheonette was no more; she had left no trace, remnant, vestige or clue. A marvel.

'I'm taking a course in History of Art,' she said, 'but unfortunately it doesn't include film. Film can be considered an art, can't it?'

'The Americans think it's an industry.'

'An industry of dreams,' she said, pleased with herself. I looked closely at her face, her carefully arranged hair, the fine gold chain around her neck. She seemed like one of those female poodles trained to display special grooming.

Finally, José arrived.

'I was in a very important meeting. The political and social situation in Brazil demands responsible action by all. We evangelists cannot refuse to make our contribution to the enhancement of democratic institutions.'

'Conditions aren't yet right for someone from your group to run for president . . .'

'We have much to give,' he said evasively.

'Great, because I came to ask for money.'

José put his hand in his pocket and took out a checkbook. 'How much?'

'I want cash.'

'I don't believe I have much cash in the house.'

'I'll take whatever you can let me have.'

'I have some,' Gislaine said. 'We women always like to have money on us,' she added, smiling. I noticed her teeth were different, better looking than before.

'I really liked your film,' José said. 'It was shown at the meeting. There was a suggestion, accepted unanimously, that you make a film for the Congregation. A film about all the evangelical churches in our Congregation. Isn't it an interesting challenge?'

'We'll talk about it later.'

Gislaine brought a wad of money, which I placed in my pocket without counting.

'I'll pay you back when I return,' I said.

'Give some thought to the new film,' José said.

I caught a cab and went to Liliana's apartment.

She opened the door wearing a short silk nightgown. There wasn't an excess ounce on her body.

'I just woke up,' she said.

How was it that Liliana could wake up so fresh, so desirable? I felt like sucking her blood-red breasts.

'I like you so much,' Liliana said, as if she had read my thoughts. 'It'd be so nice if we never fought again.'

I grabbed her by the hair, delicately, and took her to the bedroom.

'You can hit me if you want to,' Liliana said.

'I want to talk about Ruth,' Liliana said, afterward.

I climbed out of bed. 'No.'

I got my clothes and went to dress in the living room.

Liliana came after me.

'We have to talk about Ruth. You've never let me tell my side of the story.'

'No,' I said.

'I was in love with Ruth, have you forgotten that already?' Liliana said.

Suddenly she began to cry. I had never seen her cry, not even in adolescence.

'It was me who introduced you to her,' Liliana said. 'We loved each other, she and I. It was you who intruded into our lives and caused all that unhappiness.'

I felt as if I were going to faint, the same sensation as the first time I jumped from a diving platform – those dizzying seconds in free fall – the same sensation as when I woke up one day with pseudo-Ménière's syndrome.

'Ruth knew I was going to bed with you. I told her,' Liliana said. 'She never cared. All she asked was that I not tell you that she knew.'

'Don't say anything else,' I asked. 'Please.'

'I hate to cry,' Liliana said, wiping the tears with her forearm.

'Put on some clothes,' I said.

When Liliana returned, wearing the short nightgown, I took the box of stones from my pocket.

'Remember that woman who was at my apartment? Angélica, the one who was killed? The one with the box of precious stones?'

Liliana opened the box. 'Are they real?'

'Yes.'

'Aren't you going to return them?'

'Return them – who to? Angélica has no relatives. The gems were going to be smuggled.'

'The man in the raincoat! He's after them!'

'That's likely. Angélica worked for a gang of smugglers. Every year she took part in pageants abroad and took the stones hidden in her costumes.'

'How is it you know so much?'

I told her of my conversation with Negromonte.

'If I were you I'd hand the stones over to the police,' Liliana said.

'With the money I can get from selling them, I can make a film. It's been two years since I did anything.'

'Aren't you going to make a film in Germany?'

'I don't know. I'm thinking of selling Angélica Maldonado's stones. I already said she has no family. My act may be criminal from a legal standpoint, but it's not morally reprehensible. Or do you think Alcobaça is their legitimate owner?'

'You're rationalizing.'

'I'm going to sell the stones to Maurício, that friend of mine who's a jewel merchant. All of them or enough to finance the film. I'll write, produce and direct it. Why go to Berlin? I don't need either Dietrich or Dr Plessner; I can make *Red Cavalry* here. Why not? Gurian is Russian. He can be my consultant; he knows Babel better than anyone. Horses and riders aren't in short supply in Brazil. I'll make a version in English, for the international market, and another in Portuguese. If they give me a hard time I'll just make the English version.'

'I think all that's really dishonest.'

'Choose the prettiest stone for yourself.'

'Are you trying to bribe me?'

'Yes. Choose the three prettiest stones for yourself.'

Liliana re-examined the stones. While she did so, I imagined what the film would be like. I thought about the alternatives – I could film in Europe, a co-production in Poland, for example, or in Hungary; besides the technicians, they would provide extras and horses and a supporting player or two. It would be cheaper than in Brazil. Poland was a good idea, as long as they didn't give me cavalryman extras like those Wajda used in *Chroniques des Événements Amoureux* (I had seen the film in Paris, dubbed in French). Cossacks were men. In the middle of these fantasies – I had started on the casting – I was interrupted by Liliana.

'I want these. One of each color.' Pause. 'Isn't this terribly dishonest?' Another pause, waiting for my reaction. 'Shit! Of course it's dishonest. I don't want them.'

'You can throw them away if you don't want them.'

'If you screw me again, I'll take them.'

I remained silent.

In reality, going to bed with Liliana had been the only good thing that had happened to me in the last few days. Fornication – the poets are always right: 'That's all the facts when you come to brass tacks.'

'Come on, let's fool around,' Liliana said.

We spent the day in bed, until we got bored. Exhausted, actually.

'If I tell you I love you will it bother you very much?' Liliana asked. Her body was covered with sweat.

'Yes. Our relationship is merely ... uh, animalistic. It contains no noble sentiments.'

We took a shower together. She laughed and talked a lot. I neither laughed nor talked, but I wasn't unhappy.

'This animal here is hungry,' she said.

It was already dark when we went out to eat. We headed for a restaurant in Leblon.

'Do you have money? I hear it's expensive here,' Liliana said.

'I got some from my brother. I think it'll be enough.'

'Let me see.'

I slipped her the money under the table. Liliana covertly counted the bills, placing them afterward in her purse. 'It's not enough for French champagne,' she said.

We gave the waiter our order.

'Have you noticed that the things that most satisfy the spirit are physical in nature? Eating, loving, walking around ...' Liliana paused. She leaned her head forward. 'Don't look now,' she whispered in a frightened voice, 'but the man in the raincoat is sitting at the bar.'

Stupidly, I looked toward the bar. There he was, wearing the same raincoat, a drink in his hand. He made a cold gesture at me, as if offering a toast; his smile was cruel, emotionless.

'Why doesn't the creep ever take off the raincoat?' Liliana murmured. 'It's hot as blazes.'

'How did he find us?'

'He must be watching my apartment.'

'That guy is dangerous.'

'Are you afraid?'

'More or less. It's a horrible feeling to be followed by some-one who looks so sinister. He must have back-up outside.'

'You think he works for Alcobaça?'

'Probably. Know something? I have the box of gems in my pocket.'

'Are you crazy? Why didn't you leave them at home?'

'I don't know. I've fallen into the habit of carrying the box in my pocket.'

'We have to find a way to get out of here.'

With lowered voices we discussed how we could escape from the man in the raincoat and his likely henchmen. We'd have to call the police, but the police mustn't find out the truth. The truth, besides damaging me – after all, I had on me precious stones from a smuggler who had been murdered after going to my apartment – was hard to believe. 'Officer, that man over there is following me.' The only thing the policeman would have against the man in the raincoat was the raincoat being worn on a summer day without a sign of rain.

Ever since *La Sortie des Usines Lumière*, what situation had yet to be dealt with in film? I handed the box of gems to Liliana, who put it in her purse. Then she rose and went to the *maître d'*.

'The man who's with me at that table has a hidden weapon and said he was going to kill me,' Liliana said.

The *maître d'*, surprised, didn't know what to do. He didn't want a scene in his restaurant. 'Is he your husband?' he asked.

'No. Actually, I barely know him. He asked me to dinner and said he'll kill me if I don't go to a motel with him.'

'Why don't you go then?'

'Because I'm a respectable woman,' Liliana screamed. 'You think this is some kind of trick to get out of paying the bill? Take it,' she said, opening her purse and throwing at the *maître d'* the wad of bills that my brother had given me.

'Please, please, don't get excited,' said the *maître d'*, bending down to pick up the money. 'We'll work this out.'

At the bar, the man in the raincoat coldly observed the conversation between Liliana and the *maître d'*. In different circumstances I'd have asked the man to work in a film of mine. Since Widmark threw the paralyzed old lady down the stairs in *Kiss of Death* in 1947, I'd never seen a face as repugnant and terrifying as his.

'Please go back to your table and play for time while I call the police. We'll try to straighten this out without making a scene.' The *maître d'* had seen his share of films too.

Liliana came back.

'I think we've done it,' she said.

'Who directed *Kiss of Death* – Kubrick?' I asked.

'Hathaway. Kubrick directed *Killer's Kiss*, almost ten years later. What would you do without me?'

'I don't store trivia in my head.'

'You don't store anything in your head,' Liliana said.

'If I really had a weapon on me, I think I *would* kill you right now.'

'Go ahead, kill me!' Liliana shouted.

The diners at the next table looked curiously in our direction.

'Don't overdo it,' I said.

'Go ahead, kill me!' Liliana screamed again.

'Not so loud, you idiot,' I whispered. 'People know who I am.'

The *maître d'* approached, pale.

'Sir,' he said, frightened, 'would you kindly come with me for a moment?'

I followed him to the entrance of the restaurant. We went outside. Two policemen were waiting for me and I was searched.

'My wife is sick. She's paranoid. I don't mind going with

you to the precinct to clear this up. I have the prescription for her medicine here.' I rummaged through my pockets.

'Go and get the woman,' said one of the policemen.

The *maître d'* returned, accompanied by Liliana.

'He wants to kill me,' Liliana told the policeman.

'We're going to the precinct,' the policeman said, ushering us into the patrol car.

We sat wordlessly in the moving car. After a time, Liliana put her face in her hands and began to sob.

'Forgive me, darling, I don't know what came over me,' she said. 'Officer, my husband is the best man on the face of the earth, don't do this to him.'

'I'm not doing anything to your husband,' the policeman protested. 'You're the one who said he threatened you.'

'My husband is an angel, he didn't threaten anybody. He couldn't hurt a fly.'

'You need to get help,' the policeman said.

'I want to go home,' Liliana said, sobbing. A real ham. Only a couple of guys who never went to the movies would have bought her performance.

'Officer, do you go to the movies very often?' I asked.

'We're going to take you home,' he said, ignoring my question. 'What's your address?'

Which one – Liliana's apartment or mine? The man in the raincoat would find us at either place.

I gave him Gurian's address.

'Next time call a doctor,' the policeman said. 'There are some things the police can't settle.'

We went into the building.

'What the devil is this place?' Liliana asked.

'It belongs to a friend of mine who's in hospital. I have his key.'

'Let's go,' Liliana said when she saw that the police car had left.

'Go where?'

'To eat.'

'I don't have any money.'

'The *maître d'* returned the money I threw at him.'

'I don't want to go out again.'

I walked toward the elevator, which had stopped at ground-floor level. We went up.

'This place looks like a rat's nest,' Liliana said after we had entered Gurian's apartment. She went to the kitchen and I went to the library.

'Doesn't the man eat?' Liliana yelled from the kitchen.

'He just drinks,' I replied.

Liliana came back into the living room.

'You know the fridge is empty? I mean, there's a bottle of cheap vodka and a jar of orange jelly. In the pantry there's no rice, eggs, bread, macaroni, cheese, crackers, nothing. Not even a jar of heart-of-palms! We're going to starve to death.' She kicked a book lying on the floor. 'Jesus, so many books!'

'Don't do that,' I said, picking up the book and putting it on the table. 'Gurian places great value on his books.'

'When I'm hungry I don't fuck!'

'Stop pretending you're vulgar.'

'I am vulgar,' Liliana shouted. 'When I'm hungry I don't fuck!'

'Fine. I don't want anything from you anyway,' I answered as I looked for the *Mahabharata* in the bookcase.

'You conceited clown. Call a restaurant here in Flamengo and order us two steaks with fries.'

I found the book. Liliana took it from my hand.

'What book is this?'

'The kind that girls like you never read. I'm going to put the box of stones behind it.'

'There are times when the most interesting book of all is the phone book,' Liliana said, turning her back on me. She got the phone book. 'Let's see . . . restaurants . . . restaurants . . . I think this one's good . . .'

After phoning, Liliana went to take a shower while we waited for the food.

Within a short time she appeared, naked in the middle of the living room, a towel in her hand. Water dripped from her wet body.

'Does that friend of yours have some kind of skin disease? Or AIDS?'

'He's a wise, elderly man. His only disease is old age.'

The food arrived, packed in aluminium containers, along with a bottle of wine.

Liliana ate, licking her lips like a cat. When we had finished she said, 'Now I'm going to seduce you.'

I waited.

'The *Mahabharata*,' Liliana said, 'which means "great king Bharata", is one of the two great epic poems of India. The other is the *Ramayana*. They were written in Sanskrit, twelve hundred years before Christ. It's a story about the futility of war. You want more or do you already have a hard-on?'

As I caressed Liliana's naked body, her smooth, soft skin, as I felt her bones, her flesh, her warmth, her life, I was overwhelmed by great joy, a strange happiness, mixed with a kind of vertigo that for a few moments I thought might be the precursor to pseudo-Ménière's syndrome. I didn't hate Liliana anymore; maybe I never had hated her. I gave myself to that simple and primal fruition, accepting the pure contentment that she brought.

# 9

Dream. My bones ache. I'm at home alone. I'm in a large city, waiting for a letter, a phone call. I know no one in the city. I go out into a cold fog and buy two cans of a dark substance, a bunch of herbs, a bit of cheese and bread. It's already night. Along with the herbs, a magazine with naked women. In the bathroom I choose the prettiest woman (there's something of the southern hemisphere in her face, or of the Orient, a face that defies classification – she has large eyes, she's decent); she has her back turned, kneeling, and in spite of her position the hairs of her pubis stand out in a dense, dark cluster. Her hair descends her naked back and now she's in profile. I masturbate looking at her ass, her long hair, her little-girl profile, but mainly I see nothing, for my mind, my desires, my hunger are far away, piercing the air from night to day. I lie down to wait for something, the light off. I'm tired, more from waiting than from anything else. From time to time my heart skips a beat. The doctor, beside me, says it's a common thing, but it still bothers me. Nothing happens. We're in a crematorium. They didn't want to let me in so I wouldn't mix the ashes of the dead. But the ashes are mine, I say. All right then. Flames envelop my body.

\*    \*    \*

I awoke and looked at my wristwatch: six o'clock. The room was illuminated by the light coming through the filthy white curtains. For the first time I noticed the bed where we lay, felt the hard mattress. Liliana, sleeping at my side, stripped of her defensive aggressiveness, seemed like a fragile, unprotected little girl. I kissed her lightly on the forehead. She didn't wake up.

I sat in one of the tattered armchairs in the living room. I needed to take another look at my plans. I reviewed the situation:

*a*) I had in my possession gems worth a fortune, which had come into my hands through the unfathomable workings of chance;

*b*) the gems belonged to a gang of smugglers of precious stones;

*c*) I had discovered the efficient method the gang used to smuggle the stones;

*d*) jewel smuggling was a big business involving millions of dollars about which little was said;

*e*) the smugglers, besides recovering the stones, surely wanted to kill me. The man in the raincoat was in charge of this and it had probably been he who had killed Angélica and the doorman;

*f*) in other words, even if I returned the stones it wouldn't appease the criminals, because I knew too much and had to be kept quiet.

What an ambiguous sensation of fear and euphoria, knowing that someone is out to kill you! It's good to have a real basis for your paranoia!

At this point, I began to construct a script. A man accidentally gets hold of some jewels resulting from a crime and is chased by a dangerous gang of badmen. The man being chased doesn't want to keep the jewels because he has no use for them (which wasn't exactly my case), but as long as he has them in his possession he'll be pursued by the villains. And since he *doesn't want the chase to end*, he has to provoke his pursuers, etc., etc.

Then I remembered Liliana. She too was in danger of being killed by the smugglers.

I woke her up.

'What time is it? Good god, that light! It must be the middle of the night!'

'It's eight am.'

'That *is* the middle of the night!'

I told her what was worrying me.

'That's the best proof that you're getting old,' she said. 'Afraid of ghosts.'

'OK, I'm getting old, I'm getting to be anything you like. But is the man in the raincoat a ghost? Is Alcobaça a ghost?'

'From what you told me, he looks like one.'

'Liliana, I have a suggestion. Let's take a trip. Here we're both at risk, our lives are in danger. I have an offer from Germany. We can spend a few months out of –'

'I'm not going to Germany,' she interrupted. 'Not West, not East. Neither of them.'

'If you don't want to go to Germany with me, go somewhere else in Europe: England, France, Spain, Portugal, Poland, Austria, Hungary. We'll meet someplace.'

'Why Hungary?'

'It's the land of István Szabo.'

'Are you the love of my life again?'

'I don't know,' I answered.

Liliana looked at me. Then: 'Do we have the money for that?'

'We have the stones, don't we? Besides that, the Germans are going to pay me.'

'And they have to pay well. There's not a director in all of

Germany as good as you. Wait: you told me yesterday that you were going to make a film here in Brazil with the money you got from the sale of the stones, and that you wanted nothing to do with Germany. You change your mind quickly.'

'Because I came to the conclusion that if we stay here the owners of the stones –'

'Owners! If the gems belong to somebody, return them and put an end to the matter.'

'We already talked about that. They know I found out about their scheme. I can't go up to the man in the raincoat and say, "Here, take your precious stones and rest assured that I'll say nothing to the police about the method you've been using to smuggle them abroad." They wouldn't believe me. If I return the jewels I'm a dead man.'

'Also if you don't return them.'

'That's right. Pretty soon they're going to come to the conclusion that it's better to get rid of me – get rid of both of us – once and for all, even without getting the stones.'

'How are you going to sell the gems?'

'Didn't I mention that my friend Maurício is a jewel merchant? He said they're worth a small fortune.'

Liliana remained quiet for a long time, pensive.

'I think I'll go to Paris. I even know where I'll stay, at the Le Bréa, a small, modest, very nice hotel . . . I like Montparnasse. Rue Bréa has a statue of Balzac done by Rodin, where the street begins. The Jardin du Luxembourg is nearby, along with La Coupole and –'

Liliana stopped. I knew what she had left unsaid. It was in that hotel that she and Ruth had stayed when they had gone to Paris together and discovered that they loved each other. What was Liliana expecting from that nostalgic and melancholy pilgrimage? I lacked the courage to ask. I preferred not to remember Ruth.

Liliana lit a cigarette, leaned her head back against the worn armchair and fell silent, her eyes closed.

I got the phone book and called Maurício.

'Where've you been?' he asked. 'I called your apartment and no one answered. I was worried.'

'I'll explain later.'

'Has something happened?'

'I'll explain later. Look, I want to sell those gems.'

'Do you want to sell all of them?' he asked.

'No. I want to sell thirty thousand dollars' worth . . . Hold on.' I covered the mouthpiece. 'Liliana, Liliana!'

She opened her eyes. 'What?'

'You think thirty thousand dollars is enough for us to take on the trip?'

She shrugged her shoulders as if to say it had nothing to do with her, and closed her eyes again, after taking a long drag on her cigarette.

'Thirty thousand is enough,' I told Maurício.

'Come to my office tomorrow afternoon. Bring all the stones.'

I needed to pick up some clothes and my passport. But my apartment was under surveillance by the criminals, and probably Liliana's too.

'I have a friend who can do it for us,' Liliana said.

Liliana's friend showed up carrying toast, butter and English tea. She was a young Nisei named Mitiko.

'Are you from São Paulo?' I asked as we drank tea.

'I'm from Rio. Not all Nisei are from São Paulo.'

'Do you speak Japanese?'

'Not a word. At home only Portuguese is spoken. Daddy and Mom sometimes speak Japanese with each other. But very rarely. Are you directing a film? I loved *The Holy War*.'

'Let's get down to business,' Liliana said.

Mitiko noted down our addresses. We gave her our keys.
'You'll have to go in through the rear,' I said.

I explained to Mitiko where the things were that she should
bring me – the passport, Babel's book and my notes, and
a dark gray suit. Shirts, socks and underwear, toothbrush,
shaving items I could buy before the trip. 'The place is a
mess, don't be startled,' I warned.

Liliana told her where to find the things that Mitiko would
bring from her apartment.

'Is that man in the raincoat dangerous?'

'Yes. But don't worry. He doesn't know you. He's after us
for a reason I'd prefer you didn't know,' Liliana said.

'If anybody goes into my building with you, or Liliana's,
cover up by going to another floor.'

'When you're ready to leave there, phone for a taxi.' Liliana
gave part of my brother's money to Mitiko, who left immersed
in her role as a secret agent charged with a very important
mission. She was only eighteen.

I phoned Lufthansa and reserved my flight for Frankfurt
for the next day, in the evening. Because of the financial crisis
there were quite a few empty seats. I looked up Dietrich's
telephone number in my address book. I dialed the number,
thinking that I mustn't forget to reimburse Gurian for the
cost of the call.

'If everything goes well, I should leave tomorrow night on
the Lufthansa Rio – Frankfurt flight.'

Dietrich seemed excited at the news. He spoke rapidly, in
German. He quickly repeated in English what he had said:
'Plessner will be happy. He's anxiously awaiting you.'

'If you don't hear otherwise from me by tomorrow night,
it's because I'm on my way.'

'Have you thought about what we discussed?'

I didn't remember any longer what I had talked about
with him.

'We'll talk there. The day after tomorrow.'

Liliana had taken a book from the bookcase. Whenever I see someone reading, no matter where it is, I get very curious about what the book is. I've found myself in some embarrassing situations as a result. Liliana knew of my habit. When she saw me trying to make out the title printed on the book's spine – an old binding – she quickly covered the words with her hand.

'O Satan, *prends pitié de ma longue misère,*' she said.

I enjoyed reading Baudelaire, but I felt the sudden urge to get away at once, to not be in that room full of books, hiding from a criminal in a raincoat. I looked at Liliana's knee as she read *Les Fleurs du Mal,* thinking about Eric Rohmer and *Le Genou de Claire;* hell, all I could remember about the film was the title. How is it that a woman's knee can encompass so many promises, so many puzzles? – That cunt purple like a volcano – Ruth's sanitary napkin – Maybe I needed to listen to some music; where had Gurian hidden the Babel?

I remembered, shouting, as I walked about the living room: 'Liutov-Babel has to prove that – despite wearing glasses, despite knowing how to read and write – he's a true Cossack. Listen, listen: Liutov has just arrived at the lodgings of the Sixth Division, an old woman's house occupied by the Cossacks. Liutov's suitcase is thrown into the middle of the courtyard by a Cossack who insults him. He picks up the clothes and the manuscripts that fell out of the suitcase and goes to a corner of the courtyard, where he reads in *Pravda* a speech by Lenin at the Second Comintern congress. Then he gets hungry. He searches out the old woman who owns the house and says he needs something to eat. The woman, after taking a long look at him, replies that she feels like hanging herself. Liutov places his hand on the woman's chest, gives her a brutal shove, and says he doesn't owe her any explanations. He looks about and sees a sword. He also sees a goose, which he seizes and whose head he crushes with the heel of his boot, causing the animal's gray matter to gush out as it lies in the manure, its wings flapping. Liutov then plunges the sword into the bird's breast and hoists it. "Prepare this goose for me, woman," he orders.'

'Why are you yelling at me with your eyes bulging? What happened? Did you flip out?' Liliana said.

'It's a passage from my film.'

'The guy wins the respect of his fellows because he killed a goose? Is that the significance of the scene?' Liliana asked. 'Ah, you little boys!'

'Liutov is the one who gains his self-respect because of it. Still, immediately afterward, as he cleans his sword in the sand, he feels depressed. Nevertheless, killing the goose gives him the courage to go and have some collard soup and eat pork with the Cossacks until the goose is ready. Then he reads Lenin's speech to the soldiers, elated "because he has discovered the secret curve of Lenin's straight line".'

'"Secret curve of the straight line"?'

'At times I think this must be one of Babel's phrases that ended up causing him problems. Then all the Cossacks lie down in the barn to sleep, under a wooden roof full of holes through which the stars appear, warming one another by intertwining their legs. Liutov dreams, and in his dream he sees women. But his heart, stained by the shedding of blood, "creaked and overflowed".'

'Overflowed with what?' Liliana asked.

'Well, he felt a kind of euphoria . . .'

'The euphoria men always feel when they commit an act of violence? . . . And what about those intertwined legs? Hmm . . . Did such things go on among Cossacks too?'

The telephone rang, startling us. It rang again.

'You'd better answer,' Liliana said.

'Hello?'

'Who's speaking?' a woman's voice asked.

'Who do you want to speak to?'

'It's Mitiko. I'm here at your apartment . . .' She lowered her voice and I couldn't understand the rest.

'Can you talk a little louder?'

'What's the guy in the raincoat look like?' Mitiko asked, still whispering.

'He wears a raincoat.'

'I know that. Is he tall, husky, mean-looking?'

'Yes.'

'He's outside talking to the cab driver that I called.'

'You can talk louder. I don't think the man can hear what you say from down there. Are you frightened?'

'No. But I'm afraid he'll follow my taxi.'

'Do this: take the taxi and go to Santos Dumont Airport. When you get there, go to the Rio–São Paulo shuttle counter and pretend to get on board. I don't think the man in the raincoat will follow you. If he does, I guarantee he won't wait for you to board the plane. Did anyone see you go into the apartment?'

'No.'

'If I make a detective film someday, I'll give you the leading role.'

'You mean it?'

Liliana took the telephone from my hand.

'Did you get my things yet? No? Then let's leave it till later. At the airport get a different cab – a different one, understand? – and come here.'

Liliana hung up and looked at me with an ironic smile.

'Will you put me in your detective film too?'

She picked up her purse and took out a small paper package, the three gems she had chosen.

'I don't want this.'

'Because I'm a thief, right?'

'Right,' she said.

Liliana was correct. 'It's too late now,' I said.

'It's never too late.'

'When you get serious you manage to become even more unbearable . . . I prefer the sarcastic Liliana.'

'Did you ever do this before?'

'Never.'

'You're only now starting out in your criminal career?'

'Do you know what'll happen if I turn the stones over to the police? The money will go to this corrupt administration.'

'That's the justification of every tax evader, smuggler, thief and forger in the country. If the money goes to the corrupt, why shouldn't I become corrupt? Isn't that how all of you think?'

'You know very well I never –'

'If you don't want to give them back, throw them in the sea. What you can't do is keep them. You can throw them in Rodrigo de Freitas Lake, whose muddy bottom will conceal the stones until a generation more –'

'More what? More simian? Every generation that comes along is worse than the one before.'

This idiotic conversation was going nowhere. I was unwilling to get rid of the stones. It was a good thing that Mitiko appeared and we had to change the subject.

Mitiko arrived with Ruth's suitcase. Inside were my suit, the passport, Babel's book and my notes.

'What about the things that were in here?'

'There wasn't anything inside. There was a book, a vial of perfume, a packet of Modess, some clothes.'

'You didn't throw out the packet of Modess, did you?'

'No. Everything's back there.'

'What do you want a packet of sanitary napkins for?' Liliana asked.

(No, anything but talk about Ruth!)

'Your apartment is really a mess; what happened?' Mitiko said.

'I moved there a few days ago and didn't have the patience to straighten it up.'

'Would you like me to do it while you're away?'

'I think it's dangerous,' Liliana said.

'I'll tidy it up for you.'

'I don't want to put you to any trouble.'

'It's dangerous. I'm telling you it's dangerous.'

'It's no trouble. Would you mind if I stayed there for a while? I'm about to be evicted from the apartment where I live.'

'You can stay at my apartment; I'm going to travel too,' Liliana said, irritated. 'Leave the apartment messy. It's about time he learned to keep his place in order. Enough of some woman always taking care of his things.'

'I thought –' Mitiko said.

'You didn't think anything,' Liliana said. 'Give him back his key.'

Annoyed, Mitiko handed me the key.

'Later we'll come to an agreement,' Liliana said sweetly, tweaking Mitiko's cheek.

'I don't know what women see in you,' Liliana told me.

I waited for the dream to come. I'm on a street with dark air (the mixture of gases that we breathe – nitrogen, oxygen, hydrogen, helium, neon – is invisible, but I know that this air is dark) despite its being daytime. The fog clouds everything like translucent smoked glass and in the street are walls filled with books. I don't see the street, or the books, or the air that envelops the street in a blanket of transparent shadow, but I know, I know I am watched with suspicion by the passers-by, I know I feel a ravenous weariness and I know I hear barking. But it's not dogs that are barking; it's two-legged animals, their eyes covered with mud, or chocolate, or excrement.

I recognize the smells of the city and of women. A clear light transfixes me like a death ray and I disappear. I hear someone say, a metallic voice from a loudspeaker, 'For me, poetry comes out in urine. Do you know how many years I've been writing poetry? You'd be surprised. While others worked to buy a house, I worked at poetry. I didn't buy a house. See that stain up there on the wall? Good, now let's see who can piss on it for, say, five seconds.'

Liliana and I left the apartment together. Mitiko was sleeping on the sofa in the living room. I left a note telling her to close the door when she departed.

'Be careful,' I said in the street before we went our separate ways.

'I'm not a dummy like you. Don't worry.'

We agreed to meet in a restaurant at two pm.

First, still in Gurian's apartment, I picked out the same three stones I had taken to Maurício's office earlier. That is to say those that looked the most like them, or at least the same color.

Once again I confronted all the security measures of Maurício's office.

Finally, he appeared.

'Why don't you tell me what's going on? We go back a long way.'

'Later I'll tell you.' I gave him the three stones I had set aside.

'Are these the gems I examined before?'

'Yes.'

'The others were more valuable.' He stared at me in his new inquisitive way.

'These aren't worth thirty thousand?' I asked.

He laughed. 'This one is worth over thirty thousand by itself.' He paused. 'All told, how many gems do you have?'

'Half a dozen. These and those other three.'

'Where are they? The other . . . three?' For a moment I had the impression that he was looking at the bulge made by the box of stones in my pocket.

'In a bank vault.'

'It's best to keep them in a safe place. They're worth a lot of money.'

I didn't want to know how much. It wasn't the right moment.

'You only want to sell one?'

'I only need thirty thousand dollars. In American money. I'm going on a trip.'

'You told me.'

Maurício took out one of the stones and carefully rewrapped the others in a sheet of tissue paper.

'You can put these away.'

He left the room, carrying the stone with him. When he returned, he brought forty thousand dollars, which he handed me in a thick brown envelope.

'It's in hundred-dollar bills. Watch out for muggers. Don't get on a bus with this money and those gems.'

I left the building with the envelope under my shirt, held by my belt, and the box of stones in my pocket. Then I was suddenly unnerved. On the other side of the street was the man in the raincoat, accompanied by Diderot. They tried to get across, but the traffic was very heavy and they had to stand there, waiting for their chance. I started running down the street like a lunatic. I turned at the first intersection and dashed into a women's clothing store, where I remained for a while pretending to be looking for things to buy. When I left, the man in the raincoat and Diderot had disappeared.

I went into every bank along my route, trying to rent a safe-deposit box. None was available.

'They're all rented. Nobody dares keep valuables at home, with all these robberies,' an employee explained. He told of cases he was familiar with, or had read about in newspapers, of residences being broken into. 'That's why here at the bank we have dozens of account holders on the waiting list.'

It was almost time to meet Liliana. I stopped at a bureau de change and exchanged a thousand dollars for cruzados at the parallel rate, a euphemism for the black market in currency. The thousand dollars in cruzados was bulkier than the thirty-nine thousand dollars in the brown envelope. I filled the pockets of my jacket and pants with the money.

Liliana was already waiting for me at the restaurant.

I gave her the envelope.

'Go into the bathroom and take out $19,500 for yourself.'

'I don't want it,' she said.

The waiter appeared. We ordered.

'What don't you want?'

'You know very well what I don't want.'

I got up, went to the bathroom and locked myself in the stall. I took $19,500 from the envelope and put it in my pockets. I returned to the table.

Liliana was reading a book she had taken from her purse.

'Do you like Kavafi?' she asked.

I pushed the envelope toward her.

'I don't want that money,' she said.

I took a hundred-dollar bill from the package and tore it into small pieces, which I placed in my shirt pocket, the only one not crammed with money.

'Every thirty seconds I'm going to tear up a hundred-dollar bill,' I said.

'Every thirty seconds?' Liliana paused, thinking. 'Then it'll take you ninety-seven and a half minutes to tear up all the money.'

I ripped up another bill.

The waiter came with the appetizers.

I tore up two bills. 'A whole minute went by,' I said.

Liliana peeled and salted a quail's egg, and, reaching across the table, tried to put it in my mouth.

'I don't want it,' I said, turning my head and tearing up another hundred-dollar bill.

'You always liked quail's eggs,' Liliana said.

'Not anymore.'

'Are you afraid of the cholesterol? Or salmonella?'

'What I really dislike is having food put in my mouth. I used to hate it when my mother did that.'

'It's time to tear up another bill,' Liliana advised.

I tore up the bill. It's not easy to tear a hundred-dollar bill. They're made with a special highly resistant paper. Few people know that.

The waiter brought our dishes. For Liliana, grilled fish with boiled carrots. She took good care of herself. If she gave up smoking, she'd live to be a hund – oops! I tore up another bill. I ordered oxtail with watercress, plus beer.

I ripped apart another bill. My shirt pocket was full of shredded green paper.

'I'll be right back,' I said.

I went to the bathroom, threw the shredded dollars into the toilet, and flushed it. Only a few pieces went down the tube. I flushed countless times. The paper turned, swirled and still floated.

I couldn't leave the toilet full of shredded money. I reached into the bowl, picked out the pieces of paper and put them back into my shirt pocket.

When I returned to the table, Liliana was calmly eating her fish.

'You were there three minutes,' she said.
'Toilets nowadays are for shit,' I said.
'That's six bills,' Liliana said.
I tore up six bills.
'Your shirt is wet.'
'I know.'
'Come on, eat that crap there. Aren't you hungry?'
'I'm going to tear up ten bills at once so I can eat in peace,' I said.
Liliana jerked the envelope from my hands.
'You son of a bitch! You've already torn up sixteen hundred dollars!'
She put the envelope into her purse. I began to eat.
'Don't think for a minute that what happened between us was a clash of wills in which you emerged the victor. You're crazy, and crazy people like to tear up money,' Liliana said. 'It was merely a confrontation between health and morbidity, and as always, evil triumphed.'
'You really think so?'
She looked at me for a long time.
'Were you trying to subjugate me or seduce me?'
'Both,' I answered, tugging with my teeth at what remained of the fatty meat from the last oxtail bone. 'And besides that, there was the practical aspect: you need that money to travel.'
'Please. I love you. Don't dominate me the way you did with Ruth. Promise.'
'Don't mention Ruth,' I said.
'Promise you'll never again oppress and humiliate me like that.'
'I promise.'
'Go and wash your hands. And your face. You're filthy. You've got oxtail all over your face.'
When I returned from the bathroom, I told Liliana how I

hadn't been able to find a safe-deposit box in the bank and that, when I left, I planned to look up my brother and ask him to keep the gems.

At the door of the restaurant Liliana embraced me tightly. We agreed that we'd meet in Paris, at the Le Bréa Hotel, within two weeks. I watched Liliana as she walked away.

I went to see my brother at the church in Copacabana.

'I'm going on a trip today,' I said.

'Will you be away long? I'm thinking about that film, remember?'

'I'll be gone for a time, I don't know how long. I'm going to make a film in Germany, but I haven't worked out the details yet. Maybe it'd be better to get somebody else to do your film.' I paused. He waited, biting back his impatience; he knew I had a favor to ask. 'I'd like you to keep some precious stones for me.'

'Precious stones?'

I took the box from my pocket and gave it to him.

'May I see what's inside? I'm not going to keep anything if I don't know what it is.'

'Yes.'

José opened the box, took out some of the stones and held them against the light. Perhaps he'd also sold jewels in the past.

'Where'd you get this?'

'I prefer not to say.'

'I'll only keep these stones for you if you tell me where you got them.'

'I'm not going to say.'

'Then no deal.'

'It's better that you don't know,' I said.

'Tell me where you got them and I'll decide whether or not I'll keep them.'

If I told him, José wouldn't hold the jewels and would lecture me on morals to boot.

I picked up the box and put it in my pocket.

I left without saying goodbye.

I caught a taxi and returned to Gurian's apartment. On entering, I sensed the smell of Liliana hovering over the musty odor of books and shadows. I went to the bookcase, found the *Mahabharata* and placed the box of stones behind it. No one would be interested in a book like that. The danger was that Gurian might die. The address book was still where I had left it. I called Sarah.

'It's that friend of Gurian's. We were at the hospital together.'

'Yes. And what is it you want?'

'It's about Gurian's books. If . . . uh . . . if by any chance they're put up for sale . . .'

'Boris wouldn't sell his books for all the money in the world. You're a friend of his and should know that.'

I forced myself: 'But something could happen . . . understand . . . and in that case . . .'

'What sort of thing could happen?'

'Gurian isn't in good health and – not that I would wish it, as I have the greatest admiration for him – but a . . . fatality could occur . . . Understand?'

'You mean if Boris dies?'

'Yes . . . That's it . . .'

'How much will you give for the books?'

'I don't know. But I'll beat anyone else's offer. Don't sell them to anyone if that . . . misfortune . . . occurs. Leave the books as they are. I'll buy them all.'

'There are over ten thousand books.'

'I'll buy them all. I'll see Boris today, but I won't mention our conversation. It wouldn't be proper.'

'The most improper thing in the world is to die,' Sarah said. 'You can talk to him.'

I went to a Lufthansa agency and picked up my ticket. My reservation was confirmed for that evening. I had to be at Galeão Airport at nine.

I arrived at the hospital at six. I still hadn't had time to buy clothes for the trip.

Gurian was waiting for me.

'Sarah called me. Don't worry. If I die, the books are yours.'

'Thank you very much. I hope that doesn't happen soon.'

'You don't want to leave a down payment?'

'A down payment? How much? Can it be in dollars?'

'Not in dollars. It has to be in Scotch.' He laughed weakly, followed by a cough.

It was getting dark as I left to buy Gurian's whiskey. There were several brands of Scotch. I chose White Horse. I dashed back with the bottle hidden under my jacket.

A nurse was in the room with Gurian. Both of us, he and I, waited anxiously until she left.

I showed him the bottle. 'White Horse. Know why I chose this brand?' I said, pouring some into his glass. 'A homage to the white stallion that Savitski, the division commander, took from Khlebnikov.'

'A lovely story about a man who loved white horses,' Gurian said. 'Have you ever read a scene of greater despair than Khlebnikov removing his uniform jacket and tearing his naked chest with his fingernails like a madman while screaming for them to kill him, just because he was unable to recover his horse?'

'Liutov, Babel, says that Khlebnikov was a man whose character was similar to his own. "We both looked upon the world like a meadow in May – a bleak and desolate land crossed by women and horses.'"

'Babel had a great passion for horses,' Gurian said. 'Once he hid on a horse farm to write and have a chance to spend time among those beautiful animals. I don't know if that was before finishing *Cavalry*; what's certain is that after finishing the book, in 1926, he wanted to go abroad. Moscow, as he himself said, had been a horrendous and painful period in his life. Finally, the next year, he obtained permission to travel. He went to Paris, to meet his wife. But he had to return at once to settle a problem of inheritance for Eugenia, whose father had died. Eugenia stayed in Paris. Babel returned to his wife, but this time getting a visa was even more difficult.'

'What did he do in Paris?'

'He wrote a play, *Maria*, which was never produced. In Paris, he thought about Russia. He couldn't live in Russia, but he couldn't bear being so far from his country, as happens with many exiles. That's why he came and went, indecisive, unhappy, knowing that in Moscow sinister rumors were circulating about him. In 1934 he was back, taking part in the First Congress of Soviet Writers. Hold on, I think I already spoke about that, didn't I? We old people have the habit of always repeating the same thing.'

'Was that the Congress where Babel said that he was a "master of silence" and claimed, ironically, the author's right to write badly – in reality, the author's right not to write?'

'The same. Let me know when I repeat myself; I detest seeming like a decrepit old man.'

'You have a fantastic brain.'

'I forget things that happened yesterday. Getting back to Babel, did I already tell you about the Congress for the Defense of Culture and Peace, held in Paris in 1935?'

'No.'

'You're sure?'

'I'm sure.'

'The French writers protested at the fact of Babel and Pasternak not being part of the Soviet delegation. In the face of this pressure, the government hastily sent the two writers to Paris, with the Congress already nearly over. Once again, with a chance to remain in Paris, the exile's paradise, Babel went back to his own land, went back to a place close to Stalin. Eugenia did not return with him.'

The bottle of White Horse was almost half empty.

'It's time to leave. I have to be at the airport at nine and it's almost eight,' I said.

'In that year of 1935, Babel met Antonina Nikolaevna Pirozhkova, with whom he had a daughter, Lydia.'

'It's time,' I said.

'Gorky, Babel's only friend with prestige, died in 1936. His enemies now had a clear field.'

'I really have to leave, I'm late.'

'One more thing, very important. The last day, 15 May 1939. He was finishing the revision of his new book, which he hoped to give the publisher in October of that year. Babel considered it his best work. That day the police invaded his house and arrested him. Now do you want to know the worst of all the horrors that could happen, and did?'

I rose, nervously. I was going to miss my plane.

'That book, which would be Babel's masterpiece, was confiscated and destroyed, along with the other papers in his home. Everything was destroyed. Destroyed!'

A tear ran down Gurian's wrinkled face. His voice shook from effort and anger. 'According to information from his jailers, he died in a forced labor camp on March 17 1941. Probably shot.'

I gripped Gurian's hand tightly.
'I'll write to you from Germany. I have to go.'
'Leave the bottle,' he said.
Of course I left the bottle.

# TWO

## *The Manuscript*

# 10

The German stewardesses on the plane were good-looking, and the best part of the flight was watching them move back and forth. Seahorses, to take one example, are attractive animals but I quickly lose interest in them. But I can remain absorbed indefinitely by the enchantment of a woman in motion. Looking at the stewardesses helped me forget in part the trials I had just gone through in Rio de Janeiro and afforded the necessary calm that allowed me to give myself over to Babel's universe. I felt euphoric, free, perhaps because I had brought nothing with me but *Red Cavalry* and my notes about the writer, along with my passport and the money.

As soon as I opened the book, a couple in the seats across the aisle began saying things to me that I didn't understand. I tried to talk to them in all the languages I knew, without success. They were probably from some part of the Arab world. I showed them my passport, hoping they would do the same. In response the woman offered me half a dozen small, green, hard fruits. It was not usual for first-class passengers to bring food on board. I wanted to throw the fruit away, but the woman smiled at me, leaning over her seat – a sad smile, half idiotic, half apprehensive but still attractive. The fruit had an awful taste. But my acceptance of it seemed to calm my neighbors, who left me alone for the rest of the trip. I was then able to devote all my energies to Isaac Babel.

Babel had turned into an *idée fixe.* I knew that only an obsessive admirer, which surely I was not, would become so bound to a writer as was happening to me with Babel. Or else someone who was crazy. When I made *The Holy War* I acquired a deep interest in Euclides da Cunha, though in a lucid way that allowed me to perceive the shortcomings in the writer and thinker. But Babel seemed perfect to me. The idea of perfection, like its pursuit, is a dreamer's utopia. Yes, I was a dreamer who dreamed in an extraordinary manner, but I certainly wasn't crazy in the conventional psychiatric sense. I was singular (but every person is singular), odd perhaps but not crazy.

Arriving in Frankfurt, I caught the connecting Pan Am flight to Berlin.

It was snowing in Berlin. Dietrich was waiting for me at the airport.

'Did you have a good trip? Are you very tired?'

'Why was the festival postponed?' I asked.

'Do I know? Does anyone know? There are official explanations that are certainly not the true ones.'

Dietrich removed a Polaroid from his briefcase and took several pictures of me.

'They're for Dr Plessner. He's very happy that you've come. Where is your suitcase?'

'I don't have a suitcase.'

I noticed a discreet reaction of puzzlement.

'I didn't have time to pack a bag,' I explained.

From the window of the heated car, the snow-covered streets looked like a black and white film. Few people were walking.

*     *     *

The hotel that Dietrich had reserved for me was pleasant. In the bathroom there was a toothbrush and toothpaste. On the table in the bedroom, a bottle of wine and a large basket of fruit. Candies on the night table.

I drank the bottle of wine and lay down. What an agreeable sensation overtakes us as soon as we sip the last glass of a bottle of wine that we're drinking alone. I removed my clothes and slipped naked between the covers. I had never slept in the nude in my life. That is, just once, and then I woke up with a cold. I could have put on the shirt I had worn on the trip but I didn't want to wrinkle it even more; I'd have to wear it the next day.

Dream. I roll on the floor like a mad dog. Or a poisoned rat. I slam against the wall and my head bleeds. I think of taking a piece of bamboo and sticking it in my belly as Nakadai did, under Kurosawa's direction. I look at the wall, while a black American sings, and I imagine her face finally appearing, pale. 'Hey, sweetheart,' I say, 'what's that you have in your lap – a French poodle, or a bunny?' And, when I close my eyes, she, her hair long the way it was the day we went to the zoo, runs her hands along the muscles of my back. 'You're not the same,' she says. The crows (or are they jays with crows' faces?) in flight, flaunting themselves before me. She tells me there's no such thing as love; there's only orgasm, whose vitality is something like shitting, something that relieves you and then you clean yourself with a wash cloth or with water, then go about your life – buying some clothes or a house or jewelry or exercising. She says we're a pile of disposable monkeys, like used razor blades or toilet paper or Modess or empty soup cans or leftover stew or old food from summer. Maybe she's right. My heart, my blood cannot capture the subtlety of that being. I am condemned to hell and my bones ache and my flesh is so chastised that when I enter a place I am unable to speak. And my nose emits an odorless liquid, like melted ice, and I cannot pick up a piece of paper with the hand that I withdrew from the glove. In the street the last leaf of autumn, the color of dark gold, changes into her eyes. I beat my fists against the wall and leave to fight with someone. Every man I meet I tell, 'Out of my way, you sonofabitch,' and they step aside; they don't understand but they step aside anyway. Then I return home and my chin remains cold for hours, so long that I heat water in the kettle and make a compress.

I got out of bed as soon as I awoke – I am always immediately alert upon waking; I think that is the moment of the day when I am most lucid, most discerning – and went to the window. I contemplated the bisected horizon. Below, a rigid metallic gray and above, black clouds moving to the left in a compact mass, slowly, as if they were circling the entire planet. In the sky I saw the crows I had dreamed about. Or were they jays?

I picked up Babel. I think I spent many hours reading and writing. I stopped only when Dietrich showed up.

He seemed to have grown in size. He banged his body against the furniture as if he were a clumsy orangutan.

'Dr Plessner is in Munich waiting for you. Veronika Hempfel will take you to him. She'll come to the hotel shortly with the tickets. The two of you will leave at eleven.'

'Who is Veronika Hempfel?'

'She's a young scriptwriter, very competent. We're thinking of having her work with you, to help you.'

'I don't need anyone to help me.'

'It was Dr Plessner's suggestion. Veronika could be quite useful to you.'

Dietrich also said that Veronika had obtained her *magister* at university with a thesis on Babel. She knew Russian. As soon as he had convinced me with this last argument, Dietrich left.

Veronika Hempfel rang from the reception desk.

'I'm down here,' she said.

Before going downstairs I placed the better part of the dollars in my possession in two envelopes. With the envelopes in my pocket, I went down to meet Veronika Hempfel.

She was standing waiting for me in the hotel lobby, a small suitcase on the floor beside her. She came forward confidently to greet me.

I asked her for a few minutes so that I could store the dollars in the hotel safe. I asked if she spoke English, and given her affirmative response suggested we speak that language. 'My German's not that good.'

'I have to do some shopping,' I said afterward, when we were in the street.

'We don't have time; this wasn't foreseen, going shopping before our departure. We barely have time to get from here to the Flughafen Tegel. Where is your bag?'

'I don't have a bag,' I said with a calculatingly friendly smile, expecting her to be surprised.

There was no surprise. 'Do your shopping in Munich,' she said coldly.

In the plane we spent most of the time in silence.

'The people of Munich greatly enjoy festivals. They even have a lively *Fasching* . . . But it's not as . . . enthusiastic a carnival as the one you Brazilians have.'

The hint of disdain that I sensed in her voice annoyed me. I didn't answer.

In Munich it was less cold than in Berlin.

'I hope you like the hotel,' Veronika said.

Our rooms were near one another. Before going into hers, she said, 'I'm going to call Dr Plessner. Wait till you hear from me.'

I was in the bathtub when I heard the telephone ring. It had to be Veronika. Let her wait, I thought, plunging my body deeper into the warm water.

But I didn't have the patience to listen to the ringing phone for very long. I got out of the tub, my body dripping, and picked up the irritating machine.

'It's still too early to meet Dr Plessner. You have time to do some shopping now,' Veronika said.

'I don't feel like shopping.'

'Would you like to see Lola Montez? She's here in Munich.'

'Is she in a museum?'

'She's in a castle. I'll take you there.'

I had just put on the wrinkled shirt when Veronika called from the reception desk to say she was waiting for me.

'Dr Plessner arranged a car for us.'

It was a Mercedes, which she drove herself.

'The center of town was destroyed during the war and later rebuilt, maintaining its historical characteristics. Ludwig – in whose Hall of Beauties we shall soon be – said that he who has not seen Munich has not seen Germany.'

For the rest of the trip we remained silent, while I saw Germany through the window.

Veronika stopped the car in a wide square dominated by an enormous horizontal structure.

'She's there, in the Nymphenburg.'

Ludwig I's beauties were on the wall, in paintings of uniform size. We looked for Lola Montez among the innumerable lovely women in the collection.

'To me the most beautiful woman here is the daughter

of the king's stableman, that blonde there,' Veronika said. 'Whenever I come here I always look for her.'

'It must be because she looks like you. What about Lola Montez?'

'Wait here; I'll find out.'

Veronika returned with two guards, who showed us the painting of Lola Montez.

'Her liaison with Ludwig brought about the collapse of the Crown,' Veronika said.

'I don't know why Max Orphul chose Martine Carol for the role,' I said.

'Perhaps because both were mediocre actresses,' Veronika replied.

Afterward we went shopping. I bought a valise, some shirts, undershorts.

We returned to the hotel. At the reception desk there was a message from Plessner setting the meeting for the following day.

'Do you want some coffee, or tea?' I asked.

We sat in awkward silence while we waited for the tea.

'Does the stableman's daughter look like me?'

'Very much.'

'She's a very beautiful woman.'

A new silence. Veronika didn't like me, nor I her. Neither of us touched the cookies that the waiter brought with the tea.

'Dr Plessner got us tickets for the ballet tonight,' Veronika said. 'Do you want to go?'

I shouldn't have accepted the invitation.

The ballet was at the Nationaltheater München, home of the Bayerische Staatsoper. The program included *Der Verlorene Sohn*, *Les Sylphides* and *Elite Syncopations*. But I found this out only after I was already seated and waiting for the performance to begin.

'I don't want to see *Der Verlorene Sohn*,' I said.

'Why?' Veronika asked. 'It's the first one. After that we can leave.'

At that instant the ballet began.

When I saw Rouault's sets I remembered the horse at Ruth's house, the same dark, thick strokes delineating the figures, the solidity.

Prokofiev's music filled the theater. I had seen Ruth dance that ballet. Balanchine had done the choreography for her, created the irresistibly sensual movements of that dance expressly for her sumptuous body, forty years before she was born. I felt an unbearable sadness. I couldn't stand it for more than a few minutes. I didn't want to think about Ruth. I don't want to talk about her.

'I'm going to wait outside.'

Veronika came after me. We were in the theater foyer.

'What is it?'

'Just dizziness. It's pseudo-Ménière's syndrome. A chronic illness.' It wasn't the first time I had used the sickness as an excuse.

'Pseudo-syndrome?'

'Ménière, a French physician, first described the condition in 1861. The authentic syndrome is characterized by intermittent attacks of vertigo, nausea, ringing in the ears and partial deafness. I don't have the ringing or the deafness.'

'Does it happen frequently?'

'At times. The attacks can occur at intervals of days or months. I've gone a year without suffering anything. The inner ear is full of divisions, corridors, galleries, a configuration so complex that it's known as a labyrinth. These canals are filled with a liquid called lymph. Each canal has at its end a crest with sensory filaments or cilia, and floating in the lymph are small stones called otoliths that, when you move your head, press against the filaments which in turn, through the nerves, inform the brain of what's happening – which way you moved and so on. The brain then orders the body's muscles to control its balance. In my case the brain doesn't know what to do because the information it receives from the labyrinth is confused. When the brain doesn't know what to do, the body doesn't either. It's the Great Confusion, Disorder, Chaos.'

'Are you serious?'

'Yes. But this Chaos isn't cosmogonic, which preceded the creation of the world.'

'How does one get this?'

'I don't know. Some observers believe that it's connected to an allergy problem; others, the result of electrolytic imbalance.'

Veronika took me by the arm. 'Do you fall down when it happens?'

'All I have to do is not turn my head and it's fine.'

'Who built beings as complex as us and the animals that exist?' Veronika asked. I was surprised by the ingenuousness of the question.

'It could only have been the devil,' I answered.

'You have an appointment tomorrow with Dr Plessner. Don't you think you should cancel it?'

'Tomorrow I'll be all right.'

'I'm going to take you to the hotel.'

'No need,' I said. 'Go back to the ballet. See you tomorrow.'

'I just wanted to see *Der Verlorene Sohn*. Now that's not possible; they don't let you back in after the performance has begun. I'll go with you.'

We went together in a taxi to the hotel.

Veronika waited until I went into my room. 'Tomorrow at nine,' she said as the door closed.

I called the Hotel Le Bréa. They told me they had no guest named Liliana, or any reservation in her name. I explained that the woman I was looking for was Brazilian. There was no Brazilian woman at the hotel. I left my phone number, with a message for the Brazilian woman to call me if she showed up. The man on the other end of the phone spoke awful French, with an Asian accent.

Dream. A boat goes down the river that crosses the gray city. A man plays a cornet in front of a cathedral as night falls. The cold makes me cry – well, not exactly the cold, the music. Not the music either, it was she. Who? Besieged in the city, I see beyond the fallen yellow leaves the *Narrenschiff* going up and down the Rhine with its cargo of lunatics. I don't see them, I know they pass by. She says, 'I don't want you to cry, please, you never cried again after –' She stops talking. My cock is shedding skin from the cold; I only want to think about her, I can only think of her – who? – and I hadn't made my bed and had slept with my clothes on but without my shoes. A horrible dirty kitchen, fried pork chops and a broccoli and lettuce salad. I hear my voice: 'I don't want to be bothered.' She: 'Why are you so rude?' Locked in a black-walled closet in a city where it gets dark at four o'clock, I see criminals and innocents with transparent looks.

Veronika came down promptly at nine. I had just eaten breakfast.
    'Dr Plessner has a house here in Munich. It's not as imposing as the one in Berlin. We're going to meet him there.'
    'I'm cold,' I said in the car.
    'The heater is on.'
    'I need to buy an overcoat.'
    'Dr Plessner doesn't like waiting.'
    'I'm very sorry. We're going to buy it now.'

Veronika stopped at a store. I thought she was annoyed. I bought a fur-lined raincoat.

Plessner lived in an old two-story house on a quiet street. The door to the house – large, made of carved wood – opened directly onto the sidewalk. I noticed there was a gate to one side, which must go to the garage.

The door was opened by a tall, thin man with a short, blondish, well-cared-for beard and long, light brown hair. It was Plessner. Veronika introduced us.

'Finally the moment has come when we meet each other.' His English accent was affected. 'I thoroughly enjoyed your film *The Holy War*. I'm a great admirer of Brazilian cinema: Rocha, Dos Santos, Andrade, Hirszman, Diegues, Jabor, Toledo, Amaral . . . I don't know all the Brazilian directors, of course, just those whose films have been shown in festivals in Germany . . .'

What was odd about him? Was it that he said Rocha instead of Glauber, Dos Santos instead of Nelson? Amaral and not Suzana?

'It was a shame the festival was postponed. But that doesn't change our plans.'

As we talked, sitting in the living room, Veronika remained silent.

'Babel is more important than Solzhenitsyn, Pasternak, Brodsky and all the others who have become stylish here in Europe,' Plessner said.

'I think so too.'

'Dietrich said you have a synopsis to show me.'

'It's not ready yet. I plan to finish it here. I need writing equipment.'

'Tell me what you need and it'll be delivered to your hotel this very day.'

'An IBM and peripherals. Word Perfect software. Paper.'

'Veronika, have the Berlin office take care of it.'

Veronika got up and left the room. She appeared to be familiar with the house.

'Do you want to talk now about our financial plan?'

'It can wait till later.'

'I want to make an anti-Stalinist film that can be shown in the Soviet Union, that can be filmed in the Soviet Union,' Plessner said. 'That shouldn't be too hard to manage. If a film like *Pokainie*, directed by Tengiz Abuladze, can be shown, why not ours?'

'I'm not thinking about an anti-Stalinist film.'

'No?'

'My idea is to make a film that captures to perfection all the drama of *Red Cavalry*. I'm not worried about Stalin, or about the internal politics of the Soviet Union.'

'I appreciate your frankness. But Stalin and the Soviet Union are part of the drama. What do you know about Babel?'

I answered like Gurian: 'Everything.'

'Everything?' Plessner gave a long, feminine laugh. 'Veronika doesn't know everything, and she knows a lot. I don't know everything, and I know a lot. No one knows everything about Babel. We don't even know how he was killed.'

'He was shot.'

'There's one version that says it was typhus. But he could also have been strangled, knifed, clubbed to death, starved to death in a cell closed for ever. No one knows for certain what happened. And no one knows the most important thing with regard to Babel. Do you know what the most important thing is that no one knows?'

Veronika entered the room.

'Everything taken care of, Dr Plessner.'

'I do know,' I said.

'He says he knows what the most important secret about Babel is.'

Veronika looked at me in surprise.

'Please tell me,' Plessner said.

'What was in the manuscript destroyed by the police, which Babel considered his masterpiece? Could it have been a book of stories? Could it have been the novel that he, like Borges, never wrote? That's Babel's important secret: what was in that book that was destroyed. No episode in Babel's life, not even his death, is as important.'

'That's true,' Plessner said with a dreamlike air, running his hand lightly through his beard. 'The work is more important than the man.'

Then he rose and extended his hand to me.

'We're going to make a beautiful film. We'll see each other again in Berlin, in a week. Do you think you'll have something for me by then?'

'Absolutely,' I said.

On our way to the airport to get the plane back to Berlin that afternoon, it appeared that Veronika and I had overcome our mutual dislike.

In the plane I took out the synopsis, which I had written in English and in which one scene was already fleshed out – the one of Dolguchov's death, complete with dialogue – and gave it to Veronika to read.

'I didn't want to give it to Plessner because it's just an outline.'

Veronika read quickly. 'Liutov doesn't say "Today I lost my best friend" with tears in his eyes.'

'That's true,' I replied. 'The tears appear beforehand, when Afonka tells him that Korachayev will be punished. Korachayev, who commands the Fourth Division, is discredited; he fought seeking death. Since I never understood why

Liutov has tears in his eyes when he hears Afonka say this, I decided to change the placement of the tears.'

'I don't like war films,' Veronika said, handing back the synopsis.

She added that she especially couldn't stand films about the Second World War and Vietnam. She couldn't tolerate anymore Nazis, *partigiani*, marines, commandos, kamikazes, Vietcong, Vietnamese, Indo-Chinese, Americans, French and other protagonists.

'*Cavalry* isn't a film about war,' I said.

'If it's not about war, what is it about? Soldiers, blasts of artillery, combat, killings – and it's not about war? Don't tell me it's about frustration, fatigue, fear, waiting.'

It was my fate to get involved with ironic women.

'I can't take anymore of these cynical justifications for displaying violence,' Veronika said. 'And if it were about war-without-heroism, it would be like all the *Full Metal Jackets* that have passed across the world's screens in the last few years. Another thing: I don't like the phrase you put in Vitiagaichenko's mouth: "Mount up, girls!" It's a commonplace of war films to have the commander offend his subordinates by calling them girls. I find the phrase silly and macho, besides being an intolerable cliché.'

'The phrase isn't mine, it's Babel's. I think men in the Cavalry are the same the world over.'

The shrew sighed. 'There is no Cavalry anymore, I think.' Another sigh. Veronika controlled her breathing like one of those female characters of Bergman's arguing with her husband about Scandinavian marital relations. That is, like a capable actress who has learned that breathing can give emphasis and meaning to any phrase. 'I hate war films!' she said after the sigh.

'War has inspired many masterpieces, in all the arts,' I said, both defending and irritating myself as I spoke. I didn't like war films either, but the woman's provocations had made me a warmonger against my will. 'Euclides da Cunha, Goya, Stendhal, Beethoven, Tolstoy, Picasso, Shakespeare and Homer were a few of the many artists who dealt with war. And speaking of Goya –'

I was interrupted: 'I'm not convinced. If you want to do something with Babel, why not the Odessa stories?'

'The one who wants to make *Cavalry* is Plessner. Another thing: what you read, Dolguchov's death, is only a short bit of the film, scarcely more than a sequence, only a treatment, besides not having the cuts or camera angles. Strictly speaking, no, it isn't, it won't be, a war film. The war will just be a backdrop.'

'Ah, I know. It's not a war film, just guts hanging out and a mercy shot in the mouth. Is there anything else you want to tell me?' Veronika asked.

'Yes. I'm going to tell Dietrich that I don't want to work with you.'

'You're going to write the script by yourself?' She laughed.

'Why not? There are lots of directors who can write. Pasolini was a poet, a good one. Bertolucci is a poet. Kluge is a good writer,' I said. 'In Brazil many directors write well.'

'The ones you cited never wrote their scripts by themselves. The best scripts result from the collaboration of several people, including the actors.'

'I work in my own way. I don't give the script to the actors, as many directors do, or ask them to define with me the nature of the character – you're bad, you're good – or the dynamics of the film. I'm not the only one to do things that way. Forman, to give just one example, does the same: each day the actor finds out what he's supposed to do, scene by scene. The only thing worse than an actor with lots of ideas is a producer with lots of ideas.'

'You don't take suggestions from actors?'

'I take the suggestions they make at the time and I often incorporate them into the script. The best actors are the instinctive ones. The producer of *La Dolce Vita* wanted the protagonist to be Paul Newman, but Fellini wanted an actor without personality, one who was sensitive and with few ideas, like Mastroianni. The greatest actors in the world, like Mastroianni, are people who can be influenced, fragile and not very intelligent. There are exceptions of course.'

'No director ever wrote a good script by himself, and you know it.' Veronika's voice showed irritation. '*The Holy War* could have been better if you'd had the collaboration of a good scriptwriter. As for Milos Forman, he never wrote a film script on his own. *The Firemen's Ball* and *Loves of a Blonde*, done while still in Czechoslovakia, had the collaboration of Ivan Passer and Jaroslav Papousek. *Taking Off*, when he was already in the United States, was written with John Guare and Jean-Claude Carrière. In fact, in the United States Forman even stopped collaborating on scripts. *One Flew Over the Cuckoo's Nest* was written by Laurence Hauben and Bo Goldman. *Hair*, only by Michael Weller. Directors like you and Forman don't want actors to know what they're doing, in order to maintain absolute power over them. That's mere insecurity. You'll have problems with German actors. Hitchcock could never have directed here.'

What was it that irritated me about Veronika? That she was beautiful like the daughter of Ludwig I's stableman? Her self-assuredness? Her prodigious memory?

'Before we cease talking to one another – that's the direction in which our relationship is heading, isn't it? – I would like to tell you what film is to me,' Veronika said.

'Go ahead.'

She hesitated, framing her speech.

'Artaud said that if the theater wanted to find its *raison d'être* it needed to give us everything that we find in crime, love, madness.'

'Sophocles, Shakespeare gave us nothing but mad, criminal, impassioned heroes,' I said.

'May I finish?' Veronika said.

Sonofabitch, as Vitiagaichenko would say. But I controlled myself.

'Film,' Veronika continued, 'has shown wars, crimes, insanity, catastrophes, prodigious children, as well as prodigious animals and monsters, platonic and explicit sex, mysticism – everything that can be imagined – but in a superficial and distorted way, merely to make itself palatable to the passive masses who consume television with absent-minded voracity at the same time as they talk, eat and drink, go to the bathroom, or yield to light or heavy dozing. Few spectators really ever think. Film, unfortunately, has to be made for such as they.'

Veronika took a cigarette from her purse and lit it skillfully with an old Zippo, which she closed with a sharp snap. I remembered a TV film, based on a story by Roald Dahl, in which a guy bets a finger against a sports car that his Zippo lighter will work ten times on the trot without a miss. I saw by the studied snap of the lighter that she was close to losing control. She took a deep drag.

'Want to bet that your Zippo won't light ten times in a row?'

The stewardess approached and said something. Veronika put out her cigarette impatiently.

'And what is thinking?' I asked, trying to be ironic.

'Thinking is processing information –'

'A computer does that better.'

'Processing information,' she continued, 'in a way more complex than a computer, carrying out logical operations,

solving problems, but not like a computer, making deci-
sions, producing artistic expression, but not in a rigidly
programmed way. That's thinking. And more: thinking is,
especially, fantasizing, creating scenarios about desires and
ambitions. Thinking, ultimately, is dreaming.'

Truly, computers don't dream. Dogs and cats dream.

'Do you know I dream without images?'

As soon as I had said this, I regretted it. My dreams were
too intimate to be discussed with an idiot.

'I don't make films to get people to think,' I said hurriedly,
irritated. 'I don't want to make films that are prophylactic
tranquilizers, like you. I want to disquiet, cause disturbance,
anxiety, perplexity, insomnia, vomiting.'

'Does Dr Plessner know this?'

I looked at my watch. I felt like telling the woman to go
to hell.

We were silent for the rest of the trip.

When we got to Tegel, we parted without a word.

# 11

Actually, I didn't like to work with anyone when writing scripts. Being free of Veronika gave me a great feeling of relief.

The equipment I had requested from Plessner had already arrived at the hotel when I returned from Munich. I connected the micro, the printer, the video terminal. I opened the new box of diskettes.

I spent the rest of the day working. I stopped only to go and have a bratwurst sandwich at a street kiosk. In truth I went out more to see people, since I wasn't hungry. In Berlin – as in every other city I had visited – I hadn't looked, and certainly wouldn't look, at a shop window, not even if it held VCRs or books or cameras. The only thing I saw were men and women, the women more than the men. I turned my head when they passed by, unconcerned whether it seemed inappropriate or crude. The movement of people's bodies is always indicative, expressive; I couldn't reject that demonstration, that revelation of being. Now there I was, having my sausage sandwich with a glass of beer, as I observed two women eating. One of them resembled Hanna Schygulla. Hanna was trying to make a civilized act out of that gesture of weakness – which, because it is weak, is also moving –

by opening her mouth less than was necessary to eat in an efficient way, bending her head over the food in a delicate mannerism, smothering the sounds that she must emit as she chewed or sipped the food. Her posture had something animal-like about it. That's why man invented plates, glasses, silverware, etiquette – to pretend we are different from other animals. And the two women had their own liturgy, which held neither the mystic temperance of the Eucharist nor the exhibitionistic vulgarity of Trimalchio's drunken spree. Something like the way a cat eats.

I had a meeting that evening with Dietrich, at my hotel.

'What happened between you and Veronika? You don't want to work with her?'

'I prefer to work alone.'

'Shall we go down to the bar for a drink?' he asked. He seemed nervous and unhappy.

Dietrich ordered brandy and beer. He downed the brandy in a single swallow.

'You didn't like Veronika?'

'She's a tedious person. But that's not the only reason I don't want to work with her. I told you at our first meeting that I do my own scripts, remember?'

'Yes, yes.'

'She knows too much. Even for a German that's not good,' I said. 'But that's not why I don't want to work with her.'

We fell silent.

'I'm satisfied with the estimates I made of the film's cost. For an epic, I think we're spending very little.'

'This film isn't *War and Peace*,' I said. 'It can be made for not too much money.'

'Not too much money in film is always a lot of money.' He patted me on the back. 'Don't you envy writers? To create a book they use up only paper and time, the characters always work for free, and they do things that film actors couldn't do

or would refuse to do. They produce the most extravagant
scenes expending nothing but words. They kill, mutilate,
make people go mad with passion, ruin themselves or gain
paradise. An epidemic that kills millions or a handshake costs
the same for them. There was a time when I thought I'd
become a writer, but I found out that I wasn't crazy enough.
I think that an author, in principle, isn't quite right in the
head. The most megalomaniacal of directors – Griffith, Pabst,
Gance, Coppola – would not have the courage to think himself
endowed with the omnipotence of some provincial writer.'

I didn't answer.

'Do you agree with me?' Dietrich was a genteel man who
was making an effort to keep the conversation alive.

'More or less.'

'I'd like you to work with Veronika.'

'She doesn't like me either.'

'Veronika doesn't like anyone. But she's extremely competent and well informed. What does it matter if she knows
too much?' He laughed as he said this. Then, serious: 'She
would be quite useful; we would all come out ahead.'

'I'm sorry.'

'Would you like to have dinner with me tomorrow?' He
took a small pad from his pocket, wrote on it and handed
a piece of paper to me. 'If you take the U-Bahn, get off at
Kleistpark Station. Kleistpark, don't forget.'

'How could I forget a name like that?'

Dinner at Dietrich's house. An actress, Marthe, a stage
director, a poet and Veronika. She greeted me in a civilized
fashion. The guests drank wine and spoke about trivialities,
pleasantly.

Finally we sat down around the table. Dietrich, with
Veronika's assistance, served the meal.

Someone asked if I was familiar with Berlin.

'One of us should show him the city,' Marthe said.

'I'll do it,' Veronika said, to my surprise.

'I don't want to inconvenience you.'

'But it's a pleasure,' Veronika said.

'When I feel like it, I'll let you know.'

'I can also show you the city. After all, I was born here,' Marthe said, smiling.

I smiled back, without saying anything. Could she be after a part in *Cavalry*? The female roles weren't much to speak of.

Little by little the conversation drifted to the film.

'Did Dr Plessner tell you that he's thinking of making the film in the Soviet Union?' Dietrich asked.

'Yes. But my impression is that there's still some resistance to Babel in the Soviet Union.'

'Babel began to be rehabilitated at the end of the Fifties, when they published his complete works with an introduction by Ehrenburg. There's no problem. Even more so now, with Gorbachev's glasnost,' Veronika said.

'Babel's diary hasn't been published yet,' I said drily. 'As well as some stories. What was published with a preface by Ehrenburg wasn't the complete works.'

'In any case, Babel was rehabilitated,' Veronika said, irritated.

'When you direct a film, do you start from some pre-existing aesthetic concept?' Marthe asked.

'In the case of *Red Cavalry* the style of the film will be the main thing. In a conversation with his biographer, Paustovsky, Babel said that a story could be made from nothing but style – without content, plot or suspense. He was exaggerating of course. His stories have plot and suspense; any one of them could be told by a storyteller in a public square without losing its fascination. But above all else, Babel's stories have style. That's a challenge I have to face.'

'But what is style?' Veronika asked hostilely.

'A characteristic manner of expression,' I answered.

'But after all, doesn't that encompass plot, suspense – the content?' Veronika said, now aggressive. 'A film must be seen holistically, for the integrated "everything" of a work of art has a reality greater than the sum of its parts – in this case, script, lighting, editing, acting.'

Veronika's hostility had caused a certain uneasiness around the table. Dietrich's face manifested his unhappiness.

The stage director spoke of directors who have style – Fellini, Bergman, Ford, Visconti. Someone mentioned Fassbinder, which provoked a small discussion, in which Veronika and I did not take part.

The rest of the evening she and I sulked and had little to say.

I locked myself in the hotel room for three days writing the outline of the film. Dietrich called me several times. He spoke of Veronika. 'She's a good person.' I changed the subject. He asked when the outline would be ready. 'Tomorrow.' Dietrich said he'd send someone to get it.

The person who came to pick up the outline was Veronika.

She smiled when I opened the door.

'Shall we make up?' she asked.

Surprised, I didn't answer. I merely opened the door wider for her to come in.

'I think I'm jealous of Babel,' Veronika said. 'I was very rude to you. Forgive me.'

She seemed like a different woman. What could have happened? Repentance is never a spontaneous gesture; there's always some form of coercion behind it.

'I acted badly myself,' I said. When anyone offers an apology I always accept it.

Veronika extended her hand. Soft and firm.

'That scene you wrote about the death of Dolguchov was very good.'

Maybe Dietrich had been right and Veronika wasn't a bad person. What was certain was that I had always had complicated dealings with the women around me, whether I was emotionally involved with them – as was happening with Liliana, as had happened with Ruth – or in a professional relationship, or in family matters. I thought about my mother. She was a domineering woman, dedicated to her family; for her, nothing existed beyond my father, me and my brother. But we had paid a high price for that dedication, I more than anyone.

'Would you like some tea?' I asked. 'The tea here is very good.'

Over tea, which was accompanied by a great variety of cookies, we talked about the rehabilitation of Babel.

'Until 1957 Babel was considered a subversive writer and his works were proscribed,' Veronika said. 'That year a "rehabilitative edition" of his stories was published, with an introduction by Ehrenburg. But things in the Soviet Union move very slowly. Babel continued to be a virtual outcast, and a year later, in the first edition of *A History of Soviet Literature*, he rated only a few lines. Actually, true rehabilitation took place only upon the celebration of the seventieth anniversary of his birth, November 11 1964, at the headquarters of the Writers' Union. Konstantin Fedin, secretary-general of the Union, presided over the event, which had demanded a great preparatory effort on the part of some intellectuals, among them Ehrenburg, Livshits, Munblit, Nikulin. Ehrenburg gave a beautiful speech. He died three years later.'

Veronika's hair was very straight and fine; it swayed with any movement of her head.

'But all of that was possible only because of Khrushchev,' she continued. 'In 1956, as first secretary of the Communist

Party, at the Twentieth Party Congress, Khrushchev began the process of destalinization. On the literary front the principal victim of Stalin had been Babel. Even so, the rehabilitation process ran into obstacles. It was necessary for the sinister history of Stalin's crimes to be exhaustively denounced by Khrushchev before the writers and their official organization, which had always lived in terror of the system, could act, preparing the redress of November 1964.'

Veronika was a tall woman, well proportioned. She raised the cup to her lips and sipped the tea with great delicacy and elegance. Like the women at the kiosk.

'Before that, on October 15 of that year,' Veronika continued, 'Khrushchev had been forced to give up the positions of prime minister and first secretary of the Communist Party, twenty-seven days before the rehabilitation ceremony for Babel at the Writers' Union. But it was in reality thanks to Khrushchev that the posthumous homage could be made. Khrushchev never stopped being the rough worker from the coal mines, but if he had not existed there also would not have existed, twenty years later, the suave Gorbachev, glasnost and perestroika. An interesting fact: in 1964, when the seventieth anniversary of Babel's birth was commemorated, the seventieth anniversary of Khrushchev's birth could also have been commemorated. They were both born in 1894, one in April, the other in November. Don't you find these coincidences intriguing?'

Veronika's eyes were blue.

The color of her eyes made me think of Goya. I don't know what caused this association of ideas; Goya's blue did not have the clear brilliance of Veronika's eyes. I saw that Veronika had become disturbed when she sensed me looking. I explained: 'I was thinking of Goya's blue.'

'Goya's blue?'

'Not exactly his blue. Goya's colors. For *Cavalry* I would like to have Goya's colors. The shadows.'

'How did you arrive at that?'

'Several reasons. Babel and Goya were similar in many things. Even physically. Even in their myopia. That is, their portraits were similar. No good physical description of Goya exists. Actually, no good physical description of Babel exists either.'

'Are you familiar with the one that Canetti gave of him in *Die Fackel im Ohr*?'

'No.'

'The two were together right here in Berlin, at some time in the Twenties. Canetti describes Babel as a stocky man with a large head, and glasses with thick lenses that made his eyes look even larger and rounder.'

We talked a bit more before Veronika left, taking with her what I had written. She had decided to make an effort to establish a good relationship with me and had succeeded.

I left immediately after she had gone. I was tired of that hotel room. I walked along Kudamm, wrapped in my fur-lined raincoat, looking for a theater. All the non-German films being shown were dubbed into German. (Later I discovered that even Charlie Chaplin's silent films were dubbed into German. There was one theater that regularly showed foreign films in their original form. A few others had special sessions, almost always on Sunday morning, for this purpose.) Irritated, I changed my mind about going into a theater that was showing an old Kurosawa. One of the good things about Japanese film is their language. Besides which, it would be grotesque, to say the least, to hear a bunch of samurai speaking the language of Goethe. Dubbing was done as a general practice for the first time in Mussolini's Italy. A fascist thing.

I walked around the city. I had dinner at an Italian

restaurant and returned to the hotel. I watched television. The programs, those of East and West Germany as well as the French and American broadcasts, were very boring. I went to sleep.

Dream. A cool wind musses the man's thin gray hair. The woman shields herself from the wind, but not from the morning light that shines on the diamonds scattered over her body. 'What was that?' the old man asks, waking from his slumber. 'It was a dog, sir,' says the driver. 'Did we kill a dog?' 'I couldn't help it, sir.' The woman says, 'Close the window, turn on the air conditioning.' 'That's the bad thing about being old,' the old man thinks, looking back through his tears, 'filthy rich and whimpering over a dead dog.'

The next morning, Veronika appeared at the hotel.

'Dr Plessner wants to have lunch with you. In his office here in Berlin. I'll take you there.'

The skin of Veronika's face gave off a soft, uniform light. I found myself saying, 'I've changed my mind. I'd like you to work on the script with me.'

Her face turned red. I was looking at her in profile as she drove the car.

'Why did you change your mind?' she asked, timidly, staring straight ahead at the road.

I hesitated. 'I don't know.'

'You don't know?'

'I'm an impulsive person.'

'I'm afraid to work with you.'

'Why?'

'You're unpredictable.'

'Not when I'm working.'

She remained silent for a time. People were walking

hurriedly through the streets, wrapped in woolen clothing, only their eyes and noses visible.

Veronika left me at the door of the building.

'I wasn't invited.'

'You might show me something of the city tomorrow,' I said.

A receptionist took me to Plessner's office, on the twentieth floor.

'I think you've captured the essence of *Cavalry*,' he said when we were seated at a long wooden table. 'Incredible. A Latin from the tropics understanding the Russian soul so well.'

I felt uncomfortable again, like the time Plessner had spoken of the Brazilian directors that he admired.

'Have you had a chance to see anything of Berlin yet?'

'Not yet. Veronika Hempfel is going to show me round one of these days. Speaking of which, I'd like to work with her on the script.'

Plessner grasped my hands firmly in his. 'How good that you've agreed to work with her. Veronika is extremely competent. I was very concerned when Dietrich told me you didn't like her.'

'I like her now.'

Plessner looked at me, curious, a bit disturbed. He seemed to be a man who needed to understand other people's motivations.

'Come over here,' he said, leading me to the window. 'Do you see it?'

From there I could see a panoramic view of the city. 'Do you see it?' he repeated.

I imagined he must be referring to the Wall. Like a high, winding track of concrete, a great expanse of wall was visible from Plessner's skyscraper.

'There is no more significant monument to our times,' he said. 'The old spirit of Emperor Tsin reduced to petty scale. In the beginning it was barbed wire. Modern man continues in darkness.' He paused. 'Do you see that gray building?'

I said I could, but actually I didn't see anything. I just didn't want to have to ask for further identification.

'That's Checkpoint Charlie, one of the entrances to the other side. But most people cross through the S-Bahn station on Friedrichstrasse.'

'I know Checkpoint Charlie from films,' I said.

Lunch was in an intimate room, actually a large hall, where Plessner usually dined with his guests. We were served by two tall, attractive women, elegantly dressed, their hair and make-up impeccable. They looked as if they had come straight from a fashion show to wait on us. Nevertheless, by the assurance they displayed it was evident that they were used to the work.

'If you ask around in Munich someone may tell you I'm a producer interested solely in money. The truth is that my sole object is to create a good product. The money is incidental. I select the theme, read the script, make a suggestion or two about the casting and some of the technical crew, that's all. I leave the film in the hands of the executive producer, in this case Dietrich, and the director. And since I always make a very good choice of both' – a seductive smile underlined this last comment – 'my films continue to be successful. Success is money.'

When the women brought the dessert, there was a surprise in store. An enormous bowl of star fruit was placed in the center of the table. I hadn't eaten star fruit in years; it was one of my favorite fruits, with its provocative bitter taste, but it was rarely found in the supermarkets of Rio or São Paulo, despite growing readily in any back yard.

'Help yourself; they're real,' Plessner said. 'I know it's a common fruit in your country.'

'So common that you can't find it anymore,' I replied.

'Here you can find it,' Plessner said with a smile. 'At KDW. There's nothing, absolutely nothing, that you can't find at KDW.'

'KDW?'

'It's a supermarket. There are two things you must not fail to see in Berlin: KDW and the Philharmonic. Ask Veronika to take you to both.'

Plessner took one of the star fruits and placed it on his dessert plate.

'A strange fruit, very tropical.'

'But I think it was brought to Brazil from China, many years ago, probably by the Portuguese,' I said.

'That doesn't mean it's not strange.'

'True.'

Plessner looked at the star fruit on his plate as if it were some two-headed animal.

'It looks artificial. Made of dough.'

'That's the way they are.'

'How do you eat it?'

I picked up my star fruit and took a bite.

'Like this.'

Plessner picked up his fruit and tried a small bit. He chewed. 'Fibrous. Must be good for the intestines. It's a bit acidic for my taste,' he said, returning the bitten fruit to his plate.

I ate three.

While one of the women served the liqueurs, the other brought a wide, shiny wooden box with slots holding several types of cigars.

'You don't smoke?' Plessner asked when he saw I hadn't taken one.

'No.'

'I only smoke two a day. One after lunch, the other after dinner,' Plessner said, taking a cigar from the box. For a moment he said nothing, the cigar in one hand and the cutter in the other. Then he told one of the women in German that he didn't want to be interrupted.

The two women left the room.

'There's a revelation of an extremely confidential nature that I'd like to make to you,' Plessner said as he lit the cigar.

He took two puffs. He appeared to be choosing his words with care.

'Do you remember the talk we had in Munich about Babel?' he said.

'Yes.'

Another puff.

'Babel's important secret?' he continued.

'The book he was writing that was destroyed?' I asked.

'Till now it was not known what type of book it was – an autobiography, a book of short stories, a play, a novel,' Plessner said.

'And now it is known?'

'It was a novel,' Plessner said. 'It was a novel. The only novel Babel ever wrote.'

My heartbeat accelerated. A novel! What would it be like? Had Babel succeeded in writing a long text with the same concision of his stories? If there was a writer in the world capable of doing so, of creating in the novel the exactitude, the precision of the short story, that man would be Babel. Maupassant, Dostoevsky, Conrad, Lawrence – none had succeeded. Joyce, Proust had perhaps attempted it fruitlessly and therefore given up and gone to the other extreme, long-windedness. I was thinking only of writers who had tried both genres. Flaubert, strictly speaking, was never a short-story writer.

'The novel was not destroyed,' Plessner said.

'What?' The revelation left me speechless.

'Babel's novel was not destroyed. I haven't spoken of this to anyone. The information is extremely confidential.'

'Where is the book? Did you see it? Do you have it?'

'I can't say anything more about it. Not now. Remember: this information is confidential.'

# 12

I was drinking beer with Veronika at the Pressecafé am Zoo, opposite the railroad station.

'On this site once stood the Aschinger, Babel's favorite restaurant when he was in Berlin. Here he would slowly have his pea soup with pieces of sausage, watching at leisure the people around him. The Aschinger was demolished; now there's no more pea soup. Canetti, who would come with him, tells all about it in his biography. Babel didn't talk much. He preferred to watch people. Or else argue with Canetti about the Neue Sachlichkeit, the new objectivity, the new reality. Berlin was always the city for arguing new theses. Now it's the Neue Empfindsamkeit.'

Veronika took a swig of beer.

'It was here,' she said, 'that Babel taught Canetti to look at people insatiably, to understand people, without judging or condemning.'

'What is that thesis you mentioned?'

'Neue Empfindsamkeit? The new sensitivity.'

Social and political responsibility, Veronika said, should not exclude sensitivity, the individual's reflecting about himself. Subjectivity did not necessarily mean individualistic escapism. What was sought was a new, broader type of social commitment which would not negate the individual or submit him to social and political conditioning, to the dehumanization of modern society and the state.

It was a very pleasant night. Without noteworthy dreams.

Veronika came by car to pick me up. She was going to show me the city.

'You don't want to see museums?'

'No.'

'You don't even want to see Nefertiti?'

'No. My only interest, anywhere, is people. I'm like Babel.'

'Nefertiti is a person. There is even a book that says she wants to go home. *Nefretete Will Nach Hause.*' Pause. 'What about Lola Montez? You're being discriminatory.'

'Lola wasn't in a museum.'

'That palace is a museum.'

'I don't like museums. Let me tell you something: the only museums I go into are the American Museum of the Moving Image in New York and the Museum of the Moving Image in London.'

'A professional failing?' she asked.

'Could be. What I know for sure is that in the other museums I go in just to see some special thing and then leave right away.'

'I bought tickets for a rock-group *conzert*. But it doesn't begin until ten o'clock. Do you like rock? Rock is people, living people.'

'Ten o'clock? What are we going to do till ten o'clock?'

'I was thinking of seeing museums,' she said.

'I wanted to buy a radio/cassette player. The hotel just has television and I want to listen to music.'

'Then let's go shopping,' she said.

Veronika helped me choose a portable stereo radio with tape player.

'You can buy it. It's a good price, she said.

Afterward we went to a record shop. I bought Tchaikovsky symphonies, the operas *Boris Godunov*, *Sadko* and *Prince Igor* on cassettes manufactured in the Soviet Union, which were cheaper than the Western ones.

'I can only write listening to music.'

'Aren't you going to inspire yourself with some Polish music? After all, *Red Cavalry* takes place in Poland, doesn't it?'

'Who, for example?'

'Chopin.'

'Chopin lacks strength. He's too maudlin.'

'What about Tchaikovsky? Is anyone more maudlin?'

'It's Budenny's Cavalry that wins the war,' I said.

'Ah, so it's the victor's vision.'

'Not at all. It's Babel's vision. That of a Jewish Cossack.'

'And near-sighted,' Veronika said. 'Don't forget Afonka's words: "Get out of my way," he said, turning pale, "or I'll kill you. You guys in glasses have as much pity for people like us as a cat has for a rat."' Veronika laughed. 'Babel was the only myopic in Budenny's regiment, maybe the only myopic Cavalryman in all of Cossack history, at least the only declared one, one who wore glasses. Military men don't like to display their near-sightedness. Look at Jaruzelski. He wears dark glasses, as if he were some kind of playboy. It's that way in your country too. The generals wear dark glasses. And probably the captains too, but I can't say for sure because captains never get their pictures in the papers.'

'Do you think the fact of Babel's being myopic is more important than his being Jewish?'

'Let's say that both are important. The Near-sighted Jewish Cossack. Don't you think it's a good title for the film?'

'Ask Dietrich.'

'He'd kill me if I suggested it,' Veronika said.

We returned to the car. It had grown colder.

Veronika suggested we see Alexander Kluge's latest film.

'Plessner suggested I should see KDW.'

'Do you want to go to KDW?'

'No. Let's see the Kluge.'

'Are you understanding everything?' Veronika whispered in the dark theater. I felt her perfumed breath, like a child's, as if she had only baby teeth in her mouth. 'I can explain anything that's unclear to you.'

'No need,' I said.

There was a crowd at the cabaret door. Veronika had to call someone to help get us in.

It was an enormous room with many tables, all of them occupied, a packed dance floor, and lots of smoke. On a low stage a group was warming up the crowd for the arrival of the main band. Veronika took me by the hand and we made our way through to the stage. The noise was very loud. Gesturing for me to take off my raincoat, Veronika removed her coat. Then she placed both coats on the pile beside the stage.

The band was very good. Positioning herself in front of me, Veronika moved her body lightly to the rhythm of the rock music, amplified with terrible sonic brutality by the loudspeakers a short distance from us.

I avoided letting Veronika's body touch my own. I could not prevent her fine blonde hair from occasionally brushing against my mouth and nose.

When the *conzert* was over, we got our coats and left. It was around two in the morning.

'There was a lot of smoke in there,' Veronika said. 'Did you have a good time?'

'I certainly did.'

'What would you like to do now?'

'I feel like having some red wine.'

'Aren't you hungry?'

'Yes.'

'Do you like carpaccio?'

She knew a place that made a very good carpaccio.

We drove for several blocks, through streets deserted at that hour, until we arrived at the restaurant.

It was a place with few tables, some of them occupied, and a long counter with stools. Seated on one of them, a woman was drinking red wine. Behind the counter a dark-haired man with a Latin appearance was smoking a cigarette. I calculated that he must be the owner. We sat at a table near an enormous glass window that looked out onto the street. The table was dimly illuminated by the light of a candle.

'So,' Veronika said.

'A nice place,' I said.

The dark-haired man came out from behind the counter and asked what we would like.

'Carpaccio and *vino rosso*,' I said.

'I'm dying of hunger,' Veronika said.

The woman sitting at the counter got down and came over beside us.

'Are you speaking English?'

'Yes,' Veronika said.

'My name is Ellen,' she continued, in English. In the candlelight her pale face looked very pretty.

Veronika invited her to join us.

'Do you think a Cossack could wear glasses?'

'Is that a joke?' Ellen asked.

'Something like that. Not a very funny one,' I said.

'That's for sure,' Ellen said.

'You're not German,' Veronika said.

'I'm American.'

She was studying at the University of Berlin. She'd been by

herself at home when, in the middle of the night, she had felt an irrepressible urge to see people. She had gone into the first place she'd found open. By her voice it was obvious that she'd been drinking for some time before Veronika and I had arrived.

We drank and talked about film and literature. Three bottles of Chianti were consumed.

The restaurant owner, who had spoken to me several times in Italian, came up and said regretfully that it was time to close.

'What did he say?' Veronika asked.

'That it's closing time.'

'What a pity,' Veronika said. 'Why don't we all go to my place?'

'No. Let's go to mine,' Ellen said.

I wanted to pick up the tab, but Veronika and Ellen insisted on splitting the bill.

We had to climb several flights to get to Ellen's apartment. When she opened the door we found ourselves in a gigantic room that served as living room, library and bedroom. But the first thing that hit you was bookcases full of books. There must have been thousands of them. At the back, behind an immense divider, there was a wide bed. It looked like the set for a German film from the Twenties.

'The apartment belongs to a friend of mine,' Ellen said.

Ellen and Veronika made an interesting contrast. Looking at Veronika, at the rosy glow of her skin after countless glasses of wine, I thought, obviously, of Botticelli's Venus. On the other hand, Ellen, who was fiddling with the stereo system, her hair and eyes darker and darker, her skin the color of ice, seemed like a woman by Delvaux – Paul, not the director. Alcoholic thinking.

I took Veronika's hand.

'Shall we dance?'

'I don't dance very well.'

'It doesn't matter. I just want to hug you.'

We hugged each other tightly, our bodies moving slowly.

I put my mouth to Veronika's ear: 'Afterward, will you come to the hotel with me?'

Veronika didn't answer, but she tightened her body against mine.

We danced some more. I mean, we moved our embracing bodies.

At that instant Ellen grabbed me by the arm and said, 'I want to dance too.' She suddenly appeared to be drunk. She kissed me on the mouth. Veronika moved away. I saw her take a book from the bookcase and sit down, calmly, to read.

'Stay here with me,' Ellen said as we danced. 'I want you to sleep with me.'

I thought for a bit, not knowing what to do. Letting go of Ellen, I went over to where Veronika was sitting reading in the other corner of the room.

'What book is that?'

'*Frauen vor Flusslandschaft.*'

'Would you mind if I stayed here, with her?'

'No,' Veronika said, evenly.

Ellen approached with a bottle of wine and a glass in her hand. 'One for the road,' Ellen said cheerfully, pouring wine into the glass and handing it to Veronika.

Veronika took a swallow. 'Thanks,' she said, returning the glass. Immediately, she got her coat and put it on, unperturbed.

We walked Veronika to the door. We said good night to her, kissing her effusively on the cheek. Veronika opened her purse, took out a piece of paper and wrote on it. 'My telephone number.' And she left, closing the door.

Ellen took me by the hand and led me across the room to the corner where the large bed was.

'Help me take off my clothes.'

I took off Ellen's shoes, her heavy wool socks, her long pants. Then the sweater and blouse. She wasn't wearing a bra. She fell backwards onto the bed. Her loose cotton panties revealed the dark hair of her pubis.

'I like you,' Ellen said, with an effort, slurring her words.

'What's my name?' I asked as I undressed.

'Fuck you!' Ellen said, without aggression.

'Did you forget my name?'

'Fuck me!' Ellen said.

I removed her panties. Then I saw that Ellen was asleep. 'Ellen!'

I couldn't wake her. I stood there beside the bed. 'Ellen,' I repeated, dejected, in a low voice. I covered her with the sheet. I got dressed.

I took a book about Otto Dix from the bookcase and looked at the illustrations. I turned on the radio. 'Berlin, the city that never sleeps,' said the announcer of the American armed forces radio station. I turned it off and went back to the bed. Concerned, I placed my ear against Ellen's chest and heard her heart beating, a bit fast. Her body was hot and perfumed. How old was she? Eighteen? I regretted not being a necrophile or something similar.

What was I doing there with a naked, drunk, sleeping young woman? Before I could leave, however, it was necessary to solve one problem. I had just come from a violent city where doors are always tightly shut. How could I lock the door from the outside and leave Ellen sleeping safely? I couldn't take the key with me. Then I noticed a small opening in the door, for mail delivery. The key ring wouldn't go through the opening, so first it would be necessary to discover which key locked the door, then remove it from the ring. Discovering the key wasn't difficult. The problem was that the keys were on a ring with a defective clasp. 'A house containing all of Auden's books must have a pair of pliers,' I thought, rather illogically. Finally, after much searching, I found a toolbox. I broke the key ring with the pliers and removed the door key. I left the other keys on the table, with a note explaining what I'd done. I left, locked the door from the outside, and shoved the key through the letter box. Now the girl could sleep securely.

I couldn't see a taxi and didn't know in which direction to go to look for a bus. I began to walk quickly, opening and closing my arms held out in front of my body. I turned at a couple of street corners until I ran into a large wall, not very high, dark, the end of which I couldn't see either to the left or the right. It was the Wall: the modern wall of Emperor Tsin that I had seen from Plessner's office. I turned my back to it and headed in the opposite direction. I could feel my ears had hardened from the cold. Liquid began to run from my eyes and nose, which I wiped on the sleeve of my coat. I checked the time. Six o'clock, but the streets were still wrapped in thick darkness; there wasn't a tinge of light to anticipate the day. Few cars passed by. I remembered then that I had left the radio/cassette player and the tapes in Veronika's car. I felt a pain in my chest when I breathed the frozen air. I cupped my hands and started breathing in the same warm air that I exhaled through my mouth.

I walked a long time without finding a cab. I assumed it would be better to stay in one place since by moving about I might be missing taxis. Within minutes this theory proved to be correct. A taxi soon picked me up, leaving me at the hotel door.

I didn't lie down, as I knew I wouldn't be able to sleep. I filled the tub with warm water, got in and thought. I thought about many things, about the box of precious stones behind the *Mahabharata*, about Gurian, about Liliana, about Babel, about Veronika. Yes, I thought about Ruth.

Around eleven am I got out of the tub, dried off, picked up the telephone and dialed.

'What does *Frauen vor Flusslandschaft* mean?' I asked when she answered.

'Do you really want to know?'

'No. I want you to come to my hotel.'

Pause. 'Women before a river landscape. Now?'

'If it isn't a problem.'

'It'll be a little while. I'm going to take a bath and get dressed.'

'Take a bath here.'

'An hour, all right?'

She took less than an hour. Veronika was wearing long brown leather pants, a silk blouse, a wool sweater and a long blue coat, also wool.

We stood silently in the middle of the bedroom. She smiled in that mysterious way of hers. It was strange, a face with that clarity showing such a secret smile.

I helped her remove her coat.

'What a pretty comforter,' she said. 'I love comforters.' She didn't mention Ellen or the encounter of the previous night.

Without affectation, she began to take off her clothes. I liked the firm and balanced way she removed her panties, first standing on one foot, then the other, with all the elegance of a miniature art nouveau. I also admired the even color of her skin, the pink fluorescence that had earlier impressed me so. Her eyes seemed to have grown denser.

'It took you long enough to call,' she said.

I embraced Veronika's naked body. A sensation of purity

rushed over me. A sensation of bliss. She reached out her hand and grasped my dick.

I placed her on the bed. The light of her body was that of sunrise. I have to satiate her, I thought, make her come repeatedly, use my capability of maintaining an erect penis indefinitely without coming; my pleasure is secondary. The old doubt – generosity or exhibitionism? – bothered me for only a brief moment.

Veronika rested her head on my chest.

'Thank you,' she said.

'Talk to me about Babel.'

'I'll talk to you about Babel and you talk to me about yourself,' she said, kissing me now with fraternal affection.

'I want to know more about his obsessive way of revising the text.'

'Paustovsky relates that Babel rewrote "Liubka the Cossack", which is only eight pages long, at least twenty times.'

'That story isn't in *Cavalry*.'

'It's one of the Odessa stories. There is a story in *Cavalry*, also very short, like all of Babel's stories, that he rewrote over thirty times before publishing it, and even after it was published he rewrote it again for future editions. It's the story of the sacrilegious painter Apolek who uses as models for his religious paintings criminals of the city where he lives. Do you recall it?'

Veronika kissed me. The tension had become different, there was greater mutual confidence. No, on second thought, it wasn't greater confidence. We were just getting used to each other, in and out of bed.

'Make love to me again,' she said.

The scene was repeated as before: Veronika seeking to enjoy the sexual act to the maximum and me playing the role of the exhibitionist seducer or the generous giver of satiety. Of course on such occasions there came a moment (I decided when and how) in which I had an orgasm, almost always after my partner was exhausted. But this orgasm was less to give me pleasure than to leave a viscous sign which demonstrated to my partner that I was also deeply involved in the act. People believe in external signs of orgasm.

'I've talked about Babel. Now talk about yourself,' Veronika said.

'I don't like to talk about myself.'

'You already did. About your illness, about the way you dream.'

'The thing I have isn't necessarily an illness.'

'You must have an interesting life,' Veronika said. 'One sees it in your face.'

'No, no, I don't.'

'But the way you dream is interesting. Don't you even want to talk about that? You tell me your dreams and I'll tell you mine. I also have something very curious to tell you.'

'I'll sum it up: my dreams are as if I were reading a badly written book.'

'How so?'

'Most people dream as if they were watching a badly edited film.'

'Nightmares are always well edited. Full of suspense.'

'Do you have nightmares?'

'First let's talk about your dreams. Then we'll talk about mine.'

'There was a time when my relations with . . . with people were so complicated that I decided to see an analyst.'

Veronika waited for a time. 'And?'

'A woman, a Freudian. She wanted me to talk about my life and I only talked about my dreams.'

'Who made you go to a female analyst?' Veronika joked.

'It seems that Freud, and she also, believed that dreams

are linked, in their overt content, to recent experiences and in their latent content to more remote experiences. The analyst needed other data about me, besides the dreams. The translation of the dream, for my analyst, depended in part on the association between the dream and my experience – my reality, which she wasn't obtaining – and in part on the circumstances in which I related the dream to her; that is, on my reactions. I, however, described the dream in a cold, laconic way, without comment, thus denying her the revelations that she wanted, impeding the inference of hidden things, their emergence to the surface. A person who dreams a lot is a patient theoretically easy to deal with. But I didn't meet these expectations. She would ask questions and I wouldn't answer.'

'How complicated.'

'It didn't last long, obviously. She needed time. I dropped analysis when I saw that the analyst needed me more than I needed her. But I was wrong. What about your dreams?'

'I never dream. That's the funny thing about me. I mean, I never remember my dreams. My analyst (who was also a woman) said this was the result of my lack of imagination, coupled with an unconscious attitude of denial or challenge. I gave it up too.' She paused. She lit a cigarette. 'Statistics say that men are giving up smoking and women are smoking more all the time. I know, I know, there's a sociological explanation for it, there's a sociological explanation for everything, but I don't want to hear it.' She paused again. 'Sometimes I think I have no capacity for creating images, that I am without creativity, that my analyst was right, and that I developed my memory abnormally as compensation for my lack of inventiveness. I'm acquainted with a guy who knows *par coeur*, in its entirety, the *Der Neue Herder von A bis Z* encyclopedia. I once saw him give an astonishing demonstration. But the man is virtually an idiot. No, on second thought, he's a consummate idiot. There are times when it frightens me.'

But Veronika wasn't frightened. The people around me, without exception, were actors playing a mysterious role. All of them had a secret, were hiding something from the world – from me.

# 13

The phone rang. It was Liliana.
'Where the hell have you been?'
'I'm here in Paris.'
'I called the Le Bréa and they said you weren't there. Didn't you get my message?'
'It's a complicated story. I can't tell you on the phone.'
'Anyway, where are you?'
'In Paris.'
'I know you're in Paris, goddamit! Where in Paris?'
'I can't say now.'
'How can I find you?'
'At the Le Bréa. But not by phone. If anything comes up, send me a telegram. Or rather, telegraph M'sieu Casteleau Branqueau.'
'Stop horsing around.'
'I'm not joking. Telegraph Monsieur Castelo Branco, here at the Le Bréa. He knows how to find me. Telegraph, you hear? Don't telephone. I'm dying to see you.' She hung up.

I was very anxious to speak to Plessner, to find out more about Babel's lost novel. I was about to call Plessner when he called me.

'I have more to tell you about Babel,' he said.

He received me in his ample office. He told his secretary he didn't want to be disturbed. Then he went to the window, probably to look at the Wall. I sat down.

'The henchmen of Stalin who arrested Babel,' Plessner said, still at the window, 'surely had orders to destroy any papers that they found.'

'Why blame Stalin?' I asked. 'We know that Budenny hated Babel and accused him of defaming the Cossacks in *Red Cavalry*, taking him to task for cultural corruption, political ignorance. In reality it was nothing more than a military man's wounded dignity. Budenny wanted the glorification of the Cossack, Babel offered pardon. On the other hand, it's a matter of record that Stalin considered Babel a good writer.'

'Stalin had an opinion about everything, whatever it was, and was therefore the most important critic of art and literature in the Soviet Union. Budenny wouldn't have been powerful enough to have had Babel arrested. But I agree that he could have influenced Stalin, could have made him change his opinion if, as Veronika claims to have read somewhere, Stalin did indeed like Babel. It was Veronika who told you that, wasn't it?'

'No.'

He looked at me. He knew I was lying.

'In reality,' he continued, 'Stalin, the revolutionary in power, looked upon writers and artists in general with great suspicion as disloyal, indecisive people, idiotic and useless. To consolidate and perpetuate themselves – all power seeks to perpetuate itself, that's a truthful cliché – revolutions demand coherence, things that artists are unable to give. Therefore, I don't believe that Stalin needed much incentive to arrest and kill a shabby writer and destroy his pernicious work.'

Plessner looked at me appraisingly. He was hiding something; I had no idea what it might be.

'But by a miracle, the henchman sent to carry out the
crime didn't have the courage to destroy the manuscript,
perhaps because he read it first. No one reads Babel
without loving him. What is known for certain is that the
manuscript ended up in the Lenin Library in Moscow, in
the confidential documents department. A substantial part
of the Lenin Library is closed to the public. There are
thousands, perhaps millions, of documents that for one
reason or another weren't destroyed despite orders to the
contrary. Something like what happened here in Germany,
where the files relating to the slaughter of the Jews were
preserved. We killed the Jews, and at the same time kept
them alive by preserving the documentation of that heinous
act. Man needs to purge the horrors he commits, and one way
of doing so is not to forget them. Even though the Russians are
traditionally more secretive than the Germans, the memory
of Slavic horrors was also preserved.

'It appears that many people,' Plessner went on, 'suspected
the existence of the manuscript. They say that Ehrenburg,
who knew the secret, worked discreetly to rescue the book.
But Ehrenburg must have committed an error when he spoke
so vehemently at the homage to Babel in the Soviet Writers'
Union on November 11 1964. Note the date, over twenty
years before glasnost.'

I barely managed to control my impatience. I wanted
to know immediately what had happened to the novel.
I wasn't interested in the details Plessner was supplying;
besides everything else, I had already been told part of the
episode at the Writers' Union by Veronika or Gurian.

'Ehrenburg's speech has its pathetic moments. He was
moved even more by the presence of Babel's daughter,
Lydia. "I am willing to beg like a dog before the responsible

organizations for them to republish Babel," Ehrenburg said. The official explanation was that there was no paper available. "No paper to publish a little book? The paper must be found!" Ehrenburg roared. The little book was *Red Cavalry* and a few more stories, among them the Odessa tales. At one point Ehrenburg said, "Anyone who doesn't love Babel is our enemy." This must have been seen by the "responsible organizations" as an intolerable provocation. As a result, the delicate task of rehabilitating Babel and recovering the unpublished manuscript, still lost amid the immense number of proscribed documents in the Lenin Library, suffered a setback. Ehrenburg planned to put together a complete edition of Babel's works, including the confiscated manuscript. But the edition published in 1966, with a preface by Ehrenburg, besides being incomplete, did not contain the novel, which had not even been found. Possibly the book was then hidden even more carefully. The conservative bureaucracy entrenched itself also in the Writers' Union. Censorship is an unyielding cultural product. Ehrenburg's efforts came to nothing. He died shortly afterward, in 1967, perhaps thinking that Babel's novel was just a myth, suspecting logically that if the text had really existed, the rumors circulating in the early Sixties would have led some diligent functionary in one of the cultural organizations to destroy it once and for all.'

'Could you possibly forgo a bit of the bureaucratic intrigue?'

'Bureaucratic intrigue is part of life, wherever you are in the world.'

'I sense you have an important revelation to make. Do it now.'

'Be patient. We Germans have an orderly mind. And what you curiously call an important revelation is in reality something so earth-shattering that it deserves to be saved for last.'

I kept quiet, waiting.

'In 1985 the manuscript was stolen from the confidential documents department of the Lenin Library. A woman who worked there took the novel and gave it to her lover, a Soviet diplomat currently working in the West Berlin embassy. Let's call him Ivan. In the past Ivan was the protégé of Yuri Churbanov, Brezhnev's corrupt son-in-law, and I believe they were doing business together, probably currency smuggling. The fall of Brezhnev complicated Ivan's situation. May I speak briefly about bureaucratic intrigue? It helps in understanding the Russian soul, in understanding Babel. All right?'

'Forgive my impatience.'

'The fall of Brezhnev was so complete that they even removed his name from the squares and streets in Moscow, Leningrad and other cities, as well as from ships, factories, schools. The Russian way of erasing the past. Brezhnev was accused of being responsible for social and economic stagnation and for the rampant corruption during the eighteen years he was the supreme leader of the Soviet Union. As soon as Brezhnev fell into disgrace, our Ivan, a very intelligent man, won the protection of Andropov, who quit the KGB to rule the country. Upon Andropov's death Ivan sought a safeguard for himself in Ligachev, who had risen in the hierarchy with Andropov's help and become the new Suslov, the party ideologue. It did not take long for Gorbachev and Ligachev to come into conflict. In March of last year I was with Ivan in Moscow and he appeared lost to me. Ligachev, an honest Stalinist, was placing limitations on Ivan, although the latter was as conservative or anti-liberal as the old ideologue. At the time, Moscow – I'm speaking of the places frequented by foreign journalists and diplomats – was seething with rumors. Gorbachev had called an extraordinary session of the Politburo to ask for a vote of confidence on his domestic policy. Everywhere there was talk of the support eleven members of the Politburo had given the secretary-general by approving a warning to Ligachev. It was said that at the meeting the latter had defended Stalin's position and harshly criticized Gorbachev's liberal policies, calling them an "ideological jumble", claiming that they stimulated permissiveness and denigrated Soviet history. Gorbachev informally relieved Ligachev of his ideological functions, putting Yakoviev in his place, and at the same time began a process of rehabilitating Stalin's famous political victims. The all-powerful KGB chief, Viktor Chebrikov, who wound up being replaced by Kriuchkov, got into the debate, ambiguously criticizing the excessive attention given to negative facts. There then began a war of commissioned letters in the newspapers, which is a Soviet tradition, defending and attacking glasnost. You remember this, don't you?'

'I'm not a specialist in Soviet politics like you.'

'You're sure I'm not boring you with all this history?'

'No, please continue.'

'At the Nineteenth Extraordinary Conference of the Communist Party, called by Gorbachev to strengthen his policy of perestroika, the then secretary-general spoke about religious freedom, political freedom, economic stagnation and the need for dramatic incentives if Soviet society was to respond satisfactorily to the reforms of perestroika. But actually he was very clever and cautious. Other participants at the conference had the task of provoking the Stalinist old guard represented by Gromyko and Afanasiev. At the same time as speaking of political freedoms, Gorbachev, as a concession to the old communists, allowed the KGB to arrest members of something called the Democratic Union, which proclaimed itself an opposition party. He knew he had to act wisely – that Leninist thing of two steps forward, one step back.

'In October the secretary-general of the Soviet CP was elected president of the Supreme Soviet, thus acquiring the two most important and powerful positions in the Soviet state structure. Strengthened, Gorbachev forced Gromyko's resignation as president of the Republic, took away Ligachev's and Chebrikov's powers, and won the first battle.

'Ivan, our diplomat, sympathized in that internal struggle with the conservatives, who so far are losing the war. He still miraculously managed not to get involved in the trial of Churbanov. He escaped from a minor post in Africa and was sent to Berlin. Even though his involvement with Churbanov was not proven, the matter could be reopened at any time. Furthermore, he's a hopeless alcoholic. He knows he has missed all his chances.'

As Plessner had stopped talking, I said, 'And –?'

He remained quiet.

I waited for him to say what he intended to say.

I don't know how long we were both silent.

'Babel's unpublished novel is with Ivan, in East Berlin. He wants to sell it. All that's needed is for someone to go there with the money,' Plessner said finally.

My heart raced.

'That really is exciting news,' I said.

'Wait a little longer; that's not what I'm saving for last.'

What could Plessner possibly reveal that would excite me more than knowing that Babel's unpublished book was nearby, on the other side of the Wall, almost safe, ready to be resurrected?

'I asked Ivan,' Plessner continued, 'why he didn't come here, take the money, and request asylum like a good defector. The Bundesrepublik government would grant him paid asylum. With tears in his eyes – true, he was drunk – Ivan explained to me why he couldn't become a dissident. He had separated from his wife, with whom he had children, to live with his lover, the librarian who stole the manuscript from the Lenin Library. He had tried several times but wasn't able to get permission for her to travel, to come and meet him in Berlin. Ivan wants to be with the woman he loves, wherever it is. Isn't that touching? He believes that the repeated refusal of a visa, in this era of liberation, can only be because she's being watched by the KGB and the SSD. It may be paranoia, but diplomats are routinely watched by the political police. But I don't think Ivan is in any real danger because of the theft of the manuscript. It's been decades since anyone speculated about it; it's a dead issue. And there are so many documents in the Lenin Library that Ivan is probably correct that the theft has yet to be discovered. He wants a hundred thousand dollars for the manuscript, a ridiculous amount. I'd pay a million.'

'Why is Ivan asking so little?'

'Babel is practically unknown today. If you asked two hundred people here in Berlin if they've heard of him, the great majority would say no, and those who said yes would think you were talking about the tower built after the Flood. Your ordinary publisher wouldn't give an advance of even ten thousand dollars for the book. But I'm not an ordinary publisher.'

Until then I hadn't known that Plessner was a publisher. I knew he ran a business conglomerate, but not that a publishing house – one of the largest in Germany – was part of it.

'They say I built an empire,' Plessner said, 'but the problem isn't building an empire, it's keeping it. And to do that you have to be very careful. You have to align yourself with other groups, but you can't become vulnerable. Burda, the Springers, Leo Kirch, Bauer – all of them have cast greedy looks in my direction, futilely. I'm impregnable. They ended up devouring each other; they had to settle for fighting among themselves.'

'What about Babel's book?'

'As soon as Babel's manuscript is in my hands, we shall begin a huge publicity campaign that will make the name of Babel known and debated throughout the world. Along with my publishing house, others associated with us, in France, Italy, Japan, Spain, England, the United States, China, will announce that they are publishing the manuscript that escaped destruction as well as Babel's other books.'

He rose and went to the window. I followed him.

'This time of year it gets dark so early in Berlin ...' he murmured. Then he added, in a low voice, and I was certain he was telling the truth, 'I'm not doing this because I'm looking for a profit. I'm doing it for love. Babel is my passion. I want the world to take notice of him.'

We stood there silently, watching shadows envelop the city. Not a sound was heard. Plessner appeared to have finished his revelations.

'What about the film? We need to talk about it,' I said.

'The film can wait. There's something much more important I have to tell you.'

I waited.

Plessner continued to look out of the window. When I was a child, my mother used to read me stories about princes. The princes of my childhood had Plessner's face.

It wasn't yet four o'clock and the city was already covered by darkness.

'Say what you have to say.'

I waited.

'It's a request,' Plessner said finally. 'I'm asking you to take the money to Ivan in East Berlin and bring us the manuscript.'

I said nothing for a moment, my heart beating rapidly.

'How was it that Ivan offered the manuscript to you?'

'A good question ... I'm Babel's publisher here in

Germany. And also of many Russian-language writers, old ones, new ones, for or against the system . . . Ivan knew that . . . I had the good fortune to meet him at a cocktail party for the diplomatic corps on my trip to Moscow in March of last year. Chatting with him, by chance I raised the question of the mystery surrounding Babel's manuscript and said I'd pay good money for it if it really existed. I had no idea his lover worked in the confidential documents section of the Lenin Library.'

Another minute, thinking. Plessner drummed his fingers nervously on the table.

'All right. I'll go there and get the manuscript. How will I find Ivan? How will I identify him?'

'He'll identify you. Ivan already has your photo, the one Dietrich took at the airport when you arrived. When you get to East Berlin you'll go directly to the Pergamon Museum. You must enter the museum precisely at one o'clock. In the Pergamon you'll join a group of visitors being led by a guide. Ivan will decide the moment to contact you. If nothing happens after the guided tour, you must go to Alexanderplatz and wait there for a time, in front of the entrance to the television tower elevator. If no one has contacted you within fifteen minutes, you will look for the East German Tourist Information Office in the square, go in, and stand in front of the map of Berlin, as if trying to orient yourself.'

'It's like the script of a television movie trying to build up peripatetic suspense.'

'Ivan wrote this script. The man is semi-paranoid, as I said.'

'How will I know if Ivan is giving me the real merchandise and not a fake, as they did with Hitler's papers? I don't know Russian.'

'Ivan can't betray me. He needs my co-operation through

my silence. If he tries to deceive me he's through; I can bring to the attention of his enemies the serious crime he has committed. Ivan has no way out except to keep his half of the agreement. One important thing: no one must know what you are doing on this mission – not Dietrich, not Veronika, no one.'

Plessner had been surprised by the quickness of my answer. Even knowing how much Babel's unpublished novel meant to me, he was expecting a certain hesitation on my part and was preparing to persuade me, offer me a reward. Universal Recognition of High Merit for the Great Artistic and Humanitarian Rescue of an Immortal Literary Text? Money? A Career of Big-budget Films in Europe? Spices from KDW? I suspected that Plessner didn't want to make a film with me, and never had. From the outset he had just been looking for someone to smuggle hard currency to the other side and bring back the manuscript.

Plessner must have been a real idiot to think that I would risk being sent to prison without having a very strong reason. He'd have been shocked if he had known what went through my head as he recounted the interminable Slavic plot of political machinations that had led up to his proposition. I, already a thief of precious stones, was getting ready to commit another theft for my own benefit. Plessner would never get his hands on that manuscript.

# 14

I returned to the hotel. I felt as if I were in the middle of one of my dreams.

When I got to the room I lay down immediately and began to sweat. Little by little, my clothes became soaked. The room started to grow very hot. I got up, looking for some button on the wall that would turn off the heater. Finding none, I opened the window and breathed in the chilly air. Suddenly I was aware of two terrible events in the last few days: in less than two weeks, in addition to that horrible thing about which I didn't want to talk, I had become a thief, a gang of jewel smugglers wanted to kill me, and Babel had turned into an obsession. Babel! Babel! What had happened to my life? I began to tremble from cold, from anguish, and returned to bed. My tachycardia had stopped, but I felt incredibly tired.

I dream of Abel Gance. As always I see nothing – everything is always only an oneiric idea – but I know we are on the set of *Napoléon*. I ask him how he invented the steadycam. Gance replies (hiding his face from me) that the immobility of the camera bored him. 'My cameramen did everything I wanted, but they didn't like holding the camera in their hands. Look how heavy it is. Honegger, lower the music a little so I can talk with the man.' I pick up the camera and, as I roll the film, he shouts, 'Wider, faster! On Antonin! Did you see how heavy it is? That's why I invented that type of cuirass. You can walk with it!' Gance speaks as he attaches the breastplate to my chest, rests the camera on it, and directs: 'Quickly, quickly; Honegger, music!'

Dietrich and Veronika showed up at the hotel as I was in the middle of my gloomy thoughts.

'Well? Feeling good? Plessner told me he had a good conversation with you.'

I didn't understand the significance of what Dietrich was saying. What had Plessner told him? My hands trembled. I stuck them in my pockets.

Veronika looked lovely. But I felt no desire for her. Other than my appalling criminal plans, there was only beauty in my mind.

I felt a kind of fever. My hands wouldn't stop shaking. I kept them in my pockets.

'Are you OK?' she asked.

'Yes,' I replied, in Portuguese. Only then did I realize she had also asked the question in Portuguese.

There then took place between us the following short dialogue in Portuguese:

'Do you know Portuguese?'

'I'm studying it,' she answered.

'You're a genius.'

'Merely dedicated.'

'What's going on?' Dietrich asked.

'We're speaking Portuguese,' I said, in English.

'Veronika knows Portuguese? *Do* you know Portuguese?'

'A little. I'm studying.'

'Before long she'll know more than you do,' Dietrich said. 'I know the girl.'

'I want to talk to you alone,' I told Veronika in Portuguese.

'Let's stop that,' Dietrich said, good-naturedly.

Veronika went to the table. She ran her fingers over the keyboard of the personal computer.

'Shall we get down to work?' Veronika asked.

'Yes.'

'Do either of you need me for anything?'

'No,' Veronika said.

As soon as Dietrich left, Veronika asked me if I had 'that pseudo-thing'. I answered no.

'I think I have a fever.'

She put her hand on my forehead.

'You don't have a fever. Why don't you take your hands out of your pockets?'

'Why do I have to take my hands out of my pockets?'

'You don't. Just curious.'

We stopped talking.

'What did you want to talk to me about privately?'

'Can I trust you?' I asked.

'No.'

'How so?'

'If you're going to tell me you're hiding your hands because they're stained with the blood of an innocent, don't count on me.'

Were we joking?

'No one is innocent,' I answered.

A joke?

'Can I trust you?' I repeated.

'And me? Can I trust you?'

I took my hands out of my pockets. They were trembling less.

'You have a carpenter's hands,' she said.

'Is there in all of Germany a person I can trust, besides you?'

'You don't know anyone in Germany.'

'What I want to say is very serious.'

'You've already shown me your hands. Don't be in a rush.'

Where was the ingenuous woman who had spoken to me of God and the complexity of beings?

As we got undressed I was thinking that a poet would have called the color of her body nacreous. Lorca. I took her to bed, as if copulation were capable of providing elements to prove, or disprove, Veronika's trustworthiness. The moans, the stark flush of her face, the gestures of submission, the words – did it have any significance, did it prove anything?

Afterward we lay naked in bed, side by side. Veronika's eyes were closed, but she wasn't sleeping. I could tell by her breathing that she was as concentrated as an athlete before a jump. Why?

I decided to tell her about my conversation with Plessner, the offer he had made me – everything.

She listened in silence.

'And you want to keep the manuscript?'

'Yes.'

'Plessner won't let you.'

'What can he do to stop me?'

'You don't know Plessner. I do. I was married to him.'

'You were married to him? Why didn't you tell me?'

'That doesn't matter now. What does matter is that you don't know how much Babel means to him. He was telling the truth when he said he'd give a million dollars for Babel's novel. Do you know why he married me? Because he found out I received my *magister* cum laude with a thesis on Babel. When we went to bed, Plessner wasn't fucking me, he was fucking the writer. Plessner didn't want to have anything more to do with me after I'd told him all I knew about Babel. When it comes to Babel, he's capable of anything. Even killing.'

'Even marrying. Did you love him?'

Veronika hesitated. 'Yes. But he deserted me.'

'You're not going to tell Plessner that I plan to keep the manuscript, are you?'

'No.'

'I need your help.'

'Please, don't get me anymore involved in this.'

'I don't know Russian. All I need is for you to tell me whether the manuscript I'm going to receive from Ivan could or couldn't be Babel's. Plessner says that Ivan won't try to betray him, but I'm not sure. I don't want to steal a forgery.'

'You're crazy. You'll be arrested at the border.'

'Plessner promised the guards won't search me. Because I'm a Brazilian film director invited to the festival.'

'The festival was postponed.'

'It's not hard to conceal a hundred thousand dollars on your person. In this cold it's natural for a Brazilian to walk around in heavy clothes.'

'You will give yourself away. Your hands will tremble. Like just now. You think I didn't see your hands trembling? If you're caught, you'll be in prison a long time. It won't matter if you're a Brazilian or a Martian. And what's this story about Brazilians not being searched? Plessner is lying.'

'I'll take the chance.'

'And if you escape the communists, you won't escape Plessner. It won't be one of his *Schläger* who'll do the job; Plessner will kill you with his own hands.'

'I doubt it. Others have tried to kill me without succeeding.'

'You're not just a senseless idiot, you're a megalomaniacal lunatic. You're a criminal. What you're committing is theft.'

'Film began with a great theft: Edison stealing from Etienne Marey the invention of the first motion picture camera.'

'Is that true?'

'Absolutely. Just as it's true that the KGB men stole the manuscript from Babel's hands and Ivan's lover stole it from the Lenin Library. Plessner plans to get possession of it by corrupting Ivan and smuggling dollars. It's a script full of depravity. I'm no worse than anyone else.'

'Do you think Plessner is using all of us – you, me, Dietrich?' she asked. 'That we were all deceived? That he never planned to make a film at all?'

'I don't know. He didn't have to seek me out in Brazil to do that. But at this point such speculation is futile. Are you going to help me or not?'

'Yes,' she said with an agonized sigh.

I told Veronika my plan, which was quite simple.

'I go there, give Ivan the money, get the manuscript, and return the same day.'

'You'll have to return the same day. They'll probably only give you a 24-hour visa.'

Veronika would wait for me at the hotel. She would examine the manuscript. If it was real, I would flee Germany immediately.

'Where will you go?'

'Paris. I have a friend there.'

'A woman friend? Like me?'

'Different.'

'And from Paris?'

'I'll return to Brazil. I'd like you to go with me. I'm going to make *Cavalry* in Brazil.'

'I don't know.'

'Give it some thought. In Rio at this time of day the sun shines intensely.'

'I like snow.'

'Don't answer now. Think it over. We'll talk later. When I get to Brazil I'll find a way of reimbursing Plessner. That way my gesture won't be quite so dishonest.'

'A hundred thousand dollars is nothing to Plessner. He'll want revenge even if you give him ten million. What day are you going across the border?'

'Plessner will let me know. He asked for my passport to get the visa for me.'

I spent the rest of the day with Veronika. We left the hotel, went to the cinema, had dinner together.

When I arrived back at the hotel with Veronika, Plessner was waiting for me in the lobby, a small case in his hand.

Now that I knew the two of them had been married, I saw them in a different light. He called her Veronika and she called him Dr Plessner. As before. But to me they were no longer the same as before.

'I had an idea about the film,' Plessner said, 'and I was anxious to talk with you.'

'I have to go,' Veronika said.

'A pity you can't stay. I would like your opinion.'

'Unfortunately I do have to go,' Veronika said.

It all seemed pre-arranged.

Plessner and I went up to my room. He placed the briefcase on the bed and took my passport from his pocket. Inside was a sheet of official paper. 'This is your visa. You go tomorrow. You have twenty-four hours to get in and get out.'

'Does it have to be tomorrow?'

'The date and place were set by Ivan, days ago. I can't seek him out, according to our agreement. He decides on the opportunity for and convenience of the contacts. It has to be tomorrow.'

Then Plessner opened the briefcase. Ten packages of ten thousand dollars in hundred-dollar bills.

'New bills,' Plessner said. 'They take up less space.'

Each package looked three-quarters of an inch thick at most. The dollars I had brought from Brazil had seemed to take up more room.

I picked up the packs of money and distributed them about my body. Five packs went in the belt, around my waist. Two in the jacket pocket. Another two in the outside pockets. One pack was left over. I put on the raincoat. I placed it in the coat pocket.

'It's best to leave the coat open,' Plessner said, getting his muffler and putting it around my neck. 'Walk a little, so I can see.'

I walked around the room, observed by Plessner.

'There's nothing obvious. One more advantage of being thin,' Plessner said.

I stood in front of the closet mirror and took a long look at myself. The muffler, its ends hanging down the open coat, gave the outfit an informal air. There was no hint that I was carrying so much money.

'Another thing: don't wear a hat. The uncovered head will give you the fragile and unprotected look of an unprepared Latin.'

Then Plessner took from his pocket a small colored map, *Übersichtsplan*, and a booklet with the word *Stadtplan* on its cover. Putting both on the table and leaning over the map with a pen in his hand, he began his instructions.

'You go by U-Bahn and then change to the S-Bahn. Don't forget to get the ticket from one of those automatic ticket machines. We don't want you to get picked up without a ticket in the random checks the inspectors run. There are people, mostly students and Cappadoccians – as you know, we've been invaded by Turks – who never pay their fare and prefer to run the risk of paying a forty-mark fine if caught. It's a public humiliation – the inspectors are quite rude – that could unnerve you and put you off. Remember: buy a ticket.'

'Where are the ticket machines?'

'You'll see them. They're yellow. If you don't have change, the machine automatically changes the money for you. Don't forget.'

'I won't forget.'

'You catch the U-Bahn here, at Uhlandstrasse station, the corner of Kurfürstendamm, the closest to this hotel.' He drew a circle on the map. 'Get the Rathaus–Steglitz train heading toward Osloer Strasse, this orange line. It's a short run. You get off at Zoo Garten station' – another circle, now over a small square on the map beside which was written Zoologischer Garten – 'and here you take the S-Bahn to Friedrichstrasse station.' Then Plessner nervously drew a heavy circle with several strokes around the small square labeled Friedrichstrasse in black letters. There lay the border between the two Berlins which I was to cross.

'You must arrive at Friedrichstrasse at around noon,' Plessner said. 'At that hour East Berliners over sixty-five years of age, who are free to come and shop on this side, will be returning with their sacks full of merchandise. The guards waste a lot of time examining what these people are carrying. The waiting in line will be nerve-racking for you. But the guards' supervision will be less rigid. Upon leaving the station, you take this route to the museum and, if necessary, in case Ivan isn't there, to Alexanderplatz.'

Plessner marked this route on the map. Then he held out his hand.

'You don't know how much I admire your gesture. I wouldn't have the courage to do this.' A pause, while he grasped my hand firmly. He continued: 'It's of course true that the risk would be infinitely greater if I were to go instead of you.'

When Plessner had gone, I put on the raincoat again and distributed the packs of dollars around my body in several ways until I found the one that seemed best. I wrote myself a note – three packs in the front of the belt, two in the back, and so on as a reminder for the next morning.

Then I lay down and turned out the light.

I was taking a big chance smuggling dollars into East Germany. If caught, I risked spending long years in prison. But the reward was great, and worth it.

I dream of the woman with the dark false tooth, her foot over the drain. 'Now,' she says, 'tell whether or not you remember the day we danced on cold tiling.' 'You have Claudette Colbert's face,' I say. 'I want to know about dance; you never learn, boy. I know very well what my face is like.' 'You have small round breasts,' I say. 'Well, well,' she says. 'Claudette Colbert playing Cleopatra at the Museum of Modern Art,' I say. 'You went too far,' she says, taking her foot from the drain. I am being absorbed, and before entering the drain I shout: 'And full of apple blossoms!' But there is no time to save myself. The agonizing blind sensation of falling, the physical agony.

For a second, when I awoke, I thought that my pain was still an 'idea' from the dream. But even dreams devoid of images could not have that kind of physical reality. I was in the middle of an attack of pseudo-Ménière's syndrome, suffering the horrible vertigo that came with it.

I tried to get up and fell, dragging the night table and lamp down with me. I lay motionless on the floor. If I moved, it would be worse. The medicine was in the bathroom cabinet. What time was it? I must have slept a little, two hours at least.

Outside it was still dark, but that meant only that it could be any time between three and eight am. In a few hours Ivan would be waiting for me at the Pergamon. Out of the corner of my eyes I tried to detect some sign of dawn. Fortunately, all that I saw was a deep blackness outside, no indication that day was about to break. The less time that had passed since I had gone to bed, at around one in the morning, the better. I would have longer to recover.

I continued lying on my back on the floor, without moving, for some time. The worst dizziness occurred when my head was moved sideways; therefore, keeping my head rigid and my eyes wide open, I began very slowly to raise my upper body from the floor. When I sat down, the dizziness was so strong that I almost fell again. I longed to close my eyes and let myself be engulfed by the abyss, but I knew I had to keep them open in order not to lose my balance completely, even if the darkness was total and I had no visible object to serve as a reference.

I remained seated for half an hour, my eyes bulging, trying to make out the dark, blurry shape of the bed a short distance from my nose. My head was held immobilized with such force that my neck muscles were beginning to ache.

Then I kneeled down. The dizziness lessened. I stood up. Again I felt I was fainting and plunging into the precipice.

It took some time for me to recover my senses. Now, lying face down on the floor, I felt a warm dampness on my face.

A diffuse, delicate light began to come in through the window. I couldn't stay there, captive to my weaknesses. Babel was waiting for me. Keeping my head erect, as if I were a turtle, I dragged myself along the floor toward the bathroom. I could feel the cold tiling on my hands and legs. I grasped the basin and slowly lifted myself. I felt I was going to faint again. Keeping one hand on the edge of the basin,

I extended the other in search of the light switch. A fierce glare flooded the bathroom. In front of me I saw the bottle of medicine. The light, the sight of the container of pills, seemed to give me strength. I opened the bottle and took two pills. I was startled to see my blood-covered face in the mirror. I must have injured myself when I fainted the second time.

After taking the medicine, I sat on the floor and held onto the toilet, waiting for the attack to pass.

It was ten in the morning by the time I felt well enough to get dressed. I still couldn't move my head laterally; to look to the sides I had to turn my whole body, but I could now stand up and walk around the room.

The hardest part was putting on my shoes and socks without being able to look down at my feet.

After dressing, I put the allocated packs of dollars into my belt under my shirt. The contact of money against my skin repelled me. I distributed the remaining packs in my jacket pockets, following the sketch I had made. I put on the raincoat, then the muffler, without wrapping it around my neck as Plessner had suggested.

I stood before the mirror, stiff-necked, moving only my eyes in their sockets to view my entire body. The open coat and the muffler hanging from my neck gave me a casual look. I was ready to set out on my adventure.

It was eleven o'clock when I left the hotel. A fine snow, which must have begun falling during the night, covered the streets. I walked toward the Uhlandstrasse station. The cold of the snow had a stimulating effect on me. I stood for a time at the station entrance, letting the snow deposit itself on my head.

I didn't identify my train – U9 Rath Steglitz – right away. The car had just stopped at the station when I saw it and boarded with as much speed as my stiff neck permitted. And I got off immediately, just as the doors were beginning to shut, when

I remembered I hadn't bought a ticket. Seeing the train pull away, I felt the beginnings of vertigo. What kind of piss-poor criminal was I, acting so negligently? Crime only paid when it was very well planned and when the hero, or bad guy, was working for a good cause. I had seen that film several times, and I should follow the script to the letter.

I found the machine and bought the ticket. I waited for my train to come again, which took a little more than five minutes.

I stood in the car, near the door, looking outside. Even before the train came to a full stop I saw the words Zoo Garten written somewhere. I got out. I caught the S-Bahn in the direction of Friedrichstrasse.

The old men and women in the train wore threadbare heavy coats and carried sacks stuffed with purchases. I saw bottles of Metaxa in many of them. I wondered about their preference for that label of brandy. Others in the train looked like tourists.

The Friedrichstrasse station was the end of the line. The old men and women picked up their sacks. I let them get off ahead of me.

The train had stopped at a rather high platform. A set of stairs led to the ground floor, where inspectors examined passports and baggage. The old people walked slowly and I checked myself in order not to overtake them.

We came to an enormous room. The old people lined up to show their passports to the uniformed guards.

I saw that the checks were carried out by two guards in each line, first one then the other. The lines were divided into two sections: people with East German passports, and visiting foreigners. Plessner had been wrong. The old people with their sacks of merchandise were in different lines.

The guards were tall, neatly uniformed men. I looked admiringly at their beautiful uniforms, their martial stance.

I had already seen, when I arrived in Berlin, some soldiers, in shiny boots and long, well-fitting overcoats. I thought: no one wears a uniform as well as a Prussian.

But my aesthetic concerns were short-lived. The guards' gaze was hard and alert. They looked at the passport and then at the person's face, straight in the eyes. This scrutiny was carried out by the first guard, and further on the second did the same. The latter seemed to have an even more implacable face. It was part of the routine, but I began to sweat, worried. And the more I sweated, the tenser I became. Sweating might call the guards' attention to the fact of my keeping my coat on, even if it was open, and the muffler.

I remembered *The Goalie's Anxiety at the Penalty Kick* by Wim Wenders. A policeman explains to a man how a criminal can be discovered. 'We have to look into his eyes.' The man talking to the policeman is a wanted killer, but the policeman doesn't suspect him for an instant. The truth is that policemen look into a killer's eyes and see nothing. Or rather they see the same thing that they see in the eyes of the innocent. Those policemen at the border between the two Berlins, in their lovely uniforms, looked into eyes merely to intimidate, also without seeing anything, following a bureaucratic routine. If I wasn't intimidated, my gaze would have the same purity as that of the little old lady in the other line carrying her bag of merchandise.

I was no longer sweating when I arrived in front of the first policeman. He stared at me, then took my passport, opened it, saw the picture, and once again faced me menacingly – omniscient, pitiless, just as they had taught him at the *Polizeischule.*

But I had seen the film.

I let him stare into my eyes for a few seconds, enough time for him to see that I was innocent, and then averted my eyes – I shouldn't insist; innocent people don't challenge.

The policeman handed me back my passport.

Further on, the same performance was repeated. Another guard examined my passport, in a re-enactment of what had gone before. He let me pass. But I couldn't consider myself free just yet. There was still the booth, where one visitor at a time entered, the final obstacle to be overcome.

A light came on over the door and the guard ordered me inside.

It was a type of short corridor with a door at each end. The light coming from overhead was very strong. To the left of the entrance I noticed a glass-covered opening. Without doubt someone behind there was watching me, but I couldn't see through the glass.

Disturbed, I pretended to occupy myself with my passport, inside which was the visa. I slid the passport through an opening under the glass.

I waited.

'Raise your head,' said a harsh, humiliating voice.

I raised my head. I could make out a vague shape behind the dark glass. Was he, even from there, looking into my eyes?

I waited.

'Twenty-five marks,' said the harsh voice. It was the *Zwangsumtausch*, the obligatory currency exchange for all visitors. I gave him the West German money.

Time seemed to have stopped. There was not the slightest sound inside the dark booth. What could be missing?

Script: the guard sees signs of guilt in my face. He knows I'm carrying a hundred thousand dollars on me, a heinous crime in East Germany, and begins my punishment by the anguish of waiting; noting with satisfaction the first drops of cold sweat on my forehead, the tremor of my lips, he lightly places his finger on a button that, at his pleasure, will sound the alarm to expose me.

I heard a small noise. My passport appeared, finally pushed

back by the invisible hand of the menacing individual hiding behind the glass, with the visa and the East German marks.

A light came on at the other end of the booth. I opened the door and went out. I was on the other side.

# 15

I calmly climbed a short, wide stairway, fighting off the sensation of triumph that made my heart beat faster. I still hadn't left the station. I saw a café. People walking. The sooner I got out of there, the better.

It was cold in the street. I walked for several minutes. When I found a safe place, I opened the *Stadtplan* to the page that Plessner had marked.

Following the route shown on the map, I joined Friedrich-strasse and went to Unter den Linden. At the other end of Unter den Linden I quickly arrived at the Spree River canal and saw the Museumsinsel, where the Pergamon was. There were several museums on the island which was situated in a triangle, one of whose sides was formed by the Spree.

I bought a ticket and went in, perhaps too hurriedly, looking for a group of visitors with a guide.

The Pergamon building was the largest on the island. Its immense rooms were empty; there didn't seem to be a single visitor present, only guards. After walking about aimlessly, I saw that one of the guards was looking at me suspiciously. Unconsciously I brought my hands to my stomach and felt the hidden packs of dollars. There was no Ivan, no guide, no visitors in that damned museum. It was dangerous to stay in an empty place full of guards. Besides that, I didn't like museums. It was best to get out of there as fast as possible.

I saw that I was lost. But I didn't want to ask one of the guards for information, and however hard I tried I couldn't find the exit. After wandering about at random, seized by unbearable anxiety, I finally found the exit. I quickened my pace and at that moment I saw a group of people standing round a man who pointed to the walls as he spoke.

I joined the group. The guide was speaking in German, French and English. We were in a long, wide corridor formed by vitrified brick walls showing in relief lions in motion, who seemed to roar. The guide explained that this *babylonische Prozessionstrasse*, the street of the Babylonian procession, had been reconstructed using the original fragments. It was from the time of Nebuchadnezzar II, who reigned from 604 to 562 and destroyed Jerusalem five years before his death. Funny the guide should have mentioned that. In real life, things tend to take on an unexpected degree of coincidence. Áureo de Negromonte, the Carnival figure who had unforeseeably become linked to me, had had a costume based on Nebuchadnezzar's court.

As the guide went on to describe *Stiere und Drachen*, bulls and dragons, on the façade of Ishtar's gate, I made a surreptitious effort to discover which of the other visitors might be Ivan. There were in the group almost equal numbers of men and women. Ivan would certainly be a man. It's true that if this were a film, Ivan could be a woman. In any case I decided to look over the men first. The best moment to do so would be when the guide made us stop for a longer period to listen to his explanations. This happened when we came to the altar of Pergamum, which occupied the entire room in which we stood.

'This altar,' the guide said, 'is a *Weltwunder*, one of the wonders of the world. It was constructed in honor of the goddess Athena, in the ancient Greek kingdom of Pergamum, today Bergama, in Asia Minor, in Turkey.'

The altar had been discovered in excavations by German archeologists in the nineteenth century. 'It shows the struggle of the gods against the race of giants. See how impressive these figures are, biting each other, the dramatic confusion of forms, wings, muscular bodies, in fantastic movements. *Die Götter*, the gods, have human bodies, handsome and noble heads. The giants also, but with the feet of reptiles. This struggle was decided by Heracles.'

'Where is Heracles?' asked a French man, who made a point of clarifying that Heracles in France was Hercules. Until that moment I had suspected the Frenchman, for he had been acting nervously, looking to the sides and at people.

The guide explained that this was a good question, that Hercules's sculpture did not exist, that the altar, with the exception of the Byzantine murals, had been reconstructed and Hercules had been lost. 'He should be there.' The guide pointed to a place on the mural. 'The gods are grouped according to kinship, with the most important group being that originating from Zeus and Athena, but he isn't there. He was lost.'

I had begun my tour of the museum feigning interest in the booty the Germanic peoples had amassed in their wars of conquest through the years, in order to find Ivan. (Museums today in all the large imperialist nations raise interesting questions about power.) But that altar, mysteriously, awakened greater interest in me. I was no longer analyzing the other visitors as I should. I was thinking about Athena and Heracles. Athena, the goddess of wisdom, protectress of arts and handicraft, but also the goddess of military combat, a very Germanic goddess. I remembered Homer from my high-school days: 'Athena Pallas with glaucous eyes . . .' What? After all the Homer I had read, I had fixed in my memory only the color, the greenish-blue of a woman's gaze?

A tall, fat man with gray hair, carrying a black briefcase, looked in my direction. But I was thinking about Hercules, driven mad by his stepmother Hera, the hero who, after becoming immortal, was killed by a scorned wife.

Finally the tour ended and no one approached me. Little by little, everyone left the museum. I stayed a while longer in front of the altar.

When I left the Pergamon I again took Unter den Linden, which went directly to Karl-Liebknechtstrasse. The street's name raised questions in my mind: Could it have been into that canal of the Spree, which I had just passed, that Liebknecht and Rosa Luxemburg had been thrown after their murder? (Actually, the bodies of Liebknecht and Rosa had been thrown from the Cornelius bridge in the Tiergarten, in West Berlin.)

I entered Spandaustrasse. Because of the cold my eyes and nose began to produce large quantities of a liquid which I cleaned away with paper tissues that once used filled my pockets. I passed in front of Rotes Rathaus, the old City Hall, continued along Rathausstrasse, crossed the S-Bahn station, and saw an enormous TV tower. I had used a packet of tissues by the time I got to the square.

The square wasn't Fassbinder's, much less Döblin's. The TV tower sitting in the middle of Alexanderplatz was an ugly, ostensive tribute to the sovereignty of progress. Despite the cold, a good many people were walking from side to side in the middle of the square. I looked for a trash basket to get rid of the used tissues in my coat pockets.

Then I passed by the door of the tourist office. It was a low building, almost a shed; it was surely a temporary facility. I went to the tower and stationed myself near the entrance to the elevator, both to protect myself from the weather and to be seen by whoever came by from outside. Even so, my nose and ears ached from the cold.

Once again, Ivan did not show up.

I walked over to the tourist office and went in. Several tourists were asking for information and picking up brochures. I saw a large map on the wall. I positioned myself in front of it.

An older man at my side said something or other in German.

I answered, in English, that I didn't speak German.

'Have you been to the Pergamon Museum?' he asked.

'Yes,' I said.

'Is this your first visit to East Berlin?'

His pronunciation was heavily accented. But he spoke English with ease.

'Didn't we see each other at the museum?' I asked. He was the tall man with white hair who had been looking at me while I thought about Hercules. He still had the black briefcase.

'You are very observant,' he said, laughing, 'but I thought there were too many suspicious people around. Did you notice?'

'The Greek mythology bothered me.'

'Ah, you Americans are very funny.' He appeared to have been drinking. 'You are American, yes?'

Plessner, astutely, hadn't told him who I was. Ivan couldn't tell by my pronunciation whether I was or wasn't American. 'Yes, I'm American.'

'From what part?'

'New York.'

'Ah, New York!' he said. 'You like Hungarian food? You had better; at this time few restaurants still serve lunch.' He removed from his pocket the photo that Dietrich had taken of me at the airport. 'Take it. I do not need it anymore.'

We left the tourist office together.

He seemed to be satisfied that he was at no further risk. He walked beside me, holding onto my arm.

'Unfortunately, East Berlin has no American food restaurant. What is typical American food – hot dog?' Another laugh.

I laughed also. 'Mine is a hamburger.'

'From McDonald?'

Me: 'Ha ha ha!'

The restaurant wasn't far from the square.

It was a large room with old, dark furniture, Bauhaus style, and many mirrors on the wall. A pleasantly decadent appearance.

Ivan ordered a vodka immediately.

'Do you know Russian?'

'Unfortunately not.'

'The dollars are with you? One hundred thousand?'

'Yes.'

He took the briefcase from the floor and placed it on the table.

'Go to bathroom with briefcase, take the manuscript that is inside, and put the dollars in its place.'

I picked up the briefcase and went to the bathroom. I locked myself in one of the stalls. I opened the case. I took the manuscript in my trembling hands. There must have been about two hundred pages, covered with small Cyrillic characters. Babel, at last! I exhaled a sigh in relief. Babel! Babel!

I took the dollars from my body and placed them in the briefcase. I divided the manuscript into four stacks of approximately fifty pages each and put them in my belt, two over my stomach and two on my back.

I went back to the table. The sheets of papers on my stomach almost prevented me from sitting down. I gave the briefcase to Ivan. A bottle of vodka had appeared.

'I am a man without imagination. I am going to order goulash. Do you know goulash?' he said.

'Did you read the manuscript?' I asked.

'I was not interested. I read one page only.'

'What does it deal with? What is the book about?'

'I don't remember. I read one page only. What can I remember?'

The waiter came up to us and we ordered.

Within a few minutes Ivan drank two more vodkas. As he drank he became more talkative and his English got worse. He said he had been betrayed by 'that man from Tomsk' (it took some time for me to discover that he was referring to Ligachev) and by the 'secretary-general-president'. I regretted not having paid more attention to what Plessner had told me about Soviet domestic politics.

'Do you think I am bad communist? Bad citizen? No, you do not know.' He paused for a long time. 'I am poet. That is what I am. Do you know Pushkin?'

'Yes.'

'Greatest poet in world!'

Ivan recited Pushkin in Russian while the waiter served our goulash. I began to eat. Ivan had ordered a Tokay, which he drank by himself. I noticed that people at nearby tables were glancing discreetly in our direction.

Ivan said that he hadn't succeeded in publishing his verses. Nevertheless, the Soviet Union each year published close to ninety thousand titles, an overall printing of two and a half billion copies, second only to the editorial production of China. But no one read the majority of the books published; mountains of books, millions of tons of paper spent on useless, boring verbiage. 'What the people want to read they cannot find in the libraries!'

'Why wasn't your book published?'

'Petty politics . . . The popular thing these days is to speak ill of Stalin . . . Did you see Shatrov speaking of the myth of socialist revolution? Did you see Ribakov? Now he denounces the horrors committed in the time when he was enjoying life in his dacha in Peredelkino . . . Yevtushenko comes now to say enough *priterpelost*, enough servile patience, but nobody showed more subservient resignation than he did in all those years. With exception of some few, like Yuri Bondariev and Vladimir Karpov, who fearlessly attacked the terrorism of the liberals, intellectuals are not to be trusted . . . I read many poems of those traitors of the people calling Stalin little father . . .'

Gorbachev had turned Soviet politics into a hypocritical and repugnant farce, according to Ivan. He had been in Moscow most of the year, awaiting assignment to another post abroad, 'a year in which many things happened, the implacable struggle for power at the upper echelons of government, Reagan's visit, the first protests in the streets.'

Ivan had attended the ceremony commemorating the anniversary of Lenin's birth, April 22, at the Palace of Congress, when the rulers staged 'a farce for public opinion'. That day Ligachev had arrived at the Palace smiling, a rare thing for him, for 'he is a man who laughs very little' and been greeted by the prime minister Nikolai Ryzhkov, an ally of Gorbachev's, with a kiss on the mouth, as the Russians customarily do to demonstrate friendship. In turn Ligachev had applauded the speech that Georgi Razumovski had given vigorously supporting Gorbachev's perestroika and glasnost programs.

The bottle of Tokay was empty.

'Repugnant,' Ivan said. 'Boris Yeltsin took advantage of Reagan's visit to make complaints against Ligachev. Can you imagine something so humiliating happening in the Soviet Union?'

Something in Ivan's face – the agony, the suffering –

made me understand why the librarian had stolen the manuscript for him. The thief had felt sorry for that frustrated man and had sought a way to help him. Or, a cynical hypothesis, stealing the manuscript might have been a way to involve him in an adventure that would separate him from his family.

'Ligachev was right,' Ivan continued, 'when he demanded, and achieved, the defeat of Boris. Those were days of confusion. I witnessed it all. I saw the street protests in Moscow, first in history of Soviet Union, people demanding freedom for the dissidents, screaming for bigger reforms, while the police looked on in confusion. They let that old crank Sakharov appear on television and make his senile complaints to Western press for whole world to see what a nice fellow Gorbachev was. I saw Gorbachev and Raisa hypocritically commemorating at the Bolshoi theater the one-thousandth anniversary of the Christianization of Russia, to gain allies among believers and fool that idiot pope. Gorbachev thinks he is very clever but he is nothing more than a sorcerer's apprentice . . .'

Ivan was speaking in a loud voice. I noticed looks of censure from some tables around us.

'Speak more softly, please,' I said.

Ivan ignored my warning. 'I am going to tell you something: the true communist ideals were betrayed by Gorbachev and his gang. A director of KGB, Alexei Soloviov, even said that millions of people had been eliminated during Stalin era and that KGB's essential function was to find out the truth. KGB find out the truth?'

Ivan laughed loudly.

'Yakoviev came to control ideological issues and Alexandr Sukharev was made attorney-general. Did you see what Ambartsumov, of Institute of Marxism and Leninism, said? The Party and Stalin were the major ones responsible

for crimes, for corruption of Soviet society since Revolution. Ambartsumov said that! And book by Colonel Dmitri
Volkoganov, director of Institute of Military History of Min-
istry of Defense? Volkoganov says that Stalin took Russian
people to a tragedy whose consequences entire nation suffers
today. He called Stalin an insane, immoral and hypocritical
killer. Besides possessing these perverse features, Stalin, to
Volkoganov, was also stupid. A Soviet general saying that!
Is not unbelievable, American? They rehabilitated traitors
like Kamenev, Zinoviev, Radek, Bukharin. They will end up
rehabilitating Trotsky. Yuri Afanasiev, who Gorbachev made
director of Soviet Institute of Historical Archives, said that
Trotsky was condemned based on false evidence. Is the
Great Step Backward, arranged by these traitors to the
people. After lies about Stalin they turned against Lenin
himself.'

'Didn't Khrushchev do something similar in 1956?' I
asked.

'Khrushchev did not touch Lenin. His hatred was against
Stalin. Even so, did you see what happened? He was deposed
by Brezhnev.'

Ivan leaned over the table and took my hand. His face
had become very red.

'Then came Party Congress, at beginning of July. I watched
everything on TV screen they put up in Pushkin Square. A
clown named Melnikov, mouthpiece for Gorbachev, tried
to attack Gromyko, Solomentov, Afanasiev, Arbatov, who
dedicated their lives to greatness of Soviet Union, but had
to shut mouth before coldness of reception by delegates. Do
you know who was enthusiastically applauded? A delegate
who said, "Where is this perestroika? All I see are the queues;
there is still no meat, sugar, potatoes."

'But that was in July. In first days of October I was
transferred here to Berlin, on same occasion that Gorbachev

pulled his coup by isolating Gromyko and neutralizing Ligachev and Chebricov. Now he is the one gives orders.'

Ivan hit the table with his fist. 'Gorbachev and his revisionist circle want to destroy Lenin! They want to destroy socialism, they want to go back to capitalism. But the people will not let them. They have been able to deceive public till now with sordid lies. But popular frustration is growing day by day. Will emerge at any moment another Brezhnev. Remember what I am telling you.' Ivan sighed two or three times. 'But I am out of that. I want to be far away. Let them all, on both sides, sink into shit!'

I noticed that at a table near ours a man got up and went to the back of the restaurant to make a phone call. I didn't like the way the man talked on the phone, all stooped over, his head resting on his chest, his hand cupped over the mouthpiece.

'I have to leave,' I said.

'The bottle is still full,' Ivan said, indicating another bottle of Tokay that the waiter had just brought.

'But I have to leave,' I repeated. Besides being worried about the man who'd left to make a call – and had just returned to the table next to ours acting extremely suspiciously, avoiding looking in our direction, something he had earlier done openly – the pages of the manuscript were hurting my ribs.

I got up.

Ivan poured wine into the glass and said something in Russian that I didn't understand. He smiled.

'Goodbye, American,' he said.

I left the restaurant and crossed to the other side of the street. I waited. It was snowing. I was stupidly putting myself in jeopardy; it was crazy to stay there, watching the door of the restaurant. But I waited. After a seemingly interminable time, which must have been only about five minutes, a black car pulled up at the door of the restaurant. I felt like fleeing, running away. But I waited. Two men in dark overcoats and with fur berets on their heads leapt out of the car and went into the restaurant. I waited, anxious. What was going on inside?

I imagined the following scenario: the two men leap from the car and slowly enter the restaurant, looking around with hard, discerning eyes. They sit down at Ivan's table and identify themselves as agents of the SSD, East Germany's secret police. Ivan says he's a diplomat, serving in the embassy of the Soviet Union in Berlin. What are you carrying in that briefcase? Ivan's drunkenness vanishes. He begins to sweat profusely. Papers from the embassy, Ivan says, clutching the case to his chest. One of the policemen violently jerks the case from Ivan's arms. The briefcase comes open and dollars spring forth like a jack-in-the-box. Ivan shouts that he has diplomatic immunity. The waiter who served us denounces: it was an American who gave him this money in exchange for confidential documents. The American spy is carrying the papers next to his body, under a raincoat. The spy just left; he can't have gone far. One of the agents bolts for the door.

Before the waiter could finish this sentence (invented in my scenario but one that very possibly was being uttered in real life), I moved away from the restaurant at a rapid pace.

The photograph! I thought as I walked toward Alexanderplatz. I started to look through my pockets nervously for the photo that Plessner had given to Ivan so he could identify me. I had a vague recollection that Ivan had returned it. Wanting to be certain that the photo was in my possession, I searched frantically for it, slipping on the snow accumulated on the ground. Still walking, I finished going through my pockets without finding it. Could I have left it in the restaurant? At the Pergamon? No, Ivan hadn't spoken to me at the museum. In the restaurant! I had left the photo on the table in the restaurant! I was doomed.

I stopped in the middle of the square without knowing where to go. The snow chilled my head. I tried mentally to retrace my steps. Luckily I recalled that Ivan had given me the photo at the tourist office. I remembered the scene clearly: 'You are very observant,' he had said, laughing (why was he laughing? he laughed at the wrong times, like when he had uttered something in Russian as he said goodbye in the restaurant – 'goodbye, American'), and he'd pulled from his pocket the photo that Dietrich had taken at the airport. 'Take it. I do not need it anymore.' I had taken the photo and . . . and put it in my shirt pocket, under my sweater!

With great relief I found the photo. I started walking again. As I walked I tore the photo into tiny pieces that dropped in the snow, as if by tearing up that image of me I would become invisible, untouchable.

I didn't need the map to find my way back to Friedrichstrasse station.

As I went through inspection to leave East Germany, my nervousness was greater than before. I hadn't been afraid of going to prison, much less having the hundred thousand dollars confiscated. But to lose Babel's manuscript –! The very idea filled me with horror.

The guards were different, but they performed the same mime taught at the police academy. I wondered if the hearts of the old ladies with their Metaxa bottles always beat rapidly when they were pierced every week by those penetrating stares.

In front of me an American, after showing his passport, was taken out of the queue and led to a door through which he and the two guards disappeared.

Scenario: Ivan had been arrested and had told of the American spy; that is to say, me.

'Is something the matter with you?' asked the guard who was examining my passport.

'Bad food. Goulash. Goulash!' I said, hitting my belly with my hand. I made a likely face, in reality from fright, for my hand had hit the sheets of paper.

The guard returned my passport and I went through. Then it was the other guard's turn.

I finally made it past all the obstacles, climbed to the upper platform at Friedrichstrasse station, and waited for the train to arrive. When it came, I took a seat and closed my eyes. Sweat poured down my face.

Upon arriving at Zoo Garten station I almost forgot to get off and catch the U-Bahn. I left on the run before the doors closed. I was anxious to get to the hotel and find Veronika. I wanted her to read a passage from Babel's book to me, immediately.

As I approached the hotel I had a surprise. Plessner and Veronika were in front of the main door, talking. I drew back instinctively and hid in the entrance to a nearby stationery store.

I could see from Plessner's manner that he was giving Veronika instructions. She listened attentively. She was a different person. Plessner, however, hadn't changed; he spoke to Veronika the same way he had spoken to me when telling me what I should do to meet Ivan on the other side – a man who was always giving instructions. But Veronika looked different. This wasn't my Veronika.

They said goodbye, but not with a formal handshake. Side by side, their arms extended along their bodies in a quasi-secret gesture, they held each other's hands in a long clasp, saying nothing, just looking at each other intensely, a rapport of partners, of accomplices. Then Plessner got into the car parked at the hotel door and left. Veronika lifted the collar of her fur coat, to protect herself from the cold, and went into the hotel.

From a phone booth in the street I called the hotel.

'I want to speak with Frau Veronika Hempfel. She should be in the lobby,' I told the person who answered.

Veronika came quickly.

'Where are you? Did everything go well?' she asked.

'Yes.'

'Do you have the manuscript?'

'Yes. I'm waiting here at the Pressecafé am Zoo.'

'At the Pressecafé am Zoo?'

'Come right away.' I hung up.

I waited. I didn't have my watch. I counted: one thousand and one, one thousand and two, one thousand and three . . . After five minutes I left the booth and went to the hotel.

Up in my room I took the manuscript from my body. I looked at those Cyrillic characters written in ink, with a horrendous sense of impotence. I put the manuscript in the suitcase, the book with *Red Cavalry* and *Odessa Tales* which Dietrich had given me back in Rio, my papers with the outline and notes, along with the few clothes I had. I went downstairs, got the dollars from the hotel safe. I paid the bill.

The wind in the street had increased, and with it the cold. A taxi took me to the airport. An Air France flight was leaving for Paris in two hours. I managed to get a place on it.

I had been through difficult moments recently, but those two hours were perhaps the longest and most nerve-racking of my life. I couldn't remain seated for a single minute. I walked back and forth in the airport, waiting for the departure, creating scenarios in my head.

Scenario: Veronika arrives at the Pressecafé am Zoo and

doesn't see me. She sits at a table and waits a while. Then she asks a waiter if he has seen a man with a raincoat (at that point she hesitates: and a stack of paper in his hand?) – wearing a raincoat, etc., but she doesn't mention the manuscript. The waiter answers no. Then Veronika tries to remember what I said. I'm here at the Pressecafé am Zoo? I'm going to the Pressecafé am Zoo? Doubtfully, she decides to wait. She waits fifteen minutes. Her fifteen minutes waiting for me are more or less fifteen minutes of my wait for the plane; one coincides with the other. I need two hours. Veronika waits another fifteen minutes. Now I have only an hour and a half. Then she goes to a telephone and calls Plessner. Dr Plessner, she says. No, she says: Darling, the Brazilian, instead of going to the hotel, etc. Plessner replies: He's not going to the Pressecafé am Zoo. He lied to you; he doesn't trust you. It's good that you now have proof of his betrayal. Do you know where he is at this moment? Waiting for the last flight to Paris.

It was I who, with this false scenario, made those two hours of waiting tense, unbearable.

Finally, none of Dr Plessner's *komplizen* appeared at the airport. Relieved, I joined the flight to Paris, but my heart ached, weighed down with unhappiness. I had just abandoned a woman because of subjective considerations that might very well be totally unfounded. I had judged Veronika based on a scenario that perhaps was false, like all scenarios. I reviewed in my imagination Veronika at Plessner's side, holding his hand. That could very well have been nothing more than Plessner wanting to mount a conspiracy that would somehow harm me and Veronika pretending to go along with the scheme.

'We have to be very careful when we judge others,' I said aloud.

'Oui, monsieur?' said the stewardess, standing beside me.

# 16

Customs at Charles de Gaulle Airport went through my baggage with painstaking care. They were looking for a false bottom in the suitcase. They even searched me. They must have thought I was a drug trafficker. Probably because I had declared the dollars I was carrying with me.

Once free of these inconveniences, I took a taxi to the Le Bréa.

At the reception desk I was attended by an Oriental – I later learned he was Vietnamese – who spoke awful English and told me there was no Liliana among the guests.

'What about Mr Castelo Branco?'

Castelo Branco was a guest but he wasn't in the hotel at the moment.

I filled out the registration form and went up to my room in a small elevator. I took the manuscript from the suitcase and stared at those incomprehensible letters. Babel's manuscript! It was unbelievable that I had it in my possession. I don't know how long I remained sitting there with the manuscript in my hands.

I was hungry. The Vietnamese at the reception desk had told me there was a safe in the room. I opened the safe, which was built into the wall, but the manuscript wouldn't fit, only the passport and money.

I wasn't about to leave the manuscript in the room while I went out to eat. Veronika knew I had fled to Paris and must have told Plessner. They could find out I was at the Le Bréa and in my absence break in and steal the manuscript.

With the manuscript under my arm, I went downstairs to the front desk. When I gave the key to the Vietnamese, he told me that Monsieur Castelo Branco had arrived and was in the hotel's tiny waiting room.

Sitting in front of a minuscule and well-cared-for solarium, an individual was reading a newspaper. I guessed it must be Monsieur Castelo Branco. Before approaching I decided to take a good look at him. I couldn't see his face, which was partially covered, only his dark straight hair. He was dressed formally in a dark worsted suit and a tie with red and black stripes. He was a small, thin man.

I went up to him.

Standing before him as he continued to read the newspaper, I said: 'Monsieur Castelo Branco?'

He removed the newspaper from in front of his face.

'You?' I exclaimed in surprise.

'Shh!' she said.

'You . . .'

'Sit here.'

I sat down.

'Explain this to me,' I said.

'Not so loud.'

'You're crazy.'

'Shh!'

'Explain, you idiot!'

Then Liliana told me that she had always wanted to take on a masculine identity, dress as a man, like Mademoiselle de Maupin in Gautier's novel. So she had bought a false passport in the name of Euribicíades Castelo Branco and since Brazil traveled as if she were a man.

'Do you like my black hair?'

'They're going to discover you're not a man.'

'How? I have small breasts. I've already been through Customs twice, in Rio and in Paris, and no one suspected.'

'You're going to wind up in jail. Euribicíades?'

'I wasn't the one who chose it. There's a guy with that name somewhere in our country.' Then Liliana took a cigar from her pocket, rolled it between her fingers, and ran it past her nose, breathing in the tobacco smell. 'Isn't that what men do?'

'I don't smoke cigars,' I replied. I looked around to see if anyone was watching us. 'Do you know what this is?'

'A pile of paper.'

'Look at it, look at it!'

'What funny writing.'

'The Cyrillic alphabet. Do you know whose writing this is?'

'Do you understand it?'

'Do you know whose writing this is?'

'No. Whose writing is it?'

'Babel's.'

'So what?'

'It's an unpublished novel of Babel's,' I said, lowering my voice. 'Come to my room and I'll tell you an amazing story.'

We went up together, by the stairs. In the short corridor on my floor, we passed a chambermaid who must also have been Vietnamese. She looked at us with curiosity. Could she have been an agent of Plessner's?

I went into the room and turned on the television.

'This novel was apprehended by the KGB at the time of Babel's arrest and was supposed to have been destroyed . . .'

'I can't understand a thing. Talk louder or turn down the television.'

I got up and tiptoed across the room – which was totally unnecessary because the carpet drowned out the slightest noise if I walked normally – and jerked open the door.

The Vietnamese maid wasn't lurking there as I had feared.

'You're still crazy,' Liliana said.

I closed the door.

'I'm not crazy, just cautious. Listen with the utmost attention to what I'm about to tell you.'

Liliana hugged me. She kissed me on the mouth.

'Can't it wait till later?'

I pushed her away, freeing myself from the embrace. And I began to tell the story of the manuscript. At first Liliana feigned a lack of interest, lying down and rolling around on the bed, yawning and sighing. But gradually she became alert and sat up on the bed, wide-eyed.

'Is all that the truth?' Liliana asked when I had finished.

'Absolutely.'

She lit a cigarette. 'You're turning into the main character of a film noir. And now, how about a kiss?'

'A kiss? You're thinking of that at a time like this?' I said. 'It's Babel's manuscript, you wretched woman!'

'Babel is dead and nobody knows who he is. They don't even know of the existence of his unpublished manuscript with such an electrifying past. Only the KGB, which doesn't tell anyone, and Plessner, a crazy German, and Ivan, miserable and corrupt, and you, an idiotic Brazilian.'

'And Gurian,' I said.

'Who's a sick old Jew.'

'And Veronika.'

'Who's a treacherous German. Anyway, what I mean is that we have time to fool around a little.'

Liliana embraced me. In the closet mirror I saw myself embracing a man (a boy, rather) of androgynous appearance dressed in black.

'Take off those clothes,' I said.

Liliana removed her clothing.

'Do you think I should dye here too?'

'It must be difficult.'

'With a brush there's nothing to it . . .'

'No, don't dye it.'

'You like it better that way, red?'

'It's not that.'

'It's what?'

'I don't want to talk about it. I want to talk about Babel.'

'Later. Take off your clothes too.'

I undressed.

'Aren't you ashamed to be seen in that condition?'

'Liliana, I don't want to fool around. My life is very complicated.'

'Oh really? You don't want to?' she asked, coming up to me. The pointed peaks of her breasts brushed against my chest.

'Well, what's this? What progressive tumescence is that? Umm?' Liliana asked.

I said nothing.

'Didn't you say you didn't want to?'

I still said nothing.

'There's nothing in the world better than this, you know that.'

Liliana was right. It was the best thing in the world. But when it was over, it was nothing. It made you feel like doing something else.


'Do you think Gurian is out of hospital?'

'Gurian? Good lord! We've just finished making love and

you're already thinking about something else. Where's your sense of pleasure?'

'My sense of pleasure is before and during. Afterward, my desire is to phone Gurian. Do you think he's out of hospital yet?'

'Gurian?'

'That sick old Jewish friend of mine. In whose apartment the precious stones are. You were there with me.'

The hotel operator placed the call quickly.

A woman answered. I asked to speak to Gurian.

I was glad to hear the old man's voice.

'How's your health?' I asked after the exchange of greetings.

'Excellent.'

'How about taking a plane and coming to Paris to meet me?'

'Go to Paris . . .'

'I'll pay all expenses,' I added practically.

I could hear Gurian talking to someone.

'Go to Paris . . .' the old man repeated.

A woman's voice came on the line: 'Boris can't travel. You don't know he just got out of hospital yesterday?'

'Hello, hello?' I said.

'Hello,' Gurian said, reclaiming the telephone.

'Who's that woman?'

'Sarah.'

'You just got out of hospital yesterday?'

'Yes.'

'Then she's right,' I said.

'She's always right. On top of that, Sarah has no children. My bad luck.'

I could hear Sarah protesting.

'What do you want me to do in Paris?'

'Translate something from Russian for me.'

'There's no shortage of people who know Russian in Paris.'

'Do you know anyone?'

'Wait a minute.'

I waited.

Sarah came on the line.

'Boris is calmly going through his papers. He could be at it for half an hour. It's better for you to hang up and call back. This phone call is going to cost a fortune.'

'Thank you, Dona Sarah, but I prefer to wait.'

I waited.

Sarah's voice complaining again.

Gurian returned.

'Look on Rue Jacob, I don't know if it's twenty-eight or thirty, for a man named Jacques Henri-Gauché.'

'Can he be trusted?'

'Yes, beyond a doubt. Mention my name. Tell him you're my friend.'

'May I ask another favor? See if in the bookcase behind the *Mahabharata* that small box of precious stones that I showed you in the hospital is still there.'

I waited.

'Yes, it is.'

'Keep it for me.'

'When will you be back?'

'I don't know.'

While I'd been on the phone, Liliana had got dressed.

'We're having dinner at La Coupole. I already made reservations,' she said.

We walked. We passed Balzac's statue. The cold was unbearable, but there was no wind.

The restaurant was packed.

'I'm going to have only oysters with white wine,' Liliana said.

I also drank a bit.

Liliana had two dozen oysters.

'I love you,' Liliana said. 'I really do. In part because of the wine, in part because of the oysters, in part because of you. I mean, it's your fault. Sit here beside me.'

I left my seat and sat next to Liliana in the lounge chair with a red-lined backrest.

'Give me a kiss,' Liliana said.

I kissed her.

Liliana rested her head on my shoulder.

I kissed her again. Liliana's mouth had the strange taste of oysters and Chablis.

I noticed people looking in our direction with varied expressions. Some amused, others openly censorious. What the hell was happening to Paris if a man couldn't kiss a woman at La Coupole?

Then I understood the reason for the looks. I pushed Liliana away brusquely. I felt my face burning.

'What happened?' Liliana asked.

'You're dressed as a man.'

'So what? No one suspects a thing. I went through Customs twice.'

'That's just it, you idiot. Everybody thinks I'm sitting here blatantly kissing a man.'

'Nobody knows us. Forget it.'

'Don't forget the universal law of visibility: if you don't want to be seen, you will be – and vice versa. I can assure you there are several people here who know me, a journalist, a film director, my dentist – they're going to spread it all over Brazil that I'm gay.'

'So what?'

'They're going to throw us out of here.'

'We'll refuse to leave.'

'You're never going to have oysters and wine with me again.'

At the table next to ours, a man and woman raised their glasses in a toast and drank. They were a middle-aged couple. Liliana and I also raised our glasses and drank.

'Nothing beats civilization,' Liliana said.

At the other tables, however, I did not sense the same solidarity. I felt relieved when we left the restaurant.

'If I like women, why can't you like men?' Liliana asked as we walked to the hotel. A cold wind now made walking uncomfortable.

'Take off those clothes,' I said when we got to the room.

'You want to look at me?'

'Yes.'

'What about the mystery?' Liliana said.

'Tomorrow morning we have to go and find Jacques-Henri Gauché,' I said.

Carrying Babel's manuscript in a large manila envelope, I went with Liliana down Rue Vavin toward the Jardin du Luxembourg. We had decided to walk to Rue Jacob, and that was one possible route. It was not as cold in Paris as it had been in Berlin. The walk through the garden was very pleasant. Several times Liliana tried to put her arm around my waist, but I moved away; I didn't want to call attention to us. I was wearing a wool beret, but Liliana's head was still bare. She had come up with a way of walking that she thought was masculine, appropriate to the men's clothes she wore. Actually she looked like an effeminate adolescent.

We took half an hour to reach Boulevard Saint-Germain. From there we took Rue Bonaparte. Then we came to Rue Jacob.

Number 30 was an old house. We went in through a small door in the middle of a wide wooden gate and entered a large dark patio paved with stones, surrounded by tall doors, and with windows in the upper floor, all closed.

We stopped a woman and asked for Jacques-Henri Gauché. She pointed to a door.

On the door was an old plaque on which could barely be deciphered what was written. But the word Gauché could be made out. We didn't see a bell.

I knocked on the door.

We waited.

I knocked again, more loudly.

A boy with the look of a Hare Krishna opened the door halfway.

'Yes?' he said.

'We're looking for Monsieur Jacques-Henri Gauché.'

'Please come in,' he said, opening the door.

We went into a large room even darker than the patio. Old cupboards of solid wood, heavy tables and chairs cluttered the room. But what interested me most were the three people present.

Two were very young: the Hare Krishna and an ugly, pale little girl with blonde hair and large round eyes. The third was a man who must have been a hundred years old. That was surely Jacques-Henri Gauché, who knew Russian and many other things. No one lives a hundred years with impunity.

I went straight to the old man.

'Monsieur Jacques-Henri Gauché?'

'Jacques-Henri died,' he said.

I stood there for a time, not knowing what to say. Liliana recovered herself more quickly.

'Do you know Russian?' she asked.

'Do I know Russian?' the old man said. And he leaned his head back and opened his toothless mouth and gave a long laugh that sounded more like a howl. Then he extended his bony hand, reached inside my coat, took hold of my shirt, grabbing the hairs on my chest: 'I know much more than that!'

'This man is a werewolf,' Liliana said in Portuguese. 'Let's get out of here.'

'There are no werewolves in Paris, everybody knows that,' the old man answered in Portuguese with an accent impossible to place. 'Why a werewolf?' he asked, looking intensely at Liliana as if she were a shape shrouded in fog. Speechless, Liliana clutched the table.

The old man touched the manila envelope containing Babel's manuscript, which I held tightly, and said, 'Is that what you want me to translate?' He pressed the envelope, as if trying to feel the letters through the paper.

'Hahahahaha!' he said.

'Let's go,' Liliana said, frightened.

'Thank you very much,' I told the old man, making a leave-taking gesture with my head, as Liliana tugged on my arm.

'Idiot,' the old man said.

We left.

When we got to Boulevard Saint-Germain, Liliana stopped pulling on my arm. 'That guy is a sorcerer. There may not be any werewolves in Paris, but there are sorcerers,' she said. 'Or else we were hypnotized. Which do you prefer?'

'I think it's best for us to return to Rio. I need someone to translate the manuscript. You want to know my plans? I'm not going to film *Cavalry* anymore. I'm going to film Babel's manuscript.' I waved the manila envelope as if it were a rattle.

'What if it's the story of a Jewish family in Odessa in the Twenties?'

'I'll film it whatever it is. I'll build an Odessa in Rio, in Jacarepaguá.'

Liliana nodded her head, like someone resigning herself to the inevitable. In this case, to my craziness.

'Shall we have lunch?' Liliana said.

'But not at La Coupole,' I said.

'Why?'

'I've already seen everyone there that there is to see.'

'That's not the reason,' Liliana said.

'If you wanted to find a Brazilian in Paris, where would you go?'

'The Galerie Lafayette, the Deux Magots, the Brasserie Lipp, the sidewalks of Boulevard Saint-Germain, and the Avenue Champs-Elysées . . .'

'And . . .?'

'La Coupole.'

'Well? Do you want Plessner's executioners to find us? Veronika assured me he'd kill me if I stole the manuscript from him.'

We went to a Varig Airlines agency to reserve a flight to Rio for two days later.

Those two days we spent mostly in the hotel, in bed, fooling around and watching television. We didn't even go to the nearby theaters on Boulevard du Montparnasse.

It was Thursday night when we caught the plane to Rio.

# THREE

## *The Florentino Diamond*

# 17

On the plane, watching Liliana sleep, I began thinking about Ruth, for the first time not fighting my memories.

I met Ruth through Liliana. I needed someone to do the choreography for a short I was going to produce and direct. Liliana, who was sixteen at the time, said that a ballet dancer and choreographer named Ruth, with whom she was in love, could do the job for me. Liliana also told me that at fifteen Ruth had been sold by her mother to a rich man, not the way Coralie's mother sold her daughter to Camusot, but the way Marguerite was sold to the Chinese man, a more subtle thing. Ruth's mother, when she became a widow, had found that she could no longer maintain her futile, dissipated way of life unless she parted with some of her possessions. So she sold her jewels, her real estate and, finally, her daughter. She was a woman who drank a lot and ended up in a sanitarium for the mentally ill, where she died. The man who bought Ruth – and he wasn't an old man, as happens in most novels – provided her with the means to continue studying ballet. This man, still according to Liliana, also wasn't quite right in the head. He committed suicide on his fortieth birthday. Ruth was eighteen at the time. But thanks to her protector she could now earn a living as a dancer. Ruth's past, in Liliana's version, later confirmed in part by Ruth herself, was so complicated, so full of uncommon happenings, that when I thought of it, like now in the plane, I always had the impression that it was all one big lie.

I got to Ruth's house at seven am. Ruth was watering her garden, her feet wet and the hem of her skirt dirty with soil, her white blouse, embroidered in cross-stitch, spattered. I waited patiently until she had finished watering the plants. I told her of the short-subject I was directing.

'I don't know what kind of choreography could be done for a documentary about poor people in the heart of the city,' she said.

I explained to her that the characters were thieves, street urchins, unemployed jugglers, prostitutes, transvestites, simpletons from the outskirts at their leisure – in addition to beggars. I wanted her to create a choreography for a family of beggars.

'Choreography for a family of beggars? Really?'

'They've already agreed to dance for me,' I said.

'It's a documentary?' She seemed confused.

'Let's call it that if you like. But strictly speaking there's no such thing as a documentary. In film everything is edited, everything. It's fiction in one form or another.'

She told me she was more a dancer than a choreographer.

'Think of the challenge: a choreography for real beggars who have never danced,' I said.

'I think I have a good idea.' She turned off the faucet, dropped the hose. She took me to her bedroom. She put a cassette in the tape player.

'What if they danced to this music? It's the "Walk in the Tuileries" from Mussorgsky's *Pictures at an Exhibition*.'

*   *   *

I didn't let her change her clothes. We went to the city in a Volkswagen van, with the photographer and the photographic materials, the camera and other stuff.

When we got to Carioca Square, from inside the van I pointed out a family of beggars behind the savings association building, near the subway entrance. There were about twenty beggars, some lying on blankets.

A young woman, her face filthy, caught Ruth's attention because of the dignity and elegance in her manner.

Her name was Eurídice. Within a short time the beggars were ready. Ruth suggested that first we should play the music for them to hear.

While they listened to Mussorgsky, Ruth asked Eurídice to watch her. Ruth danced briefly and then asked if the other woman thought she could repeat the same movements. Eurídice answered that she would try.

Then something wonderful happened, a mixture of the grotesque and the sublime. All the beggars decided to imitate Ruth's movements, each face with a different expression, each body with its own peculiar interpretation. That day I discovered, fascinated, that every human being has the ability to dance, the capacity to create meaningful bodily movements.

Ruth suggested that the scene would be beautiful if all the beggars were naked. 'We could take them to one of those deserted downtown streets where we could film without being disturbed.'

A naked beggar is no longer a beggar. Especially in film, where the characters' dress is very important.

'Just imagine if in *Casablanca* Humphrey Bogart walked around in a short-sleeved shirt? The film would be a failure. Bogart is interesting because he wears a raincoat with pockets he can stick his hands into. And he wears a hat. And the other characters *are also dressed.*'

Instead of undressing the beggars, we covered them in rags. Ruth agreed with me. Especially because some of them were fat. The idea of poverty suggests thinness.

'It's because they don't diet,' I joked.

In the film the scene looked even better. I had improvised a kind of dolly, using a handcart with car tires on which I mounted the camera. I wanted the camera to move the entire time, sometimes in the opposite direction from the dancing beggars, and this could be accomplished by pushing the cart slowly backward and forward. Meanwhile, I wanted to zoom in and out, always extremely slowly.

The photographer operating the camera thought this was impossible. I told him that the great conquest of the 'impossible' in terms of camera movement had been achieved by Allan Dwan in 1915, filming *David Harum*. For the first time the camera, freed from the tripod, followed the character down the street. After that it never stopped. I also told him that Altman, in *The Long Goodbye*, had done what I was proposing. He replied that we weren't in Hollywood but in Carioca Square, not on top of some sophisticated crane but on a handcart. How could he correctly tilt, raise and lower that goddam camera?

We filmed not only the dance but almost everything in that way. The effect we achieved was sensational. My short, *The Beggars' Ballet*, won rave reviews the world over, and I never told anyone the secret of its intriguing cinematography. Actually I got better results than Altman, who, despite the availability of better technology, worked under the restrictions imposed by studio sets and never achieved the aesthetic effect he was looking for: to make the spectator feel as if he were a voyeur, an eavesdropper. Working outdoors, in a wide square surrounded by skyscrapers, I wanted to put the spectator not only in the position of voyeur that he is always in, but in that state of attraction-repulsion assumed by people faced with a shocking vision that, contradictorily, both rebuffs and entices – the posture, for example, they display upon seeing a naked corpse lying on the sidewalk. In reality, human beings have an ambiguous attitude toward sex, power, madness, poverty, pain, death.

'It was the most beautiful dance I ever saw in my life,' Ruth said later as we were having a beer. She bent over and kissed my hand.

For a few moments I didn't understand what was happening. I had presumed she wasn't interested in men, only in girls like Liliana, but Ruth's look said otherwise. We got in the van and went to a motel.

It was an apartment full of mirrors. Not knowing what to do, I went to the window and opened the curtains. The outside landscape was a cement wall.

She came close to me. I embraced her from behind. We remained this way for some time, looking at the cement wall. I sensed her arrested breathing, a perfumed smell of shampoo in her hair. Ruth turned around to face me. I saw she was afraid – of not coming, of being disappointed? For my part, I was calm. I knew what I wanted: to give her pleasure, mainly. It wasn't difficult, since I knew how to control my coming. Did that make it an imposture? An astute way of confronting the superiority of women? That mirror-filled apartment was a proper setting for all deceits. Even the wall appeared false. But there was no lie in me, only my self-control creating an image, one I did not seek, of an ardent lover when in reality I was merely generous.

Generous? Or a blusterer? I had invented for Ruth a man who didn't exist and who therefore could last only a short time. Especially after that had happened. But I didn't want to think anymore. I impatiently rang the bell for the stewardess.

'Whiskey,' I said when she came. 'I want whiskey.' I wanted to forget. I was once again struggling against my memories.

# 18

It was hot in Rio the morning we arrived from Paris. The temperature in the taxi that took us along Avenida Brasil toward the city's south zone was unbearable. We didn't know if we were going to my apartment or Liliana's, as we were afraid the man in the raincoat was still looking for us.

'Let's go to Mitiko's place,' Liliana said. 'Her eviction is going to take two years, according to the lawyer she hired.'

Mitiko received us with displays of affection. I didn't remember her being so white or having such dark hair. It was the color of Liliana's wig.

Liliana hadn't mentioned her disguise and Mitiko had never seen her dressed as a man, with her short hair dyed. But none of it seemed to surprise her. She wanted to know what it was like to pass for a man, what type of sensations Liliana had experienced, if women propositioned her, made amorous advances. Liliana replied that the ones who propositioned her, when she was dressed as a man, were men. And that she had come to the conclusion that at least 30 per cent of men were homosexual – open, in the closet, or latent.

Mitiko said she'd like to assume a false identity as a man herself. She had small breasts, a small ass like a man's, and was tall and thin.

'All Chinese boys look like girls,' Liliana said.

'I'm not Chinese,' Mitiko protested.

'It's all the same thing,' Liliana said. To me: 'Don't you want to disguise yourself as a woman?'

'I'll give it some thought,' I said.

'He wouldn't make a good woman,' Mitiko said.

'You never know,' Liliana said.

'I want to dress like a man and make a woman fall in love with me thinking I'm a man,' Mitiko said.

'What I want is for a *man* to fall in love with me thinking I'm a man,' Liliana said.

I had no intention of staying and listening to the conversation of those two idiotic girls.

'I have to go. I don't know when I'll be back.'

'Rest a bit,' Mitiko said.

'I can't; it's urgent.'

I picked up the manuscript and left.

The traffic in the streets seemed to have become worse. Pedestrians looked uglier in the midst of that oppressive heat.

Gurian opened the door for me.

'Are you OK?' I asked.

Before he could answer, I added, pointing to the manuscript in my hand, 'See this?'

'Yes,' Gurian said. 'Come in, come in.'

'This,' I said, entering the apartment, 'is Babel's manuscript that was confiscated by the NKVD when he was arrested.'

I told Gurian everything. As I talked, Gurian shook the manuscript frantically against his face, stamped his feet, kicked things on the floor – there were always things on the floor at his place, besides the books – and shouted unintelligibly.

Finally I understood what he was saying: 'I broke my glasses! I can't read!'

'You can't read?' I screamed. 'What do you mean you can't read?'

'I broke my glasses this morning. I stepped on them.'

'How can you step on your own glasses? That's crazy.'

We yelled at each other for some time, exasperated, he because he couldn't read immediately something as provocative and extraordinary as an unpublished text of Babel's, and me for being dependent on a crazy old man.

'What are we going to do?' I asked when we had calmed down. 'Don't you have a friend who can read it for us?'

'No, no, no, no, no,' Gurian said, growling like a rabid dog, 'I don't want anyone in the world to reintroduce this text in my place.' (I had told him that after Babel's manuscript was confiscated and hidden in the Lenin Library it had most likely never been read by anyone, not even Ivan or his thieving lover.) 'Leave this with me,' Gurian went on, clutching the papers to his chest. 'Nobody in the world is better qualified than I am to take care of this precious item.'

I left him grasping the manuscript. I took the *Mahabharata* from the bookcase. I removed the box of stones hidden behind it.

The stones were all in the box. I didn't remember how many there were before, but I was sure none was missing.

I had planned to take the gems with me. But I changed my mind.

'May I leave the stones here? Just for a few more days?'

Gurian said yes. I put the box back where it had been before.

'When will you get your new glasses?'

'I don't know. They're special lenses. Maybe even today.'

'Call the dentist and ask for them no later than today.'

'He's not a dentist. He's an oculist.'

'I didn't say dentist. I said oculist.'

'You said dentist. I heard you clearly.'

We began another heated argument. I called him a deaf old visionary. He called me a stupid young man.

Afterward we finished off a bottle of whiskey that Gurian had hidden from Sarah beneath the bed.

I left the manuscript with Gurian, along with Mitiko's phone number.

Liliana wasn't there when I returned.

Mitiko sat down beside me and gave me a smile.

What attracted someone to another person? What made me take Mitiko's hand at that moment? Casanova, according to Schnitzler, wanted to give pleasure much more than to receive it. I was also like that. Was that giving of pleasure a form of exhibitionism? A kind of vainglory? I had acted the same way with Ruth.

'Do you think I'm a Casanova?'

'You don't seem like one,' Mitiko said. 'Do you want me to kiss you?'

'I don't know.'

'Why did you take my hand?' she asked.

'If you were a cat I'd have done the same thing.'

'Cats have hands?'

'I'd have taken the cat in my lap.'

'Is that what I am to you, a cat?'

'A mystery.'

'Now you're becoming a professional seducer, calling a woman a mystery.'

'Women and cats.'

'I want to kiss you,' she said.

She kissed me. We heard the door opening.

'People are really crazy in this city,' Liliana said, entering.

Mitiko got up from the sofa where we were sitting. Her face was flushed; she nervously straightened her blouse.

Liliana recounted that she had been in the bank, waiting in line for a teller, when she noticed that a well-dressed gentleman was staring at her. As she was about to leave, the man came up to her and, in a polite and gentle voice, commented how beautiful her ears were. Liliana thanked him, and the man asked if her ears were pierced. Liliana answered no. Then the man asked how much she wanted, in dollars, to let him pierce her ears. Startled, Liliana asked if he was joking. The man answered that he was serious and that, if Liliana so desired, they could sign a contract in her lawyer's office prior to the operation.

'How was it he was going to pierce your ears?' I asked.

'Ear fetishes are a form of semi-sublimated sadism,' Liliana said.

'Or worse,' Mitiko said.

'People are really crazy,' Liliana repeated.

'Gurian broke his glasses,' I said.

'I think we're going crazy too,' Mitiko said.

After that no one said anything.

'I'm going to call my brother.' Those two women together made me nervous.

José said he wanted to see me immediately.

'Where are you? I'll stop by and pick you up in the car.'

Mitiko had produced a manicure kit and was doing Liliana's nails.

'My brother's coming round for me.'

'Will you be gone long?'

'No. I'll be back shortly.'

José arrived in a large dark-colored car driven by a chauffeur.

I got in.

'What did you want to talk to me about?'

'Later,' he said, with a meaningful glance at the driver.

We went to the church in Copacabana.

'I've acquired a television station,' he said when we were in his office, inside the church.

'Acquired how?'

'I acquired the franchise. That is, the Church did. But I'm the president and chairman of the board. I don't have to spell out to you how important this is for my plans, I mean, the Church's plans. You know better than I the power of the mass media.'

'Yes, I do. But what's this got to do with me?'

'I need you. I want you to help me.'

'I don't know anything about TV. You know more about it than I do.'

'Don't be modest. Modesty has always held you back.'

'A guy wrote in the newspaper that I was arrogant.'

'Let's not discuss that now. My proposal is that you handle all the non-evangelical programming for our TV station. You'll get a good percentage of the gross.'

'I want to direct my film.'

'What film? You've been trying for two years to find the money to direct a film and haven't been able to.'

'Why do you want a TV station too?' It was a stupid question; I knew that José, or the Church of Jesus Savior of Souls – a legal corporation duly registered as a tax-exempt civil entity – already owned a record company, a publishing house and a radio station.

'We need to spread the word of Jesus and plan to make use of the same resources as the wicked, to fight with the selfsame weapons of the heretics.'

'The same reasons that make you get elected to Congress?'

'Yes! Brazilian society has come to its state of moral decay from lack of faith. Depravity, corruption, narcissism, conspicuous consumption, violence, moral degradation, environmental pollution, unbridled ambition, social conflict – all from lack of faith.'

It seemed like *Il Generale della Rovere* by Rosselini. A con artist passes himself off as a man of integrity, adopts the latter's code of honor, and as a result ends up sacrificing his own life. Could my brother have been a scoundrel like the character played by De Sica, who in the end redeems himself by believing in his own lie? I looked closely at his face.

At that instant a woman opened the door.

'José –' she began, and stopped when she saw me.

'My brother the film director,' José said. 'This is our sister – sister in Christ – Dalva. Yes, Sister Dalva?'

'It's not important, reverend. It can wait till later. If you'll excuse me . . .' said Sister Dalva, leaving hurriedly.

'We live in new times,' José said. 'Don't you see? We're no longer those "believers" ridiculed by the Catholics and segregated in ghettos on the outskirts of large cities. Here in Rio alone there are two hundred denominations, hundreds of evangelical temples, two million of the faithful. You have no idea how much we take in each month just from tithes.'

It wasn't hard to calculate, assuming the number of followers mentioned by José was correct, bearing in mind the ecclesiastical tax they were charged.

'Eight million dollars,' I said. 'Eight million dollars a month.'

José smiled. Could I have underestimated?

'Does your group plan to make it to the Presidency?'

José smiled patiently. 'Our objective isn't the Presidency. But what if it were? I ask you: why can't a member of an evangelical church be president of the country? We've had ranchers as president, lawyers, military men, doctors – why not an evangelical pastor? What could an evangelical pastor do that would be worse than all those who've already held the position?'

'The same crap then?'

'You must learn to control your anger.' He paused. 'Forgive my saying so, but I've listened carefully to what many of our followers – who have no idea, of course, of our blood ties – have to say, and all of them – all! – hated *The Holy War*. Pardon me for saying this, but I think they're right. It's an anti-religious, anti-Christian film.'

Looking me in the eyes, he continued: 'You're my brother, but Jesus Christ is my father, my family!' He tried to grasp my hand. 'Don't give in to depression. Since you were a child you've gone through these phases.'

'Fuck you, José.'

'May Jesus give you peace!'

José extended his hands toward me.

'My brother –' he began, in a voice filled with caring and forgiveness.

I turned my back and left without hearing what he said.

As I walked I felt a kind of uneasiness, as if I were being followed. I stopped and looked behind me. My heart froze. The man in the raincoat was standing in the street. He smiled in that twisted, repressed, Widmarkian way of his. I went toward him, resolved to ask, as Raymond Burr had done in *Rear Window*, 'What do you want from me?'

I came to within a short distance of him, not too short, about twenty-five feet.

'What do you want from me?' I shouted. (Burr had said it almost in a whisper.)

The man in the raincoat approached calmly, with slow steps.

'You know what we want from you.'

'Fuck you too!' I shouted.

Another smile. That bastard should be in film.

'You're throwing away all your chances.' He talked like a Hollywood heavy.

I left him standing in the street and walked away without looking back. I had the strength, the power. I was owner of Babel's unpublished manuscript, the only novel by the greatest short-story writer in the world. What could some bad guy who did a hammy imitation of a forgotten actor do to me, who had defeated the ghost of Joseph Stalin?

Mitiko and Liliana were talking and holding hands on the living-room sofa when I arrived.

'Your friend called,' Liliana said.

'What friend?'

'The old man. He said he'd received the glasses. He urgently wants to talk to you.'

'He received the glasses?' I said, dashing to the telephone.

Gurian's line was busy.

I called dozens of times and Gurian's phone was always busy.

'Wait a while,' Liliana said. 'You're very nervous.'

'I think he left the phone off the hook. Gurian is very absent-minded.'

The busy signal continued.

'I'm going to his place,' I said.

'You've been in and out all day. I want to talk to you. It's serious,' Liliana said.

'You've sold your ears, is that it?'

'Idiot. It really is serious.'

'When I get back. When I get back we'll talk.'

'I'm going to dress as a man too, for at least a year,' Mitiko said.

'When I get back. When I get back we'll talk,' I said.

In the corridor two men were waiting for the elevator. One of them had something in his hands that looked like a piece of folded black cloth. The other came up to me and said, 'Can you tell me what time it is?'

I didn't have time to do anything. They violently pulled a hood over my head. I tried to defend myself without yelling; I didn't want to show cowardice to Liliana and Mitiko, who would surely be the first to hear my screams. But I was immobilized, gripped forcefully, and was being pushed. Besides that, the fact of being dragged, of having to walk blind, left me stunned; for a time I was more afraid of falling than of the singular attack I was being subjected to. Then I felt metal handcuffs close around my wrists.

I heard the noise of the elevator arriving. Inside the elevator I continued to struggle to break free of my captors. The elevator descended.

'Help!' I shouted.

The elevator stopped. I must have been in the foyer of the building. Maybe in the garage. My head struck a hard surface. A car? I struck my head again; now I knew it was the top of a car. I lowered my head in an idiotic reflex that helped my kidnappers. I heard the car door slam, then another.

'Let's go!' a voice said.

I heard the roar of the car as it pulled out.

'Help!' I screamed again.

A gag was stuffed brutally into my mouth.

I moved my body. There was space where I lay. It was probably a van, perhaps a Volkswagen microbus.

'Didn't I say it'd be easy?'

'Shut up!'

That one must be the boss, I thought.

The sound of rock music. The car radio. Music usually had a relaxing effect on me, but this struck me as aggressive, filling me with fear. The gang of smugglers was surely behind the kidnapping. They would kill me if I didn't give them the gems. They'd kill me anyway.

In a short time I'd be a dead man, like Babel. The idea that Babel was dead and that I was about to die seemed absurd and wanton to me. I wasn't thinking about the immortality of the soul, in which I didn't believe. Strictly speaking, my feelings about Babel the man weren't much different from those I had experienced when a dog of mine died. After they took the dog away – it's almost as complicated to cut ties with a dead dog, a dog you love like a friend, as with a dead human being – I thought, how could the sweetness, intelligence and elegance of that being have disappeared? All that was left of him was my memory and a collar – nothing. What was left of Babel? Words, like my dog's collar – nothing? Where was Babel's pain at seeing his father lick the Cossack's boots? His happiness when he first met Eugenia Gronfein? His fear as he faced his executioner in that prison in Siberia?

And me? What would be left of me? Where would my wonder at seeing Liliana's red pussy be? My happiness upon reading one of Drummond's poems?

'That music irritates me,' the leader of the kidnappers said.

I briefly heard the sound of various stations being tuned. The roar of the motor was very loud.

Ruth.

Now I wanted to think about Ruth again. And it was good I had that hood over my head, for that way they could not witness my pain.

Every time I remembered the accident, I told myself it wasn't my fault. A dancer with a great future becoming paralyzed in a senseless automobile accident seems like one of those tear-jerking films on afternoon TV. But it happened. And I wasn't to blame.

I had gone to pick her up at the theater after the show.

Usually it was Ruth who drove. 'Driving a car is a woman's job,' I used to say. To tell the truth, she drove much better than I did. But that day she said she was tired and asked me to drive. A skid, a light impact against a pole – that was all that happened. But Ruth was dozing. On impact, her unprotected head was violently jerked forward then back, causing a break in the spinal column that damaged the medulla. Her nervous system was affected.

Ruth was dozing. Ruth asked me to drive. How was I to blame? Before, I hadn't thought about the accident in those terms. My rationalization had even led me to blame Ruth for what happened.

'I was always an indecisive person,' she had told me that cursed night. 'In doubt about being a classical ballerina or a modern dancer, I attempted each style and only managed to be mediocre in both. I waited so long to decide whether or not to have a child that now it's too late. I'm a cripple with no alternatives.'

I embraced her, bending over the wheelchair where she sat. I felt Ruth's tears dampening my neck. 'Don't talk like that,' I begged.

'I was asked to dance with Béjart, but I was never able to decide if I should leave Brazil or not. Now it's too late. We make our destiny, and I didn't know how to make mine. But now I know what I want.'

*Now I know what I want.* Oh, how stupid I had been.

'That's good,' I said.

I put her to bed, as always. We still slept in a double bed, even though, through my doing, we were no longer a couple. I was unable to feel desire for Ruth. Every day I massaged her legs, atrophied from paralysis. Her strong legs, which before were full of warmth and life, had been transformed into two rickety members wrapped in dull, rough skin under which I felt, in my fingers, the tibia and the fibula as if I were touching the bones of a skull. We were no longer a pair of lovers. I felt no desire for Ruth; there was only pity in my heart.

'Would you love me if my legs weren't withered from the paralysis?' she asked.

I didn't answer. In reality my desire for Ruth had ended long before the accident. Why? Who can explain why the desire for a beautiful woman can come to an end? I shouldn't, I mustn't go on lying. The accident had provided the excuse for not having to go on making love to her. I loved her, yes, I loved her and wanted to go on living with her, as one lives with a sister, with a friend. As a lover I wanted Liliana.

That awful night Ruth took an entire bottle of sleeping pills. When I woke up, she was dead beside me.

And where was the joy Ruth felt when she danced *The Prodigal Son*? Where were the movements she made so brilliantly in the space around her? Her sweetness? What was left of her – the sanitary napkin?

# 19

I tried desperately to get the hood off. I wanted air, light – the light that would free me from thinking about Ruth. I rolled back and forth in the cramped space where I lay. I tried to break the handcuffs gripping my wrists. Finally I stopped, exhausted, feeling pain in my entire body. My hands were wet with blood. I tried to count the passage of time. One thousand and one, one thousand and two, one thousand and three, one thousand and four – each count equalled a second – one thousand and five, one thousand and six . . . I gave up at nine thousand and one.

I felt a painful sting in my arm. I slept.

The squadron, in formation on the plain, ready for the charge, the horses reined back, side by side. We await our orders. Each of us holds in his right hand, in an upright position, a lance topped by a green and yellow pennant, the colors of Brazil. Across our backs, the barrel pointing upward on the right side, the bandoleer about our chests, we carry a Mauser rifle. The horses are starting to become restless and rub against each other, pressing our legs painfully despite the protection of our boots. The leader shouts the order to march. We urge the horses forward with a light touch of our spurs.

The horses, on a short rein tightening the bit in their mouths, raise their heads, for they know what is about to happen. The leader rides forward, alone. He turns and shouts the order to trot. The reined-in horses twist their necks and open their eyes wide. I try to see the enemy, without success. The leader raises the arm holding his sword and orders, 'Squadron! Charge!' in a hoarse, shrill voice. An electrifying force takes hold of men and animals. Our lances are lowered into horizontal position and the spurred horses rush onward in an impetuous gallop, their heads leaning forward. One of the riders issues the first shout of euphoria and instantly all the men are yelling crazily and every horse is snorting without restraint. I know that if I gallop faster than the others I'll be the winner – 'Come on! Come on!' I urge my mount, who heeds my desire and lurches forward in violent spurts. At one moment the horse turns its muzzle rearward, in full gallop, and fixes its wild eyes on mine. This is just before we come up almost upon the tail of the squadron leader's horse, Captain Mário Slackjaw. 'Go!' I shout at the horse, 'charge!' The horse, still in full gallop, leaps forward and I am able to plant my lance in the captain's head. The lance enters through the nape of his neck and exits through the nose, and the green and yellow pennant flutters in the wind, red with blood. My momentum is such that after severing Slackjaw's head I overtake his mount and display to the decapitated captain, who rides elegant and erect as ever, the trophy at the tip of my lance.

I awoke from my first dream with images to the sound of the car motor. We must have been going up a hill. The noise lasted for a long time, what must have been hours. Then we went onto an unpaved highway. We were probably on a dirt road, full of bumps that shook the car roughly. I didn't know how long I'd slept, as I'd been doped and unable to orient myself. My wrists ached. I felt like throwing up. I knew that if I did, the gag would drown me in my own vomit.

The car stopped.

I was removed from wherever I was. I couldn't stay on my feet, so the kidnappers helped me. We went down a set of stairs. I felt cold. We were probably in a cellar. They sat me down in a chair.

'You can take his gag out,' the leader said.

I tried to say something but didn't succeed. My words came out garbled.

'What the hell's he saying?'

I repeated it.

'Talk straight, goddamit.'

I repeated it again.

'He's asking us to take off the hood,' the leader said. 'Not yet,' he continued. 'The boss'll have to decide that and he's not here yet.'

I heard footsteps receding. Had they all left or was one of them still there, quietly watching me? The idea of another person in that cellar, watching me in silence, filled me with panic.

'Is there anyone there?' I asked.

Silence.

'Answer me.'

Silence. What was that noise? The sole of a shoe crushing a bit of dirt? A tiny gust of air sucked lightly between teeth? It could also be a rat. How nice if it were a rat, I thought. I heard a bird singing in the distance. And rock music.

They weren't going to remove the hood from my head. It was a way of coercing me. I mustn't panic. I needed to occupy my mind with things other than fear. Fear would be the end of me.

I decided to re-create in my mind – and in my heart; didn't the ancients believe that the heart was the seat of memory? –

the stories in *Red Cavalry*. First, the one Budenny hated most, 'The Cemetery at Kozin'. It couldn't be more than twenty lines; how could so few words have inspired such great hatred? We're in the cemetery of a small Jewish village, with tombstones bearing crudely sculpted inscriptions and carvings, three centuries old. Lambs and fish above a skull, rabbis with woolen birettas. Beside an oak splintered by a bolt of lightning is the tomb of Rabbi Azrael killed by Bogdan Khmelnitsky's Cossacks. Four generations are buried there, and the gravestone speaks eloquently of them; it says that they fought against oblivion: O death, O greedy one, O covetous thief, could you not spare us even a single time? Was that the entire story or was my mind deceiving me? If that's all there was, what caused Budenny's hostility? There was one more thing, which I had forgotten: one of the dead was a rabbi from Krakow. Was that the reason for his hatred? Because the protagonists of that elegy were Polish Jews? Because Budenny believed that the story made it clear that Babel was above all a Jew?

I recalled an interview I'd given to a journalist.

'What's your greatest material wish?' she asked.

'To believe in God,' I said.

'Would that change anything?'

'My style, perhaps. My language is asyndetic, full of missing conjunctions. Faith would make my style hyperbolic, polysyndetic.' And so on. At the time I'd thought I was joking.

'If Brazilian films,' the journalist wrote, 'were as interesting as the interviews with their directors, Brazilian cinema would be the best in the world.'

My greatest material wish, I now knew, was freedom. In actuality human beings are characterized by great stupidity. They only discover that a good is fundamental when they no longer possess it. Imprisoned in that cellar, I discovered that the most important of all freedoms was the freedom to come and go, freedom of movement. A prisoner there in the cellar, I had all the other freedoms – to think, to curse my captors, to have a religion (if I wanted one), to choose my political beliefs. I had the freedom to dream. But what good did that do me if I was a prisoner in a cellar?

'Is anyone there?' I shouted. 'I want to urinate.'

Footsteps.

'You wanna piss?' A male voice.

'Yes.'

Someone helped me stand up. I felt dizzy and supported myself against the person next to me.

'Take the guy for a piss.' It was the voice of the leader.

I was being led somewhere. Fearful of falling, I shuffled my feet along the ground. It's not easy to walk with a hood over your head and handcuffed on top of everything else. We stopped.

'Open his fly,' the leader said, laughing.

'I'll open it and you give it the three shakes,' the other one said.

Laughter.

'Either take care of it yourself or do it in your pants.'

Despite the handcuffs, I managed to open my fly and pull out my flaccid member. I stood there holding my penis, unable to urinate.

'Well?'

'I can't,' I said, 'I'm inhibited. It's difficult for me to urinate in front of other people.'

'Let's give the guy some space.'

I remembered a certain occasion when I'd been hospitalized for a suspected bleeding ulcer in my stomach, which in the end was not confirmed. They confined me to bed with strict orders not to get up. A beautiful nurse came into the room carrying one of those metals receptacles called a 'parrot' for patients to urinate in while lying down. 'Time to wee-wee,' she said, smiling. She immediately lifted the sheet and, before I could defend myself, placed my penis in the mouth of the receptacle. Having done this, she stood there looking at me. 'Through?' she asked after a time. 'No.' Ten minutes later I still hadn't managed to. Half an hour later, the same story. 'We need your urine,' she said. She got a glass of water and wet my wrists. 'Sometimes that works.' It didn't work. She turned on the tap and let it run. 'Hear that noise? Think about running water. Sometimes it works.' I desperately thought about running water. Futile. 'I'm inhibited,' I said. 'I'm going to call the doctor,' she said. When she had gone, I thought I would be able to urinate. But something had happened, some kind of block; whatever it was, I couldn't. The doctor, a fat, pleasant sort dressed in white, took a long time to arrive. 'Well, what's going on? You can't make peepee?' 'I'm inhibited.' 'Have you been trying to urinate for very long?' 'Almost an hour,' said the nurse. The doctor picked up a glass of water. 'I already wet his wrists,' the nurse said. 'There's a better trick,' the doctor said, handing the glass to the girl. 'Here, wet his thing.' With the glass of water in her hand, the nurse reached for the sheet, to lift it. But I refused to let her, clutching it tightly to my chest and shouting, 'I don't want you to do that!' Jesus, couldn't they understand that my urinary blockage came precisely from the fact of that beautiful woman planning to witness my micturition? 'We need your urine for tests, we really need it,' the doctor said. He had stopped being a friendly and pleasant fat man. In reality he never had been a friendly and pleasant fat man; his look had turned angry, his voice cold and menacing: 'We'll have to administer a catheter!' And the worst of all was that nothing was wrong with my health, as I learned afterward.

Now here I was in this cellar, suffering from the same thing. 'Is anyone there?' I shouted. My hood stank. I heard steps.

'Well?' asked the leader. 'We left you alone and it didn't do any good?'

'I can't.'

'Then put that piece of shit back in your pants. The boss is coming to talk to you.'

I put away my penis. They took me back to the chair and sat me down.

I heard very light footsteps, like those of a child.

'Leave me alone with him,' said the boss.

'Yes, sir,' said the gang leader. I heard footsteps retreating.

The hood was removed from my head.

Before me stood Alcobaça, the very pale man who was the brains behind the smugglers.

'Nice to see you, Mr Alcobaça.'

He looked at me. There was no feeling in his gaze. At most, perhaps, a slight curiosity.

'I want those stones,' he said. My skin crawled when I heard him: his voice was that of a person unable to feel hunger, hatred, love, fear. Olivier would have been overjoyed to find a voice like that for the ghost of Hamlet's father. 'I need them . . . Where are they?' he asked.

I couldn't tell him where the stones were. I would put Gurian's life at risk and, besides that, put Babel's manuscript at risk. Further, if I said where they were, I could be killed.

'I won't tell. You can torture me if you want.'

'Torture you? How? Why? I abhor violence.'

I was standing up. 'If you don't mind,' Alcobaça said, 'I'm going to sit in your chair. I'm very tired.'

'You killed the doorman. You killed Angélica, the fat woman.'

'That was an act of stupidity on the part of Ricardo. He's been punished for it.'

'Who's Ricardo? The guy who always wears a raincoat?'

'That's the one.'

'He's called Ricardo. Richard. Incredible.'

'Where are the stones?'

'I can't tell you.'

'Listen. I'm going to leave you without food or water until you tell me where the stones are.'

He started to put the hood back on my head.

'Can I ask a favor?'

'A favor?'

'Leave off the hood. It stinks.'

Alcobaça stared at me. He smiled, showing his white gums.

'All right.'

He left, walking slowly. I heard the sound of the door being bolted.

I examined the cellar. When I was a child, before we moved to the place over the millinery shop, I had lived in a house with a cellar like this. I spent all the time I could in the cellar, watching the rats, the centipedes, the spiders, the scorpions. I considered those animals – yes, they're animals like us, not insects – my only real friends. The cellar where I was being held prisoner was very much like the cellar of my childhood, which gave me a certain nostalgic comfort. Its walls were stone and it had a dirt floor with an enormous rock in the middle. That was all there was in it, besides the chair where they had bound me earlier. The door was made of solid wood and didn't move an inch when I placed all my weight against it. On the window, heavy iron bars. Through them, I could see a great stony, bleak landscape.

In one corner a rat scurried and disappeared through a crack in the wall. I also saw, feeling a melancholy pang, a large hairy bird spider walking along the floor. These spiders, errant wanderers, don't spin a web like the others. The bird spider's bite is a bit painful but does little harm. As a child I had been bitten by them several times. I bent down to examine a centipede. I remembered the day I had tried to find out for sure whether they really had a hundred legs. Only on that occasion did I kill one of the animals – out of, shall we say, scientific curiosity, if an ignorant layman like me may use that solemn phrase.

When it saw me bending over it, the animal raised the poisonous claws behind its head, ready to fight. Its tropical poison could kill me. I shouted to scare away the centipede. I didn't want to hurt it, and I would suffer very greatly if I killed it. The centipede stayed where it was, en garde. I stamped my foot on the ground, and only then did it flee, moving all its legs like some fantastic mechanical creature from a Japanese monster movie.

Surely there were scorpions in the cellar. When I was a child, my mother, in an effort to get me away from the cellar at home, kept telling me stories about people who had died from the prick of a scorpion's stinger. I always played with them cautiously, differently from the way I played with rats and spiders. I saw many females give birth to live baby scorpions and walk about the floor with them on their backs, until the family ties were cut and the young, their stingers already filled with poison, went off into the world on their own. For the scorpion is a solitary creature, the most misanthropic of animals, approaching another of its kind only to fuck or fight to the death.

I looked in the corners, searching for them. The cracks in those stone walls were suitable for their development. I finally discovered two enormous black scorpions; they must have been over seven inches long, and they were there to court. I had already seen some matings of those dangerous friends of mine. The male, which is more slender and has a longer tail, was at that moment offering his suit, grasping two of the female's claws and rubbing his erect tail against hers. Then they began to copulate. I knew what was going to happen as soon as the act was over. The female would kill the male, unless he managed to get away, which was rare, and then devour him, or rather, suck him. Scorpions kill their prey by wounding it and injecting a neurotoxin that causes a type of poisoning similar to strychnine. They then inject into the wound digestive enzymes that liquify the prey's internal tissue. After which they suck it out, leaving only a dry husk.

My two scorpions were motionless, their copulation finished. Suddenly the female attacked the male with her two great pincerlike claws and began to crush him. The two animals thrashed about in a deadly ballet; in her destructive task the female used her two claws as well as her chiliceras, two smaller but very powerful pincers. The male struggled as long as he could, but in a short time he was dead.

The female set about devouring him, absorbing him. I looked on in fascination and she looked back at me. I knew she was looking back at me; from childhood I had known that scorpions looked at me too, especially when I spoke to them in the cellar of my house: scorpions can have up to twelve – twelve! – eyes, and anything with that many eyes has to be very sharp-sighted.

It would be night before long. I went to the barred window and looked at the world outside. Yes, night was falling rapidly.

I tucked my pants inside my socks, improvising a kind of boot. Soon it would be totally dark and I had no desire to feel a scorpion crawling up my leg. It was an animal that did that sort of thing; I also knew it had an unpredictable nature, and if one of them did that I'd have to kill it. I remembered the parable of the scorpion and the frog, recounted by Orson Welles in *Mr Arkadin*, in which the scorpion is presented as an ignoble character capable of all kinds of treachery. Poor animals. The story had even been dreamed up that they commit suicide when threatened, which is a sordid slander. I sat down in the chair with my legs crossed like a yogi, trying to see the animals that kept me company. Then it got so dark that I couldn't see anything.

I was happy, despite being handcuffed, for I love the dark. It would bring me the peace and solitude I desired. As a child I used to wait until everyone in the house had gone to sleep – I would bite my fingers, press the nerve in my shoulder, mortify myself physically so the pain would keep me from dropping off and I'd have the way clear to go to the cellar with a flashlight to see my nocturnal animals. Unfortunately, I had no flashlight now.

Twice during the night – a beautiful ebony night, so black that with my eyes shut the darkness was less opaque – I dozed off and fell out of the chair. From time to time I got up and stamped my feet on the ground; then I slammed the chair down, always with care so as not to hurt any of the animals. Then I sat down again with my legs crossed and returned to my reminiscences of the happiest time of my life.

I heard roosters crowing, and day began to break, entering slowly through the iron bars on the window.

At once I heard a grating noise, very loud, unbearable, that made my flesh creep. It was a sound I had never heard before. What the devil could it be?

The cellar door opened and the man in the raincoat came in.

'What's that noise?'

'It's a grinder.'

I identified the voice of the man who had led the kidnapping. Of course it could only have been him.

'What are they grinding?'

'I don't know,' he lied, with a twisted smile. 'You gave me

a hard time. It took a lot of work to get you. Where were you these last few days?'

'I was away.'

'Ah! That's what I thought . . .'

The Man in the Raincoat wasn't all that bad, I thought.

'I came to tell you you're not going to get any food. At least until you hand over the stones. If you give us the stones I have orders to make you a nice roast suckling pig.'

'Thank you very much.'

'Think it over carefully. Don't be fooled by the boss's appearance. He looks like a poet, but he's tough. I don't know anybody as tough as him.'

'I'll think it over.'

Another smile. Widmark playing the nice guy.

No, I wasn't going to take a liking to the Man in the Raincoat. Shit, I wasn't one of those idiots who get kidnapped and after a time come to see their kidnappers as nice guys just because they haven't been killed or had their teeth and fingernails yanked out with pliers. The scorpions were better.

Diderot came in as soon as the Man in the Raincoat left.

'You see what a mess you got yourself into because of that fat woman?' he said. 'A good-looking man like you . . . This is for your needs.'

It was a roll of toilet paper.

'Where's there a toilet for me to use?'

'There isn't. You're just like the man in the iron mask, you can't leave the dungeon. The man in the iron mask did everything inside the dungeon, there in the Bastille.'

'How do you know?'

'I did some research. When I used to compete – did you know I used to take part in costume pageants before I became a promoter? – one day I suddenly felt like making a costume of the man in the iron mask, so I read everything about him.

Know something? He wasn't a prince, or a duke, or a count, or anything. He wasn't even French. He was Italian, a petty noble. But that wasn't why I didn't make the man in the iron mask costume. You know why? Because he took care of his needs inside that same Cimmerian dungeon in which he was kept prisoner. Filthy, repugnant. That's why I gave up the idea.'

'Cimmerian?'

'I graduated in liberal arts. My mother was a piano teacher. An uncle of mine was a candidate to the Brazilian Academy of Letters,' he said with a superior smile.

'Could you get me a glass of water?' I said.

'No. You can't eat, you can't drink. I'm not about to second-guess the boss. He'll kill me if I do that. And he's going to kill you, from hunger and thirst, if you don't return the stones.'

'And if I do return the stones?'

'That's up to him.'

'Will he kill me if I return the stones?'

'What did he tell you?'

'What do you mean?'

'What did the boss say he'd do if you returned the stones?'

'He only told me what he'd do if I *didn't* return them.'

'The boss is a man of his word.'

'Get me a glass of water.'

'You're crazy,' he said.

'One last thing: who's in the habit of listening to rock?'

'That's Ulisses. A jerk.'

I hadn't met Ulisses yet.

'What's that noise?'

'You don't know?'

'I do know. It's a grinder. But what's it grinding?'

'You don't know?' Diderot repeated.

'No. Tell me.'

'Me?'
He left.

When I see a film, I think things like: why did the scriptwriter have the character say such-and-such? When I read a book I also think the same thing: why did the author write that? The guys are professional phrasemakers; they should know what they're doing. And I also pay a lot of attention to people talking on the street corner. The Man in the Raincoat had spoken of roast suckling pig. That must have some relevance. At least it told me I was someplace where roast suckling pig was eaten in celebration. Since I had been drugged during the trip, I couldn't say for certain how long I was in the car, but I don't believe it could have been more than five hours. Traveling five hours, let's say, in a van, which isn't a very fast vehicle, I could still be in the State of Rio, if my kidnappers had taken a lot of twists and turns to throw me off – which wasn't very likely – or I could be somewhere in the states of Minas Gerais, São Paulo or Espírito Santo. Was roast suckling pig a custom of Minas or of São Paulo? I knew it was a rural delicacy. In some large region of Brazil, I didn't remember where, the people sometimes ate roast suckling pig at Christmas instead of turkey. Yeah, and so what? So nothing. In fact, it didn't matter in the least in which State of the Union I was. Then the noise stopped.

That same day I had a visit from Alcobaça. He entered in the company of a large man carrying an armchair. It had to be Ulisses.

'You may go,' Alcobaça said after the man had placed the chair on the ground.

Ulisses retired and Alcobaça sat down in the chair, his eyes closed. He was paler than ever.

He sat there for two minutes looking like a dead man.

Then he said: 'I am driven by a strange pathology, a break in my body's inner harmony, of unknown etiology.' A pause. 'My life would make a film.'

Whenever I hear that, I know my interlocutor wants to tell me a long story. I made myself comfortable. It didn't cost anything to try to get onto the good side of the man known as Boss by the criminals who had kidnapped me.

Then Alcobaça began his story, speaking softly like someone who suffers from emphysema. Until the age of thirty he'd been a very healthy man. Then he began to feel bad, a very great weakness, insomnia, loss of appetite, diffuse pains throughout his body. As he belonged to a very rich family, he could consult doctors in the finest clinics in the world in search of a diagnosis. He was subjected to all the tests known to modern medicine, but they found no cause for his illness. His condition couldn't be attributed to heredity, for his parents and all four grandparents were still alive and enjoying perfect health; or to an unhealthy physiology, as all his organs and glands functioned properly; or to parasites, trauma, tumors, infections, viruses, bacteria and so on. His immunological system was flawless.

Even without knowing what he was suffering from, several of the many doctors that Alcobaça consulted attempted various therapies: chemical, biological, diathermic, radiological. He took dozens of drugs.

Then someone suggested he try alternative medicine. The best healers, classically, are the lame, the blind, priests and hysterical virgins. They recommended to him one who was simultaneously a priest (albeit *défroqué*) and a hunchback, which seemed to Alcobaça a guarantee of legitimacy.

'You're dying,' the Hunchback told Alcobaça when he went to see him.

'I don't want to die,' Alcobaça said. 'Give me some medicine; there has to be a medicine.'

'I don't believe in modern drugs produced by multinational pharmaceutical houses,' the Hunchback said. 'The cure, as Hippocrates said, is in Nature – the Nature that is within and outside the man.'

The Hunchback then expounded a theory, based on the age-old Greek medicine of Erasistratus and Galen in combination with ancient Chinese medicine, which Alcobaça summarized for me as follows: life was a vapor, a subtle gas, a breath, a pneuma – in sum, a spirit that permeated the organism, feeding it and causing its movements. The human being was a system of veins, arteries, nerves that together made up tissue. Blood and two types of pneuma, one called *vital spirit* and the other called *animal spirit*, were the wellsprings of existence. The blood transported by the veins and the air passing through the lungs to the heart were transformed into the vital pneuma that sustained the organism; immediately thereafter, they were sent to the various parts of the body by the arteries and upon arriving at the brain were transformed into animal pneuma, which initiated movement. This eclectic medical concept of the Hunchback's combined the use of herbs with minerals, not simultaneously and cumulatively but in successive phases.

First the Hunchback tried herbs, without result. He changed over at once to minerals, prescribing for Alcobaça the use of China clay, what the Chinese call kaolin, a term meaning high hill, a white clay used both for the treatment of diarrhea and also in ceramics for the production of porcelain. But, like the herbs, the kaolin did not produce the therapeutic effects that the healer hoped for.

The Hunchback looked upon Alcobaça's disease as a challenge. He moved into the patient's mansion in order to monitor the treatment better. Of one thing the Hunchback was sure: lithotherapy, the medicinal use of stones, was the correct treatment for that mysterious illness. He decided to try a stone that came not exclusively from the mineral kingdom but boasted a more complex make-up, a mineral conceived in the animal kingdom. The first stone with such a structure, which he knew existed and which he prescribed for Alcobaça, was alectoria, a stone formed in the liver, or intestines, of the rooster.

'*Alektor* in Greek means rooster,' Alcobaça said. This stone was administered in powdered form, in small quantities such as occurs in homeopathic medicine. Thousands of roosters were slaughtered to yield it in sufficient quantities, for only rarely did poultry possess it. Alcobaça's rich family built a chicken farm to supply the necessary alectoria.

For a year and two months Alcobaça took the alectoria manufactured by the Hunchback and enjoyed good health. He traveled about the world, for he was now able to walk again without having to sit in a wheelchair every two hundred and twenty steps as before.

But after those fourteen months, the alectoria powder lost any effect. The Hunchback became very worried, not knowing what to do. He sought the answer in alectoromancy, a form of divination consisting of a rooster eating grains of corn placed on letters. In the reading, the rooster first pecked the letter *b*, then *e*, then *z*, then *o*, then *a*, and finally the letter *r*. Bezoar. Bezoar! The Hunchback, through magic, had discovered a new medicine. The word (*bazahr* in the original Arabic) referred to a calcareous concretion that forms in the intestines and urinary tract of quadrupeds and men, held to be an antidote in medieval medicine. How could the Hunchback have forgotten that oval – sometimes spherical – stone so laden with therapeutic properties?

The treatment was similar to that of alectoria, the difference being that the bezoar stone was easier to pulverize. For a year Alcobaça was kept alive by the administration of bezoar powder. Until once again he began to waste away, to become ill, to be threatened by death, for the bezoar powder, like the alectoria before it, no longer produced any effect. The Hunchback, who had given up all his other patients to dedicate himself to Alcobaça, did not lose heart. In spite of being defrocked, or perhaps because of it, he possessed a great faith in God. He prayed for an entire day, and by praying received the answer to his doubts: why not try a simpler treatment, making use of a purely mineral element, rather than more stones formed by animals like alectoria and bezoar, minerals formed under great pressure and at high temperatures in the deepest reaches of the earth's crust? It was in this manner, the Hunchback later learned, that diamonds are crystallized before the eruption of their primordial rock projects them to the surface through volcanic chimneys.

Until the beginning of the twentieth century, Alcobaça went on, gems were used not only as amulets and talismans but also as medicine against diseases, having the ability to effect a cure in several ways: *a*) by their mere presence; *b*) by being placed on the diseased or painful part of the body; or *c*) by being ingested, in keeping with classical lithotherapy. Even in the twentieth century, in Japan, calcic pills with pulverized pearls were sold for medicinal purposes. But the Hunchback knew, through divine inspiration, that only the diamond would do to cure his patient.

First was a small diamond, which the Hunchback served his client in powdered form, in small doses. Alcobaça's recovery after two weeks was impressive. His resistance increased considerably, and he began eating better and sleeping well. After two months, the man who had been at death's door even began riding a horse again.

'That was when I decided to become a prospector, and I bought this piece of land here in Mendanha. My health was so good that, while looking for precious stones, I myself hammered apart the agglomerates I found.'

'Agglomerates?'

Alcobaça explained that agglomerates were rocks made up of angular volcanic fragments, randomly fused together and easily found in the region. Precious stones could be encrusted in agglomerates. He never found a gem that was worth anything, but his health improved from the exercise.

'Do you know I became fascinated by prospecting? It's a fantastic gamble. I bought this land because I'd heard that a company in the area, the Tijucana, had mined eighteen thousand carats in a single year. I, however, only managed to find diamonds of such low quality that I couldn't even use them in my treatment. They said that in the stream running through the land I'd find diamonds and alluvial gold and that on the crests of the hills I'd find ores full of diamonds and gravel bearing pure gold. I wasn't interested in gold, but I'm sorry I didn't find the diamonds.'

Diamond lithotherapy had freed him of his mysterious illness. He was a cured man. The only thing was that he couldn't halt the treatment; he continually needed diamonds of excellent quality, pulverized, to stay alive.

Only the powder of a colorless diamond produced the beneficial effect. Colored diamonds were useless. Other precious stones, pulverized, even if colorless and of adamantine brilliance, like cassiterite, colorless sapphires, zircons or cerussite, were harmful to him.

The pulverizing of the diamonds, because of their extreme hardness, was done by a special grindstone, a gadget invented by the Hunchback. First the diamond was crushed, then ground. The sharp, grating noise I'd heard was Alcobaça's last diamond being crushed and reduced to powder.

'After a time I'd gone through the entire family fortune. All I have left is this house, in the middle of nowhere, as the Americans say,' Alcobaça continued. 'One day my supplier of precious stones, after denying me even one more stone of any kind if I didn't first pay him what I owed, suggested I smuggle for him. I accepted the offer. I smuggled the stones and he paid me in colorless diamonds, much like what happens with some addicts, who work for traffickers and receive drugs in payment. In the beginning I always took the stones abroad myself. Then I had the idea of smuggling the stones in Carnival costumes. I need an ever larger quantity of powder to stay alive. I need those rubies, sapphires, emeralds that the fat woman stole from me and you now have, to pay my supplier. It's my life that's at stake, understand? I still have one diamond, a stone of great purity and unsurpassed beauty, a family heirloom, but I don't want to destroy it. I'll only do that as a last resort. Within thirty days I must prepare another dose. I hope you can't go without eating for that long.'

I said nothing, thinking about what he had told me. I felt sorry for Alcobaça, but I was disinclined to sympathize with my captors or allow myself to be intimidated by them. They had committed an unforgivable act of violence against me.

'I'll think about it,' I said.

'I don't have much time,' Alcobaça said. 'A month.'

'Where are we? What place is this Mendanha? I've heard of it, but I don't remember.'

Alcobaça stood up.

'Your ignorance astounds me,' he said, leaving and bolting the door. One more person who called me ignorant.

# 20

A scorpion can go a year without eating. A Siberian salamander, which has an average life span of ten years, was frozen for ninety years in a state of anabiosis and came back to life when placed in a receptacle of cold water. We human beings lack the slightest resistance to privations. In reality we are an animal with few resources.

I had gone without eating for five days now and no longer felt hunger. I had with me an aluminium canteen covered with green felt, like those used in the army, full of water, which had come to me unexpectedly.

On my second day of total abstinence Ricardo, the Man in the Raincoat, had come into the cellar carrying the canteen.

'The boss told me to give this to you. He doesn't want you to die of thirst. He said death by thirst is horrible.' He laughed. 'He wants you to starve to death.'

This said, he took off my handcuffs and left.

Twice a day one of the kidnappers traded the empty canteen for one full of water. My urine, which had become dark and had a strong odor, returned to normal. My salivary glands were working again, allowing me to spit, which I did several times, recalling a classmate in high school who used to wander around the streets spitting unceasingly until his mouth was completely dry from thirst and he could drink water with great eagerness and enjoyment.

I'd had only one bowel movement, a hard and cracked stool that I suffered greatly to expel. Strangely, it had no smell. I made a mental note to mention the fact to Diderot.

On the fifth day of abstinence I felt the muscle walls of my digestive tract contract in vermiform movements, trying to evacuate a content it did not have. Poor *ieiunum intestinum,* with no mass to absorb and push onward in its unrelenting peristaltic rhythm toward the ass, frustrated because it couldn't supply the blood and lymph their allotment. Poor body, whose cells continued, in a disturbing automatism, to secrete mucus and enzymes to digest what didn't exist.

The body, however, does have some intelligence, like a sophisticated robot directed by a well-written piece of software. Thus my body began to make some very interesting adaptations and adjustments. First it reduced my physical mass so that, with less tissue, metabolism could be carried out with greater economy of energy. My pants began to fall down my legs and I had to add several notches to my belt. Then my body made me feel a kind of lethargy that forced me to avoid useless muscular effort, like going to the window to look at the trees, or going to observe a rat excreting in a corner of the cellar, or a hairy spider running erratically along the ground. My pulse rate became slower and slower. I counted one thousand and one, one thousand and two, one thousand and three, one thousand and four, one thousand and five, one thousand and six, and my pulse beat four times in those six seconds, which gives a pulse rate of forty beats a minute. I remembered reading – or had I dreamed it? – that in the concentration camps, women subjected to extreme lack of food suffered from amenorrhea, that is, their menstrual flow stopped; probably one more demonstration of the body's wisdom. I remembered Ruth's sanitary napkin. Where had I put it? I didn't ever want to lose it. Enormous apathy had taken hold of me. The only emotion I felt was a tremendous desire for food.

Ascetics believed that prolonged fasting led to the development of virtue and spiritual perfection. To them, the sharp hunger I felt at that time should be viewed as a great struggle against myself, which would enable the liberation of the divine spark within me, domination of my impulses, renunciation of the world, and betterment of my soul by preparing it for the contemplation of God. I recalled Babel's stories, while I still could. Until one day I began feeling too lazy even to think. I didn't want to renounce the world, but the world had become tiring. I was so tired I didn't even have the strength to pick my nose. The best thing was to sleep.

At a certain moment I heard a voice, like my brother's, saying, 'Accept this privation and martyrdom with joy, for you are being purified.' Other than José's tedious voice, I heard nothing. I had no visions, I liberated no divine spark; an overwhelming sleepiness was taking hold of me. I was going to die because my body wasn't wise enough to stop working at full speed for a period of time, like a polar bear, for example, or a salamander, or a good machine.

Dream. People in silence. The girl with the damp gums licks me with her mouth of pearly teeth. Other women, with ample busts and bleached hair, walk around the square beating on the scaffold. It's hot, although it's winter. 'He's just a blasphemer,' one of them says. The nauseating silence is broken by the sound of splitting bones and the howls of the prisoners asking to be finished off at once. The executioner's hands are small and white. The condemned man's body is covered with piss and shit, which begin to dry. The women look on with disgust and attention, industriously. Discipline, horror, power, reward and punishment – such is the world, they say in chorus, covering their noses.

I awoke to see a figure standing beside me. An enormous man – it's true I was lying on the ground and my point of view increased his stature – crouched at my side.

'You're crazy,' he said. 'You're going to starve to death for no good reason. Give him the stones.'

It was the Hunchback. I tried to get up off the ground. The Hunchback helped me into the chair. He truly was tall, the tallest hunchback I'd ever seen in my life.

'I don't like being threatened.'

'I'm begging you,' the Hunchback said.

I didn't remember any hunchback in *Red Cavalry*. The only one that came to mind was Charles Laughton, fat, short, ugly, saying 'Water, water!' (which he receives from the beautiful Maureen O'Hara) in *The Hunchback of Notre Dame*, directed by William Dieterle.

'Water,' I said.

The Hunchback got the canteen that was lying on the ground and put it up to my mouth. I took a small swallow.

'I have to make a film,' I said.

'Yes, make your film. You'll be free if you return the stones. You can make one, two, three films, as many as you like.'

The Hunchback and I looked at each other, in silence. In his gaze I saw his compassion for me.

'Will he really die?'

'Yes, he will. He's a good man,' the Hunchback said.

'All right. I'll return them. But tell him I want him to come and apologize to me.'

I said this very slowly because of the lethargy I felt.

'He'll come,' the Hunchback said.

At that instant a boom, similar to a shotgun, sounded. The Hunchback ran towards the door and disappeared.

I heard shouts, voices giving commands. More shots. Screams. Shots. Footsteps. More shots. It's my turn, I thought. I remained seated. There was a silence, then voices, softer.

The cellar door was opened and a man came in. He was wearing a dark blue suit and pointed a shotgun at me. My time had come.

'Who are you?' he asked.

I told him my name.

'Get up. Place both your hands on the wall.'

With difficulty, I did what he ordered. I was searched. The man took my billfold from my pocket.

'Stand still. Don't take a step. I'll be right back,' he said, leaving at once.

I got tired of leaning my hands against the wall and went back to the chair. If I was going to be killed, it was better for it to happen in some comfort. Dying, in fact, wasn't such a painful idea at that moment. When a person gets as weak as I was, life loses its zest.

Three minutes later the man reappeared.

'Stay here for five minutes, then you can leave. If you come out before that, you'll be shot, understand?'

I remained seated on the chair.

I heard footsteps of people leaving.

The sound of an automobile starting. Immediately there descended on the cellar a silence so great that I had the impression I could hear the spiders walking along the floor.

I calculated that five minutes must have gone by and made my exit.

The cellar stairs led to a pantry. At the foot of the stairs was the Hunchback, a fatal wound in his head. He had a nice profile; if he weren't so hunchbacked he could have been the leading man in a romantic film. Further on, in a large room with dark colonial-style furniture, I found the body of the Man in the Raincoat. He had died in character; all he needed was a hat on his head to look like the lead in a Republic B film. He had a revolver in each hand and his clothes were soaked with blood. Immediately afterward I came across the bodies of Diderot and Ulisses. They had died in an embrace.

'Alcobaça?' I shouted.

I heard a moan, which appeared to be coming from above. Then another.

I slowly climbed the stairs, gripping the carved wood handrail. The moans were coming from one of the many rooms on the upper floor, whose doors opened onto a long corridor with walls displaying portraits painted in oil. I opened several doors before finding the source of the sound.

Alcobaça was lying in a large bed covered by a canopy. He was holding a sheet against his chest. He looked at me and said, with melancholy and despair, 'He took the Florentino.' Then his head fell forward. He was dead.

I went downstairs to the pantry. I opened the refrigerator. Inside I found an aluminium container, a milk pan with round holes in its lid, filled with a thick white liquid covered with golden-flecked cream. I drank the milk straight from the pitcher, spilling it on my face and clothes. I felt like vomiting.

I took the pitcher to the living room and lay down on a sofa. On the living-room walls were more oil portraits, old paintings with peeling gilded frames. Who were those men and women? Relatives of Alcobaça's?

The slaughter and my movement around the house had left me more fatigued than ever. I have to recover my strength to get out of here, I thought. Lately all I did was run away.

I don't know how long I lay there, drinking milk. I felt like going to the bathroom to move my bowels. The milk had had a purgative effect. I had to climb the stairs again, since I didn't find a bathroom on the ground floor. In reality, the lower floor was too full of corpses for me to get around easily.

Sitting on the toilet, I thought back over my life of late. A woman I loved had killed herself. My father had died some time earlier after a long agony. I had become a thief. I had stolen the precious stones of a poor fat Carnival figure killed by gangsters, who were now dead themselves. And I had become a currency smuggler. So what? Truthfully, all I wanted at that instant was to satisfy my desire to defecate.

Afterward, I did something repugnant: I searched the bodies looking for money. I didn't find money, documents or any papers that might identify them. The killers must have cleaned up after themselves. The only thing I could find was a credit card in Diderot's pocket.

In front of the house I came across a garden of red and white flowers. I turned to examine the building's façade and my heart beat a bit more quickly, to the extent this could happen to a ravenous man who had just drowned his torment in a bit of milk. The front of the house displayed 'between two repulsive gargoyles, a half-moon overhang in which was carved the date 1831'. I remembered the phrase, and who had said it to me. I also saw the stained-glass windows, the enormous wooden door, and the mountains of stone on every side. Good thing my memory had started working again.

The landscape I saw was rocky; everywhere I looked there were piles of stones, mountains of stones. The car that had brought me here had disappeared.

I sat on the steps of the colonnade of the house and waited for the milk to give me the strength to flee.

# 21

Night was falling by the time I felt strong enough to make an excursion around the house. I briefly hoped to find a car hidden in one of the two sheds at the back. In the first, I discovered only wooden panning troughs, small sledge hammers and unrecognizable tools. And the grindstone where Alcobaça must have pulverized the diamonds.

I didn't find the car in the other shed either. But there was a cart for a horse and two saddles, one with a high saddle horn, the other English. In the same wooden rig was a harness with twin bridle, one a bit, the other a bridoon. A bit like that couldn't have been for any greenhorn rider or some nag. The rural horses of the interior – I didn't know where I was, but it was the middle of someplace in the backlands, maybe of purgatory, judging from those rocks – wore only the bit and weren't hard to ride. I remembered on one occasion, at a ranch, betting Ruth that I could ride a horse like that using only a halter.

I went looking for the horse. It had to be a headstrong animal if it needed a double mouthpiece. It was in a stall, and even from a distance I could see that it was a large specimen of the crossbred *manga-larga* stock, with intelligent eyes, a dapple-gray with a lustrous shiny coat, indicating it was well cared for. I patted him on the forehead. I was so happy to find a horse, an animal with such a good nature, something that hadn't happened recently – I wasn't comparing it to the scorpions who had kept me company in the cellar but to the people I'd been dealing with – that I gave him a kiss on his cheek, feeling the large, hard bones of his mandibles. Patting him gently, I caressed his neck and shoulders. I ran my hand along his lightly curved back until I came to his hindquarters. I felt like singing. Like crying. Like dancing.

I did none of these things. With a rope from the stall I improvised a halter. I led the horse to the shed where the saddles were kept. I chose the saddle with the pommel, the high saddle horn, even though a horse like that deserved to be ridden with the English saddle. But I was in a very weakened condition and might need to hold on to keep from falling if the dapple was highly spirited.

While I put on the harness, using my own nose as a reference, I calculated the horse's height to be about sixty-six inches from withers to ground. He must have weighed at least thirteen hundred pounds. He had an A branded on his haunch.

Next I was careful to check the length of the stirrup straps, since the stirrups seemed very high to me. I had to lower the straps three notches. This must have been the horse Alcobaça rode, and he was quite a bit shorter than I.

OK. It was time to mount. I put my left foot in the stirrup but didn't have the strength to raise my body.

'Be patient, dapple; it's your fault for being so tall,' I said, patting the horse. He looked at me with patient eyes.

I led him to a footstool, on which I stood and got into the saddle.

The saddle, despite the horn being somewhat toward the rear and hitting against my thigh, was very comfortable. The dapple's gait was firm and his pace more relaxing than a rocking chair.

I went down a dirt road, with tire tracks, between stone-covered mountains. I soon came to a highway and a kind of crossroads. I stopped, not knowing which way to go. One of the roads was level. The other went up a hill of black stone. I was lost. I chose the level path and felt a very subtle resistance on the horse's part. I loosened the reins. The horse headed for the steep path. I allowed it to lead me.

The darkness of the night made the countryside completely disappear. I don't know how long I wandered without knowing where, letting the horse choose the way, always ascending. His shoes made a metallic sound on the rocks.

Several times I dozed on the moving horse. I remembered a story of Babel's in which a Cossack (Savitsky, Vitiagaichenko, Liutov-Babel?) falls asleep on his horse after a bloody battle. I had thought that to be an exaggeration on the author's part. Suddenly I was surprised by a lighted cross looming in the sky ahead of me. I'm starting to see things, I thought. As I approached the cross it became more real, more tangible. I finally neared two large wooden beams in the form of a cross, studded with glowing light bulbs, atop a hill. Below, not far away, thousands of lights flickered. It was a city, which appeared enormous.

What city could it be? The illuminated cross told me nothing; every city I knew of on the edge of a mountain had a cross on top of it. I regretted not being better at geography so I might know where Mendanha was. I really was very ignorant.

The horse began to descend toward the city. I would have to abandon him sometime; the A branded on his flank could give me away. Once again I was in a difficult situation. I couldn't go to the police and tell the story of my kidnapping. No one would believe me; the truth was too absurd. Scenario: officer, I was kidnapped by a smuggler of precious stones hooked on high-purity diamond powder. Ah, says the officer, hooked on diamond powder, interesting. Did he snort it or mainline it? Actually I don't know how the powder is administered, I say. Go on, go on, says the officer, making a cryptic gesture to the cops in the precinct. One policeman stations himself at the door, his hand on the holster of the revolver at his waist; another goes to the window and makes a show of inserting a shell in a .44 rifle. The men held me prisoner in a cellar, with scorpions, centipedes and hairy spiders – not that it bothered me; I was already bitten over a hundred times by hairy spiders – and since I was imprisoned in the cellar, I didn't see the killers arrive. Hear that, boys? the officer says. He was bitten over a hundred times by spiders. You sonofabitch, says the policeman with the rifle, hitting me on the head with the gun butt, you think we're hicks? We know all about the bad things you've done here in this area, says the officer. Let's bury him alive under a pile of rock.

The scenario concerned me. I dismounted, removed the harness. I kissed the horse's muzzle. 'Go home, dapple!' I shouted, giving him a slap on the haunch, over the A. The horse galloped away. I threw the harness down a ravine. Then I sat down and waited for day to break; I wasn't about to enter a city like that late at night. A stranger on foot can only show up at the time of some bus arriving. Usually buses arrive early in the morning; night trips, over long routes, were very common, and despite having been drugged when I was kidnapped, I knew that my journey had taken a long time.

A cold wind was blowing, even though it was summer. I bent forward, hugging my body. Despite the cold, I dozed a little. When I awoke, day was beginning to break. A very red sun appeared in the distance, lighting hillsides of black stone that went on for ever. The hill where I stood was completely covered with enormous stones of strange and varied shapes, of different sizes, some of them immense, polished, weathered, sculpted by the wind. From cracks in the rocks sprouted a sparse yellowish vegetation. It was a (real) film set of extreme aridity. A path of dark earth and pebbles, which I judged to be about three miles long, descended toward the foot of the mountain.

I walked slowly toward the city, while the sun flooded with light the collection of colonial houses and churches crossed by steep streets paved with large dark stones; its Baroque look resembled Ouro Preto, but I was familiar with that city in Minas Gerais, and it had a different topography. What the hell city was I in?

I finally ended my descent. I looked back and saw the mountain I had just crossed, a dark, grayish wall of stone. I began to see houses and a man passed me without showing signs of curiosity, which eased my mind.

I asked a woman passer-by: 'What street is this?'

'Areião Street.'

Every small town has a square with the main church: 'How do I get to Church Square?'

'Church Square ... Look, go this way, take Rio Grande Street, then Burgalhau ... Then up to Barão de Guaicuí Square, then you take a narrow street, off to the right, then you go up and you'll see the church.'

I felt enormous weariness. The right thing would be to get a room at a hotel, phone Liliana, rest a while. I didn't have any money, but I had Diderot's credit card.

I began climbing Burgalhau Street, paved with those large dark-gray stones that, I now saw from up close, had an irregular shape. I heard the roar of a motor, a sound like that of the car in which I had been forced to travel with a hood over my head. I looked back in fear and saw, climbing the street toward me, a black van with dark windows. It's them, the killers, it's no use running, I thought. The car came closer. I leaned back against the stone wall of a house. I opened my arms, giving up.

The van passed me by. Inside was a man in a cowboy hat who didn't even look in my direction. On the car's license plate was written Turmalina. Could that be the name of the town, Turmalina? What a funny coincidence. I continued my walk through the steep, narrow streets. Everybody's Drugstore, State Savings and Loan. Another car, Gouveia plates. Still another car, Datas plates. Shit, Turmalina, Gouveia, Datas, where the hell was I? Scenario: I go into a store and ask, Please, just where am I? One moment, says a young man. A policeman comes toward me . . .

At that moment, in the midst of my anxiety, I saw a police car, a paddy wagon, gray and white, with an arrow like a bolt of lightning painted on the door and the words Radio Patrol, MPMG. My heart beat rapidly, but the car slowly passed me by and disappeared.

Finally I arrived at Church Square. My fatigue had increased. Every city has a Church Square and a Metropole Hotel. I stopped a woman on the street. It was always better to talk to women.

'Where's the Metropole Hotel?'

'Go up this street, then take a right. Then go up. That's Quitanda Street. Right away you'll see the Metropole Hotel.'

Always climbing, a city of steep inclines. On Quitanda Street I saw cars going by with Diamantina license plates. I finally knew where I was: in Minas Gerais, Diamantina, a city of Baroque houses and stone streets. Another car with Diamantina plates. I no longer felt lost. Alcobaça's land was in Diamantina, a city that had got its name from the abundance of diamonds found there, an ideal city for a man who ate diamonds. Elementary.

*    *    *

I entered the Metropole Hotel by climbing a narrow stairway with two flights of stairs. There was a small patio with three cars, Belo Horizonte plates, and an enormous bougainvillea full of scarlet flowers.

The center of the hotel lobby was occupied by a wooden ephebus dressed in a Greek tunic, its hands raised and a fern on its head. In the corners, two small wooden columns with a spiral shaft held silver cachepots containing floral arrangements. In one corner, serving as support for a vase of flowers, was a wooden item looking like a large candle holder from a church. There were flowers all over the place. Also pictures on the walls: a man holding a wooden trough full of gravel, looking for diamonds in the river; two men and two women having a picnic, in a composition similar to *Le Déjeuner sur l'Herbe*, without the nude woman and the men in black; colonial rooftops of Diamantina.

A young man behind the reception desk stood up when I came in.

'I want a room. Do you take credit cards?'

'Yes. With bath?'

'With bath.'

He placed a registration card before me. I had put Diderot's credit card in my pocket and I didn't know his full name.

I took the card from my pocket.

'Do you want me to put the credit-card number?' I asked, as I read Diderot's full name. Diderot de Sousa.

'No, that's not necessary.'

I filled out the slip. Diderot de Sousa, Brazilian citizen, teacher, married, residing at 242 Barata Ribeiro Street, Apartment 101. I was impressed by my cunning, and by my crafty calmness as I unhesitatingly forged the data. In fact it would be easy for me to pass as a high-school Portuguese teacher; surely I wouldn't run into anyone in that hotel who would ask embarrassing questions about our language. Barata Ribeiro Street had hundreds of buildings. Being married would inspire greater confidence. The only problem would be if the card was on the blacklist. But I didn't believe that hypothesis; Diderot wasn't the kind of person who didn't pay his bills.

'What about your luggage?' he asked.

'I lost it,' I said.

'Lost it?'

'In Belo Horizonte. When I changed buses.'

I added a long story, told in part with his assistance. I thus found out the name of a bus company that could have taken me to BH and another that could have brought me from that city to Diamantina.

'The worst part is that all my money was in the suitcase. Could you arrange some shaving equipment for me?'

'I'll take it to you right away. Your key. The apartment's on the second floor.'

I took the key. I began climbing the stairs, covered by a red runner, that led to the upper floor.

'Breakfast is only served till ten o'clock,' he said.

'I'm just going to take a bath and get some rest. Where is Mendanha?'

'It's over that hill with the large cross on it.'

There was no telephone in the room. I opened the window. I could see the time-worn colonial roofs, lit by the morning sun, and the stone hill over which I had come, with the cross on top. There beyond lay Mendanha, the Sítio Velho, the Old Ranch, with its dead.

The safety razor that the doorman brought had a blade that was almost totally dull from so much use, but even so I managed to shave. My face looked better now. I showered and lay down to rest, knowing that I couldn't go to sleep. The sooner I got out of there, the better. The dead men at

Alcobaça's place could be discovered at any moment, and the police would be sure to take an interest in people like me. After breakfast I would devote myself to the task of finding a way to get a bus ticket to Belo Horizonte.

I dream of a vertical tunnel, a sort of chimney, through which I slowly plunge, gliding in a kind of reverse levitation. The tunnel, all of black stone, is encrusted with diamonds that sparkle to light my way as I descend, floating. I see the diamonds, I think, in the dream. This moves me so much that I wake up.

How long had I slept? I got up, startled, and opened the window. Calmer, I saw the colonial rooftops receiving the same morning light from the sun. Certainly it wasn't ten o'clock yet. I must have slept an hour at most. Yet the nap had left me completely recovered. I was hungry.

I went down to the room where they served breakfast.

In the dining room there were even more flowers than in the hotel lobby. I could smell the strong odor they exuded.

Only one table was occupied, by a man.

The breakfast table was set with great care. The tableware appeared to be silver. There was bread of several kinds, cookies, jelly, toast. Ham and cheese. A glass with purple beet juice. And a floral arrangement in the center. Flowers everywhere. Anthuriums, rhododendrons, Easter lilies, dahlias, chrysanthemums, daisies.

A man came up to me.

'My name is Odilon. I'm the owner of the hotel. May I sit down?'

He sat down.

'I see by your registration card that you're a teacher.'

'Yes. I'm a teacher of Portuguese. And history. I'm doing a

small historical study here in Diamantina. I'm taking a break from Portuguese.'

The man who was drinking coffee at the next table got up and came toward us.

'Sit here, Gaspar, don't run off,' Odilon said.

'When did you get to Diamantina?' Gaspar asked, sitting down at our table.

'This morning,' I said.

'Not today, yesterday,' Odilon said.

'Today,' I said.

'Yesterday. You slept twenty-four hours. João, the boy at the desk, said you went up to your room yesterday at eight-thirty in the morning and didn't come out till today.'

I felt the blood drain from my face.

'What's the matter?' Gaspar asked.

'I couldn't have slept so long.'

'Why?'

'I had to call Rio. I don't have any money. Didn't the boy mention that I lost my suitcase and –'

'João told me. Putting money in a suitcase! Where was your head?' Odilon said.

'Right. I want to see if they can send me some money.'

'Then make your call, make your call.'

I'd have to call from the front desk. João, behind the counter, looked at me with a smile. I dialed direct, collect, to Liliana.

'Give your name and the city from which you are calling,' said the recording.

'Diderot, from Diamantina,' I said. With João listening I had to give the same name as on the hotel register.

I waited a bit. I heard Liliana's voice – 'Who?' – then the sound of the phone hitting the cradle. Of course. Liliana didn't know anyone named Diderot.

'No one answers,' I said to João. 'I'll try again later.' I

looked around me. There was a room off to one side, with a television set, two sofas and some armchairs.

'Are you planning to have lunch at the hotel?'

'Yes,' I answered. 'Where is the bus station?'

'You don't know?'

'Of course, of course, I don't know what's with my head, ha ha! It's where I arrived, of course. Ha ha.'

Did the boy suspect something? Or was he looking at me like that simply because he thought I was a fool?

I left.

After walking for a time I asked a woman passer-by where the bus station was.

'Go this way, take Mercês Street, and just keep going up,' she said. This was no city for a guy suffering from starvation.

I did as the woman said. Finally I came to the station: a bus stop with some benches, a news-stand and a ticket window.

'Do you take credit cards?' I asked.

'What?'

'Do you take credit cards?'

'For what?'

'To pay for the fare.'

'To pay the fare?'

I showed him the card. He held out his hand. I slid the card through the opening in the window. He took the card and looked at it closely.

'Just a minute,' he said, leaving his chair.

He came back at once, with the card in his hand. He smiled, showing a cavity between two nicotine-stained incisors.

'We don't take it,' he said.

I took another route back, descending Francisco Sá Street, which curved and left me on the cross-street A. Nelson, near Quitanda. How was I going to get out of this damned city? I had to get away, fast. Begging? Stealing? Asking Odilon. I stopped and looked at my reflection in a pharmacy mirror. I was all wrinkled, my shirt torn. I imagined myself to be the ruined, ragged Oscar Wilde, meeting the opera singer Nellie Melba in a Paris street and saying: 'Madame Melba, don't you know who I am? I'm the famous writer and I'm going to say a horrible thing to you . . .' No, my face wasn't that of a supplicant; it was more that of a killer. It would be better to hold someone up to get the bus fare.

I climbed Quitanda Street toward the hotel, trying to imagine what would be the best place to stage my hold-up. I chose a narrow little street to the left of anyone going up to the hotel, with a few crannies that would do as hiding places. I had a heinous plan, which I would be incapable of executing. The alternative was to call Liliana at a time when no one was at the hotel desk. Beg, never.

I stopped in a store that accepted credit cards and bought some jeans, two pairs of undershorts, two shirts and a cheap watch, bargaining shamelessly with the man who waited on me so he wouldn't suspect my card was stolen. I asked for a receipt. My object was to reimburse him later, but the ass didn't want to give me a receipt, saying that he'd already come way down in the price of the merchandise.

'Diderot? That's really one odd name,' he said.

'He was a philosopher,' I said.

'Like Socrates?'

'More or less. Except he was French. His first name was Denis.'

'Denis is prettier, isn't it?'

'I think so too.'

'Why didn't your father name you Denis?'

The guy wanted to talk. I talked as long as he wanted to. I told him my story about being a teacher who'd lost his luggage, and so on.

It was eleven am. I returned to the hotel, went up to my

room, took a shower and changed my clothes. I was hungry. I went downstairs, but the dining room was closed; lunch was served at noon. I went into the television room beside the reception desk.

The television set was on. I sat down, dejected, glum. Suddenly I felt someone watching me. There were three men in the room, but none of them was looking at me (or at the television); they were looking at a brunette woman sitting with her legs crossed. The one looking at me was the woman. She was smoking a cigarette, which is all I saw because I quickly turned my glance away from her.

The young man from the reception desk came in and said that lunch was about to be served.

I got up, looking at the floor, walked toward the stairs leading to the restaurant.

I sat at one of the tables, as carefully decorated as it had been at breakfast. Someone stopped beside me. I raised my eyes.

It was the woman. I noticed she was tall.

'May I sit here?'

'Of course,' I said, rising and pulling out the chair for her.

She sat down.

'I was in the television room, being stared at by those awful men, when you came in. I saw right away that you were a sensitive and unhappy person. It wounded me in the heart. So different from the others.'

At that instant the men who had been in the TV room came into the dining room. They were surprised to see the woman at the same table with me. They looked spitefully in our direction. They had an aggressive air about them. Could they be the killers from the Old Ranch?

'I know that type of man,' the woman said, looking at the backs of the men after they'd passed by. 'You have no idea how. Where are you from?'

'Rio.'

'My name is Dália. I'm from Curvelo.' Pause. Ironically: 'The heart of Minas.'

Odilon appeared at the door of the dining room. He smiled at Dália, said something to the waiter, and came hurriedly in our direction.

'You've already met? How nice; I think you have a lot in common.'

'We just met a moment ago,' I said.

'You know what this beautiful lady once was?'

'None of that, Odilon.'

'She was Miss Curvelo. And the only reason she wasn't Miss Minas Gerais was because she didn't want to be. Actually, because of that dog.'

'Let's change the subject,' Dália said.

'All right. But don't be mad at me; a woman as pretty as you never has reason to get mad. You know what I like about her? The way she takes care of herself. Dália always smells nice and elegant.' He wrinkled his nose and smelled Dália. 'Ah . . . You know, I'm like that myself. Before I go to sleep, for instance, I dress up as if I were going to a party. I put on silk pajamas – they may be satin, depending on the sheets; my pajamas always go with the sheets – I brush my hair, put on some cologne, and lie down and stretch out. On the days when I have my feet done, I rub one foot against the other . . . It's so good. I really like myself. I love myself.'

'Why do you rub one foot against the other?'

'When I have my feet done they come out smooth. It's so nice to rub one smooth foot against the other . . .'

A man in a coat and tie appeared at the door of the dining room. He looked at the diners one by one, then came slowly in.

'Detective, what a pleasure. Did you come to join us for lunch?'

The police detective didn't respond. He sat down. He stared at me.

'This is Professor Diderot, from Rio. He's doing some historical research in our city. You know Dália.'

'I want to see the registration cards of those men,' the detective said in a low, hard voice, indicating the men who had been in the TV room. 'Now.'

Odilon rose indignantly. He clearly did not like the detective's tone.

The detective went with him.

'Are you OK?' asked the former Miss Curvelo.

'No. I'm not OK. I lost my luggage.'

'I can tell when a person is suffering,' Dália said. 'I've been there. I'm still going through it.'

I ordered chicken with okra, one of the items on the menu. Dália chose pork chops, refried black beans, a dish of manioc flour and collards.

Dália might have seen something in my face, but it was the detective I had to watch out for, not her. Dália wasn't interested in me. She was involved with her own problems and merely wanted someone to listen to her confidences.

I asked the question she wanted to hear. 'Why are you suffering?'

'Ah! I'd rather not talk about it.' And she began her story. In less than two minutes I knew everything. The ex-Miss Curvelo was the lover of the richest man in town, who was married. The wife had found out – a stupid note forgotten in his pocket – and forced her husband to put an end to the affair.

'I didn't expect that from him,' Dália said, about to cry. 'You live with a man for two years and suddenly you find out he's really a rat. He doesn't need her money; why does he stay married to that cow?'

'Yeah,' I said.

'I could have been Miss Minas Gerais, but he wouldn't

let me. I was the leading contender. You can ask anyone in Curvelo, Belo Horizonte, Juiz de Fora. The girl from Belo was pretty but – pardon the immodesty – I was a real panther. That's what I was called: the panther from Minas. They gave me that name when I won the Miss Summer contest in Rio.'

Dália began to eat with gusto now that she had let off a little steam. She cut a piece of pork chop, mixed it with a bit of beans, a pinch of manioc flour, a small mound of collards, in quantities that appeared precisely equal, and put it into her mouth. She chewed vigorously. Her teeth were large.

'After being Miss Minas I would've easily been Miss Brazil. It was two days before the contest and the press was all over me, television inviting me to be one of the girls on "Fantástico", radio, magazines, all you heard was my name, and he got jealous and made me withdraw. If I'd been Miss Minas Gerais I'd already be on my way in a career in entertainment, or at least a model. But no, he didn't let me, he wanted me subjugated, dependent. I sacrificed myself for him and that's what I got in return.'

Odilon came back to the table.

'Did you ever see such a rude man? Just because he's a police detective he thinks he can treat other people like dirt. He made me feel like crying, but I controlled myself. Imagine, crying because of a coarse policeman. I only cry over love. And when I cry, my dear' – addressing himself to Dália – 'the tears come gushing out so hard they hit the wall.'

'I cry like that too,' Dália said. 'Large drops that spurt out.'

'How about you?' Odilon asked.

'I never cry,' I answered.

'He doesn't know what he's missing, does he, Dália? Crying is good, such a relief.'

'What did the detective want?'

'I don't know if I should say ... He asked me not to mention it to anyone before he questioned the suspects.'

'Suspects?'

'No need to get nervous. After we confirmed that you were a teacher from Rio, the detective lost interest in you. He thinks the killers are thieves of precious stones.'

'Killers?' Dália asked.

'Oh lord! I shouldn't be telling this.'

'How did the detective confirm I was a teacher from Rio?'

'I told him I'd known you a long time, that you always came to Diamantina for your research. You don't have the look of a killer and I wanted to get that gorilla off your back.'

'Killer?' Dália exclaimed again.

'Blabbermouth,' Odilon said, giving three light taps on his mouth.

'Was somebody killed?' I asked, trying to sound uninterested.

'You both have to swear you won't tell anybody.'

'Come on, Odilon, let's hear it.'

'Well, if you insist ... In Mendanha, a district here in Diamantina, at a place known as Old Ranch, there was a massacre, five men killed. Nothing like that's happened in this neck of the woods for many years.'

Odilon recounted everything the detective had told him, which wasn't much.

'I think whoever did that awful deed is already a long way from here. But the detective doesn't think so.'

I tried to eat, without success. I pretended to put a forkful in my mouth.

'Don't you like the chicken?' Odilon asked.

'I have a bad headache,' I said.

'I have some very good headache medicine,' Dália said.

'Thanks. I have a painkiller in my room. If I lie down a bit it'll go away.'

I lay down without taking off my clothes. I felt anxiety, an uneasiness that left me unable to breathe. What if they identified Diderot? They'd track me down immediately. The name wasn't very common, not even in France. Get away, I had to get away. Babel was waiting for me!

I slept.

Dream. Burning in flames, drowned in blood where rose petals float under an unexpected purple morning light, she (who?) says to me: 'Fire is better than mold.' 'Wait,' I shout, 'don't let yourself be consumed before my answer.'

# 22

I awoke startled by a knock at the door.
'Who is it?' I asked.
'Dália.'
I opened the door. She had changed her clothes.
'Do you feel any better?'
'Yes, thanks.'
'Don't you want to go out? This city is also very pretty by night. That's why it has so many bohemians, so many serenaders.'
I hesitated.
'I'll wait for you downstairs,' she said.
She must have noticed that I had just woken up and thought I would like to straighten up before going out. Straighten up what? 'Let's go,' I said, grabbing the room key and closing the door.
As we descended the stairs covered with red runners, I was thinking. Madame Dália, don't you know who I am? I'm Diderot and I'm going to do a horrible thing – I'm going to ask you for money.
'When I get nervous I get an awful appetite,' Dália said. 'All I can think about is eating. That contemptible cur on top of everything else is going to leave me obese. Are you like that?'

'Like what?'

'Do worry and unhappiness make you hungry?'

'They have the opposite effect.'

'Then you're unhappy and worried.'

'Something like that.'

'Do you mind keeping me company at dinner?'

'Of course not. It'll be a pleasure.' Madame Dália, don't you know who I am? I'm Diderot and I'm going to do a horrible thing – I'm going to ask you for money. I mulled this over as we walked, Dália's heels striking loudly on the sidewalk.

There was almost no one in the street. The bohemians that Dália had mentioned must have been at home watching television.

The small restaurant was on Beco do Mota, a nearby side street. We went up some stairs, under the gaze of a black waiter on the upper level. The dining room was empty.

Food in Minas Gerais is for someone who's really hungry. Dália studied the menu, not sure what to choose. Finally she narrowed the options to chicken in brown sauce or taro with cornmeal mush and cracklings. We ordered the chicken in brown sauce. I was famished.

Before the food arrived, Dália had two servings of rum.

'I'm so nervous I had to stop myself from ordering the taro and cracklings too. You see what that louse is doing to me. I have a twenty-inch waist and weigh 132 pounds, which is very good for a woman almost five feet eleven. But a year from now I'll be as big as a house! All because of that rat.'

Dália said this while holding the chicken thigh in her hands in order to suck up the dark, bloody liquid still on the cartilage that she had not been able to get at with the knife and fork. She then filled her mouth with a forkful of rice saturated with sauce the dark brown color of blood. I recalled the German women eating at the kiosk in Berlin.

Was Dália's unabashed ease a lack of manners or was she acting out a scene?

'Odilon and I are good friends, you know, despite being acquainted only a relatively short time, since I was elected Miss Curvelo. He went to Curvelo the day of the contest, and we were introduced and suddenly discovered that both of us had had to overcome tremendous obstacles to get ahead in life. He started working when he was twelve, took a job in a textile mill, where he made it to manager. My life was even harder than his. Odilon had a mother, who was his idol as long as she lived. I was an orphan without mother or father. I doubt you can guess what job I had. I really do.'

'Factory worker.'

'I should've been so lucky as to be a factory worker. Try again.'

While I thought, Dália cleaned her plate with a piece of bread. It was so clean it looked as if it had been licked by a cat. I wasn't interested in Dália. The only thing that I wanted was to get to Rio, sit down with Gurian, and listen to the old man read me Babel's novel.

'Give up?'

'Garbage collector?'

'Worse. Know what I'm going to order for dessert? Glazed papaya. Have you ever had it?'

'Worse than garbage collector?'

'On your way here, your bus stopped at a barbecue restaurant, the Caverna de Maquiné, right?'

'I don't remember . . .'

'Of course it did. It's an obligatory stop. It's a little before the turn to Cordisburgo.'

'Ah yes, now I remember . . .'

'Did you go to the rest room?'

'Uh . . . no.'

'There's a rest room for men and another for women. I

took care of the women's rest room. I was ten years old. But I wasn't paid a salary. I lived off tips, off the small change the women who stopped to pee would give me. When each bus arrived I would run inside the rest room and sit at the door by a box with some coins in it, to see if people caught on, since it wasn't required to pay anything; you gave something if you felt like it. I lost the ability to smell urine, did you know that? Excuse my mentioning it over the dinner table, but that rest room, the more I cleaned it, the more it smelled. Until one day it stopped smelling – to my nose.'

We ordered the glazed papaya with white Minas cheese.

'How did you get out of the rest room?'

'A woman from here in Diamantina took a liking to me and took me into her home to look after her children. It was another kind of suffering. She would beat me for any reason at all, if I ate a cracker without asking permission, and if I asked she'd say no, if I had a soft drink, if I laughed – what are you laughing at, girl? – if I cried – what are you crying about, girl? – she'd come at me with a belt, or paddle my hands with an old paddle that must have dated back to when the city was founded, probably one of those used to beat runaway slaves. And I ended up becoming a runaway slave. I took the paddle with me when I left, out of spite. I still have it. When I feel myself weakening, I get out the paddle and hit myself in the palm with it. I walked to Curvelo, I walked an entire day and night. I got a job there packing groceries in a supermarket.' She paused. 'You were looking at me funny while I ate. What was it?'

'Eating is a secretive act. But not for you. You're not ashamed to eat.'

'Why should I be ashamed to eat?'

'It's a rather groundless theory.'

'I'm not ashamed of anything. You know I was a whore, before I was a Miss? I wasn't a cheap one; I even went out with a governor and a cabinet member. At the time I was living in Belo Horizonte. When I had lots of money I went back to Curvelo.'

'*The Visit of the Old Lady.*' A story of Dürrenmatt's ruined by Bernhard Wicki.

'I wasn't all that old. I'm thirty.'

'I was joking.'

'In Curvelo I didn't continue in that life. I opened a boutique, exclusively for items from Rio, or imported from Paris, New York . . . I set the tone for fashion in Curvelo. The short, fat, varicose-veined matrons of the city were so envious of me it nearly killed them. And furious, since their dear husbands melted like butter every time they saw me. I didn't encourage any of them; I led a serious life, never left the house. All the men were desperate; even the priest fell in love with me and attempted suicide because I refused to go to bed with him. That was when I started entering beauty contests. The women's hatred increased even more, but they didn't have the nerve to confront me, or even look me in the eye. I was chosen Miss Curvelo. Then I met that cur. The rest you know.'

'It'd make a film,' I said.

'Don't I know it,' she said.

Dália drank another rum.

'I was the one who had to do everything – if you know what I mean . . . Túlio would just lean back like a pasha, and I had to find some way to give him pleasure . . . The son of a bitch. I was the most faithful person he ever met in his life. While I was with him I didn't go to bed with anyone, not even the priest! And the money wasn't even his, it was his father's . . . But I don't need Túlio's money, I have a lot put away, stocks, dollars, a savings account, an entire building in Belo.' She paused. The rum was starting to take effect. She grabbed my arm tightly: 'Take me back to the hotel and fuck me.'

Madame Dália, do you know me? I'm . . . Diderot and I'm going to say something horrible to you – I'm going to ask you for money.

'What are you waiting for? There are men who would give their lives to screw me.'

Madame Dália, you don't know me. I'm not Diderot and I'm going to do a horrible thing – I'm going to ask you for money.

We left, her arm intertwined with mine, supporting herself.

When we got to the hotel, Odilon and Gaspar were whispering at the front desk, an air of collusion between them.

'Ah . . . Our professor got hooked . . . What was it, Gasparito, that Elizabeth Taylor's husband said about the beauty of the women of Diamantina?'

'Not the actress's husband,' said Gaspar calmly. 'It was a guy with the same name, a traveler who visited our city in the last century. He said that the men were the weakest' – at that instant Gaspar looked into Odilon's eyes and both smiled – 'and the women the prettiest and friendliest that he had found in Brazil.'

Madame Dália, I'm going to say something horrible to you.

'Odilon, have João bring a bottle of wine to my room,' Dália said.

We went up the stairs with the red runner. Behind us I heard Gaspar and Odilon whispering between laughter.

Madame Dália, I'm going to say something horrible to you – I'm going to ask you for money and I'd like to say it after screwing you, but I'm so tired that I'm afraid I'll play the deplorable role of poor Pasqualino, who can't manage to screw Shirley Stoler in Wertmüller's film.

From the window of the room the illuminated steeple of the church was visible.

'If there's one person I hate,' Dália said, taking off her clothes, 'besides that no-good Túlio, it's the former bishop of Diamantina, Dom Joaquim. He had them tear down the old church – which was lovely, I've seen photos of it – and built that piece of crap.'

Dália was naked.

'Is my nose smaller?' Dália said. 'When I get mad my nose gets smaller. I feel a twitch alongside the nostrils and it contracts. When you see my nose getting smaller, watch out!'

Her body was beautiful and made me feel a tug in my viscera. It wouldn't have been hard to get my libido going.

There was a knock at the door.

'You go,' Dália said, hiding in the bathroom.

Odilon handed me a bottle of white wine with two glasses.

'It's on the house,' he said. 'A bit of advice: don't drink much; let her do the drinking. A woman functions well drunk, but it's more difficult for the man. Trust me, I know what I'm talking about.'

He closed the door delicately.

I knocked at the bathroom door.

'You really preferred the old church?' I asked when Dália came out.

'What irritates me is that they tore down the old church. Dom Joaquim could have built a new church for his glory, but why tear down the old one?'

What she said helped me get hard. My good fortune was to like people.

Dália filled the glasses with wine. She downed her drink in one gulp. I moistened my lips.

'Lie down,' she said.

The alcohol excited her, and she was avenging herself. From time to time Dália stopped to take a drink. The bottle was empty. Her desire grew greater and greater, and I began simulating. After all, I had immense problems to solve, I had undergone physical privation recently, and I was tired. And Babel awaited me!

'I have to talk to you about a very serious matter.'

'In the middle of screwing?' she asked.

'We're not in the middle. We're nearer the end.'

'It's the middle for me,' she said.

'But it's a very serious matter.'

'Life and death?'

'Death.'

'All right. But first I'm going to the bathroom.'

A rooster crowed in the middle of the night. What does that mean? I thought.

Dália returned from the bathroom wearing a white lace nightgown open at the sides. She got into bed beside me.

'My name is not Diderot,' I began. I told her a condensed version of my kidnapping, without mentioning the precious stones, claiming ignorance about the reason behind everything, and the death of my kidnappers at the hands of unknown persons.

'That would make a film too,' she said.

'Now I'm going to say something horrible to you.'

'Say it.'

'I'm going to ask you for money.'

'I've heard that before.'

'I'll pay you back.'

'I've heard that too. This is the first time it's me doing the paying. How much?'

'The cost of a Diamantina–Rio bus ticket.'

'You don't even have that much?'

'We left the restaurant without paying!' I suddenly remembered.

'Forget about that. You don't even have money for the bus ticket?'

'I don't have a nickel to give the boy who takes care of the bathroom at the roadside restaurant.'

She embraced me, moved by this. 'Come on, a little more. I'll pay for the Belo–Rio plane fare.' She took her lips from mine to say, 'From here, there's only the bus.'

I didn't manage to sleep a second. As soon as Dália began breathing deeply I disengaged myself from her arms, got up, and went to look at the mountain of stones outside. The mountain showed the marks of various dark tones, black hollows, grooves, cracks caused by the winds of many, many centuries.

I waited at the window for day to break. It was the second time in Diamantina that I had seen the sunrise. Was someone else awakening like me, anguished like me, watching the sun appear?

The light entered the room. I sat down in the chair and watched Dália sleeping. I felt great shame at doing this, invading her secrecy; people sleeping should be respected in their vulnerability. With the thumb and forefinger of both hands, I framed for a hypothetical camera Dália's semi-nude body. I'd never had the courage, the hardness to do that with Ruth; I always averted my eyes from the secret weakness of her flesh in the moments in which she revealed herself to me.

Dália awoke and stretched.

'You're looking at me as if I snored during the night.'

'It kept me awake,' I said.

'Liar. Nobody ever told me I snored.' Pause. 'Do you like me?'

'Yes.'

'A lot?'

'A lot – considering the short time we've known each other.'

'I've decided to go to Rio with you.'

'There's so much I have to do in Rio.' I felt my voice shaking. 'Abominable things. I couldn't give you any attention.'

'Even at night?'

'Even at night. Not any time.'

'What do you have to do that's so important?'

'Read a book,' I said.

Dália got out of bed. She looked straight at me.

'Your nose is about this big,' I joked, showing the tip of my little finger.

Actually, she seemed about to cry.

'I'll come back, to take you with me.'

'I've heard that before too. I've heard every phrase a man can tell a woman.'

I hugged Dália. She began to cry, her body trembling silently.

'I'll be back, you'll see. From wherever it is, I'll come back to get you.' Her weeping had left me so sad and unhappy that I came to believe the lie I was telling. She too, feeling that I was telling the truth, stopped crying.

'I want to see if I can catch the first bus.'

'The first bus already left. In any case we have to wait for the bank to open so I can get the money.'

I had to be very persuasive so that Dália would get dressed quickly and we could leave the hotel at ten. She wouldn't let me pay the bill with the false credit card.

'Don't stick Odilon with it; he's a nice guy. I'll pay your bill.'

At a branch of the Bradesco Bank, Dália got the money.

'Here's money for the airfare, the taxi and the restaurant. I don't want my man going unprovided for.'

I felt my face burning. I said nothing, took the thick

wad of bills. I jotted down the number of Dália's bank account.

Dália insisted on taking me to the bus station. The bus for Belo Horizonte would leave at ten forty-five.

I kissed her cheek.

'See you soon,' I said.

'I'll wait for the bus with you.'

'There's no need.'

'I want to,' she said, sitting down on a bench.

I sat down beside her. My heart was beating rapidly. There were still a few minutes before I would leave that place, get away from the corpses at Alcobaça's, from the police, from fear.

A gray and white Fiat passed by slowly, the words Radio Patrol and a red arrow in the shape of a lightning bolt painted on the door. From inside the car the patrolmen looked our way, chilling my heart.

'What square is this?' I asked, as if I were completely at ease. 'What building is that over there?'

'Sacred Heart Square. That's the seminary. Can't you read?'

'I don't mean that faded blue one. I'm talking about the other one, that one the color of the south-end-of-a-donkey-going-north, with the two Ionic columns in front.'

'All that's the seminary.'

'What about that television antenna?'

'Seminarians watch television too, priests watch television, everybody watches television.'

The police car had disappeared.

A thin priest, with gray hair and wearing a very black cassock, appeared in the square. Who, I wondered, ironed the priest's cassock with such care? He could have come out of the seminary or else from the church with the rose window in the middle and an incongruous loudspeaker in the belfry. The only place he couldn't have come from was the fire station, which was one of the other buildings in the square, or from a ruined shed on whose walls was written TRACK PERSONNEL BARRACKS. The fire department was installed in the old railroad station.

Dália held my hand, our fingers interlaced.

The police car returned, passed slowly in front of us, the policemen looking in my direction – where was that damned bus? – and stopped up ahead.

A policeman got out and came toward us. It was better to get the whole thing over with once and for all.

Scenario. In the Diamantina police station the detective is giving a television interview. 'The accused,' he says, 'who behind the respectable façade of an artist hid a vile and twisted soul, first killed the Carnival figure and smuggler known as Fat Angélica, to steal precious stones; later, knowing that Angélica's criminal cohorts had more gems at the ranch at Mendanha, he came here accompanied by hired assassins whom we expect to apprehend within hours, killing five men, the greatest slaughter in Diamantina's history, the kind of horror unseen in these parts since the execrable Marquis of Pombal created the notorious Royal Intendancy in the eighteenth century.' The television shows clips from *The Holy War*. Plessner is interviewed in Berlin and says, '*Ich sah sofort dass er ein übler Ganove war und liess ihn aus der Bundesrepublik Deutschland ausweisen*'; that is, he'd seen right away that I was a common thief and had had me expelled from the Federal Republic.

The policeman passed close to us and continued walking. He went through a door marked MEN. The bastard was just going to the bathroom.

The bus finally arrived, a large eight-wheeler sporting the words GREEN BIRD.

'This is your bus,' Dália said.

'Where can I phone you?' I asked.

'At the Metropole. It'll be my home till you take me to Rio.'

I got onto the bus. From the platform, Dália waved to me.

As we left the city I saw an enormous billboard: WELCOME TO DIAMANTINA – THE JEWEL OF NORTHWEST MINAS. Goodbye, Diamantina; goodbye, Dália; goodbye, corpses, mountains of stone, mild-eyed dapple; goodbye, police detective; goodbye, Baroque. I was so euphoric that I got up from my seat and walked from side to side. Still near the city, I saw luxurious houses, many of them still under construction, but we were quickly swallowed up by the gray mountains of stone, with small intervals of skimpy vegetation in a soil dotted with itacolumite. The piles of stone took on singular shapes, one looking like a camel, another a man's face, another the head of a zebu bull. An arid and disquieting landscape, frightening and fascinating.

At eleven twenty-six we pulled into Gouveia. The bus stopped to let off some passengers and pick up others. The stop was only fifteen minutes but it seemed like an eternity to me.

The rocky landscape continued. In certain stretches there were large cracks displaying slabs and sheets of white itacolumite. I heard a man say loudly behind me: 'There are no reliable statistics.' The bus stopped again, in a small town. An arrow indicated the road to Presidente Juscelino. I heard more clearly the voice of my neighbor behind me: 'But it is known, with relative certainty, that for the coffers of the King of Portugal, between 1770 and 1821, 1,320,000 carats of diamonds were taken from the land around the mining camp of Tejuco.'

The voice of the other man: 'A shitpot full of diamonds!'

It was four minutes before one pm when the bus entered

Curvelo, the heart of Minas Gerais. I still had four hours of travel ahead of me. The driver told us that we would make a ten-minute stop. I got out to have some coffee. Once again, as had been the case lately, my pockets were full of money, even though it was a devaluated currency I was carrying.

From the bus station it wasn't possible to see what kind of a city it was where Dália had experienced such exciting moments, but as the bus pulled out of Curvelo and crossed its streets, I could see it was a rather prosperous town, with wide streets and clean, comfortable houses.

We drove past the Raros Motel at one-thirty. That was where Dália's romance with Túlio must have begun. At two-ten we passed through Paraopeba, fortunately without stopping. It seemed the journey would never end. In the middle of the highway I began seeing signs saying WE HAVE MINHOCUÇU. These ads repeated themselves countless times. Some said 'We have Minhocuçu DAY AND NIGHT.' Whatever minhocuçu was, there were people who got up at night to eat, drink or ride it.

It was two-twenty and people were sleeping in the bus when my euphoria began to subside. I saw the sign for Cordisburgo, a place where important people are born, but that wasn't the reason; Cordisburgo could only make me happy. My sadness began when the bus stopped at the Caverna de Maquiné barbecue restaurant and I remembered Dália.

'Ten minutes,' the driver said.

I got out and went to the door of the women's rest room. A woman was going in, and I said to her, 'Would you please ask the girl inside to come out?'

A skinny little mulatto girl came timidly to the door.

'Do you want to talk to me?'

'A girl who used to work here sent this for you.'

I gave the girl half the money Dália had given me.

She stood there with the money in her hand, puzzled.

'The money is yours, understand? Yours. Nobody else's. It's yours.'

At two-fifty – I knew because I was looking at my watch the entire time, awaiting the moment to meet Babel! – I began to see along the road immense black, smoking sheds that looked like something out of Fritz Lang's *Metropolis*: Itaminas, Interlagos, pig iron-producing steel mills pouring smoke into the world.

We passed through Esmeraldas.

There was a moment when I slept.

Dream. I know I am dreaming, and I decide to watch myself watching myself dream. 'That's me,' I say, in front of a screen, a black screen. This repeats itself, and repeats itself, several times.

I woke up at three thirty-five, by now close to Belo Horizonte, and the motels began to appear – Status, Le Premier – and the housing projects.

As soon as we arrived, I asked a man where I could get a taxi to the airport.

'A taxi? It'll cost a fortune. Take a São Jorge bus; it leaves right here from the station.'

In less than an hour we got to the airport of Confins, which means limits – a name worthy of Minas – at the far side of town.

At eight pm the plane landed at the airport in Rio. I was anxious to hold Babel in my hands again. And there was also another important matter to take care of.

# 23

From the airport I went straight to Gurian's apartment.
A woman answered the door.

'Is Mr Gurian in?'

'Who?'

'The owner of the apartment. Who are you?'

'I'm the cleaning lady.'

'You're the cleaning lady and you don't know who the owner is?'

'Dona Sarah was the one who told me to clean up. Let me tell you, I never in my life saw a place this dirty.'

I brushed the woman aside and went in.

Babel's manuscript was spread on the living-room table, the pages covered with notes in red pencil, unintelligible scrawls, probably in Cyrillic. That crazy old man . . .

I gathered the pages, my hands trembling. Happily, I pressed the manuscript forcefully to my chest. The cleaning lady was looking at me, not knowing what to do. I looked back at her with an ugly expression, so she'd be afraid and not bother me with questions. I couldn't waste time on explanations. I had too much to do.

I went to the bookcase and looked for the *Mahabharata*. I got the box of stones and stuck it in my pocket. I carefully placed the manuscript between the *Mahabharata* and *Les Fleurs du Mal.*

I called Sarah.

She told me that Gurian was in hospital again.

'He can't drink, he knows he can't drink,' Sarah said.

'I'm at his place. I picked up some things of mine that were here,' I said. 'Did he tell you anything about a manuscript he was looking at for me, by the writer Babel?'

'Was it you who brought those papers to him? You're to blame for Boris having a relapse.'

'Why?'

'Isn't it some sheets of paper in Russian?'

'Yes, that's it.'

'I went by his apartment one day and Boris was drunk, as always – that wretch is going to drink till he dies – reading those papers and making notes, and I asked, "Boris, are you drinking again?" and he said, shaking the papers in my face, "This calls for even more drink." You're to blame, for giving him that to read.'

'They're very important papers.'

'It's nothing to do with espionage, is it? Boris is too old to get involved in adventures. Don't talk to him anymore, understand? You're a bad influence.'

Gurian was in St Matilde Hospital, which only had visiting hours on Thursdays. It was Tuesday; I didn't want to wait two days to see him. I had another very important thing to do; but first I wanted to see Gurian.

I went to St Matilde. In the reception area there was a young woman in uniform.

'Is Mr Boris Gurian a patient here?'

She consulted a file in front of her.

'Yes.'

'I'm his cousin. I arrived from Germany yesterday. Could I possibly see him for just a moment?'

'No, I'm sorry. He's in the ICU.'

'Thirty seconds.'

'St Matilde has very strict rules, for the patient's own good.'

'But I'm a doctor.'

The woman thought a bit. She picked up the telephone. 'Dr Paulino, there's a doctor here who's the cousin of a patient in the hospital. He wants to visit him.'

While the receptionist was talking on the phone, I noticed a guard posted by the elevators.

'Dr Paulino is on his way.'

There was a mirror in the reception area. I looked at my reflection. I looked like anything – except a doctor.

Dr Paulino was a man of about fifty, well preserved, pleasant. He greeted me, calling me doctor.

But he was no fool: 'I thought at first I recognized you, that we might have been in medical school together, but you're quite a bit younger, doctor.'

'I studied in Campinas,' I said.

'Ah yes, Campinas. They have a good medical school. What's your specialty? Maybe it's the same as mine.'

He didn't have the courage to ask to see my identification before being certain I was an impostor. Whatever specialty I chose, Paulino would be sure to ask me embarrassing questions. But my desire to see Gurian was so great that I didn't care about being unmasked. After all, which of my masks would be removed? It was worth a try.

'I doubt it,' I said.

'What?'

'Your having the same specialty as me. It's a new field that for the time being exists only in Campinas.'

'What is it?'

304

'Lithotherapy. In Germany it's already offered at several universities, such as Berlin, for example. Lovely city, Berlin; I was there recently. Berlin was the first, but Campinas was the second in the world to create a chair of lithotherapy.'

'Lithotherapy . . .'

'The use of stones for medical purposes, as the name indicates.'

'Interesting. Please, tell me more about it.'

'We began by using bezoar, then alectoria, from *alektor*, Greek for chicken, as you know, doctor. But recently we were testing certain minerals expelled by volcanic chimneys.' I said this tripping over the words, as I didn't remember very well what Alcobaça had told me.

'May I see your identification?' he said, gently. The guard came toward us. Paulino must have given him a signal.

'I have to speak to Mr Gurian. Just one minute. Please.'

'You had best leave,' Dr Paulino said persuasively. He must have thought I was mad. Crazy people are fond of pretending they're doctors.

In the mirror I looked at my image and the image of Paulino. Paulino looked like a doctor from an American film – clean, handsome, reliable. I really did look like a madman, from a French film in which the line between eccentricity and madness is not well defined.

The guard took me to the door. I glanced back and saw the doctor looking at me and saying something to the receptionist. They both laughed.

From a phone in the street I called Maurício's house and said I'd be at Florentino within half an hour.

'Now, in the middle of the night?'

I hung up the phone without replying.

I was received immediately. A man was waiting for me at

reception and led me through empty corridors straight to Maurício's office.

'Where've you been?' he asked.

'You know where I've been.'

'Me?'

We looked at each other. How would I have presented this scene in a film? Both of us tense, and curious? A certain displeasure in my gaze? And in his too, why not? And weariness in both faces.

'You did a dirty job, or had it done, at the Old Ranch in Mendanha,' I said.

'I don't know what you're talking about.' Weary, weary.

'You and your assassins went there to kill Alcobaça.'

'You're dreaming.'

'You made a mistake. You forgot you had described to me the house at Old Ranch. The gargoyles, the 1831 inscription . . .'

Maurício sighed. Weary, resigned, unhappy.

'You had spoken to me of the Florentino. Alcobaça, dying and miserable, told me you had taken the diamond.'

'Dying, miserable?' Weary, resigned, unhappy, curious. A difficult scene.

'You did a sloppy job of butchery. They left him to suffer, before he died.'

We fell silent.

'Why did you kill him, you sonofabitch?' Displeasure in my voice, sadness, without shouting.

'Alcobaça was going to pulverize the Florentino to ingest it, thinking it would cure him of his illness,' said Maurício, sighing.

'He would only have done that as a last resort. He was proud of possessing the Florentino.'

'I know. But above all else he wanted to survive. I ask you to let me tell the story from the beginning. Please, sit down.'

Maurício removed a painting from the wall. From the safe he took out a black velvet box. He placed the black box on the table. We sat facing each other, the table between us.

'Alcobaça's grandfather, the commendator, who was a very rich man,' Maurício began, 'bought the Florentino in Europe, probably in Austria or Hungary, sometime in the Twenties. Alcobaça was raised in Europe, a spoiled child who never worked a day in his life. For that matter, his father never did a thing either. The Brazilian bourgeoisie of that period considered work degrading. Alcobaça's father spent his life having affairs with sly women in various parts of the world who helped relieve him of a substantial portion of the money his grandfather had accumulated. What is beyond dispute is that through prodigality, incompetence and negligence the family fortune was drying up. The young Alcobaça, ours, was not a wastrel but by way of compensation he suffered from a serious illness that the doctors couldn't diagnose and which ended up becoming quite expensive.'

'He told me about the disease,' I said. 'You can skip that.'

'Some years ago the Hunchback, a kind of guru-healer, came to me to buy diamonds for Alcobaça. He told me of the disease and the strange treatment of his client. I took an interest in the matter and came to know Alcobaça personally. He spoke to me of the Florentino. I already knew the mysterious history of the gem, and when I saw it I fell madly in love with it; I even changed the name of my firm to Florentino. I dreamed about the stone constantly; I think I already told you that. To stay close to it, I became Alcobaça's friend. At times I would go to his house just to have him show me the gem.

'Alcobaça's disease demanded an ever larger number of diamonds of great purity. He bought the Mendanha land to see if he could find diamonds, but he found only quartz, itacolumite and carbonate, what the French call *diamant concretionné*, which has very little value and was useless to him as medication. I furnished Alcobaça with the diamonds but he didn't pay me. I purposely let the debt grow, and one day I made him a proposition: if he gave me the Florentino I would provide him with the diamonds necessary for his treatment for the rest of his life. He agreed. But he didn't deliver the Florentino, despite my continuing to give him all the diamonds that the Hunchback asked for. Alcobaça always came up with some excuse. Finally, I decided to go and get the gem. I knew he lived surrounded by dangerous hired gunmen, and I took some security men from my firm. When we got there they attacked us and we were obliged to defend ourselves. That's all. I'm very sorry things ended as they did.'

Maurício opened the black velvet box before us. He put his hand in and took out an enormous glittering stone which he held between index finger and thumb. As his hand moved, the gem sparkled intensely.

'See, the Florentino flashes as if the noonday sun were imprisoned within . . . Even at night, in the most absolute darkness, it doesn't stop shining . . .' said Maurício, placing the diamond between my face and his own.

'You're a goddamned liar,' I said. 'Alcobaça was an invalid and was killed in his bed. The Hunchback also would never hurt anyone. Neither of them had to be killed. Or Diderot either. You were rubbing out witnesses.'

Impassive, Maurício carefully put the Florentino back in the box. Then he rose, opened the safe and placed the diamond inside.

'Listen to me, you fucker. I haven't finished talking to you!' I screamed.

'Control yourself,' he said.

I took out the box of precious stones that I had picked up at

Gurian's house and shook it in Maurício's face like a rattle. I opened the box and, with the stones exposed, rubbed it in his face, causing two of them to fall to the floor.

He pulled away, taking two steps backward.

'When Alcobaça couldn't pay any longer, you suggested that he smuggle precious stones,' I said. 'Everything was going smoothly until Fat Angélica decided to rob you and one of Alcobaça's gunmen killed her. You got worried. That could draw the attention of the police, arouse suspicions.'

'No, no. You can keep those stones for yourself. It all happened because Alcobaça didn't keep his promise. He was going to pulverize the Florentino.' Maurício grabbed my arm forcefully: 'No one can destroy a masterpiece of nature to save his own rotten skin!'

'Because of a diamond you killed five people.'

'I'd kill a thousand for the Florentino.'

'You're crazy.'

'I spared you, didn't I?'

I remembered Maurício at the age of eight, playing with dolls and the rest of us children ridiculing him. For several moments I stood there with the box of stones in my hand, not knowing what to do. Then I closed it and put it in my pocket.

I walked toward the door. I went out into the corridor.

Maurício came after me: 'You have to understand ... The Florentino is the clearest and most brilliant diamond that ever existed ... It's unclassifiable, far above the highest rating in the HRD table, exceptional white plus ...'

The hospital was empty.

There was a man at Admissions. I went up to him, took out the box.

'This is an aquamarine. I don't know how much it's worth,

certainly a fortune. It's yours if you let me visit Mr Gurian in the ICU.'

The man took the stone in his hand and looked at it against the light.

'It'll cost me my job.'

'Nobody will find out a thing. Tell them I'm a doctor. Tell them whatever you like. Work something out.'

'This way,' he said, putting the stone in his pocket.

We went up in the elevator and into an empty corridor. We came to a door. ICU NO ADMITTANCE.

'Here it is,' he said. 'I have to get back to my post.'

Gurian had a tube in his trachea, a needle in his arm feeding him glucose. His eyes were open and he smiled sadly when he saw me. He gestured for me to come closer. He said something or other that I didn't understand. I bent my head and brought my ear close to his mouth.

'I won't make it this time,' he said in a hoarse voice, speaking a little from the mouth, a little from the hole in his trachea. 'Where have you been?'

I couldn't waste time.

'What about Babel's manuscript?' I asked.

Gurian gave a laugh that emerged solely through his trachea.

'The manuscript isn't Babel's,' he said. 'I've lost the will to live.'

I grasped the bed to keep from falling to the floor.

With great difficulty Gurian said that the book was by a neophyte writer, A. Kulikov, a friend of Babel's, younger than he, and that he had probably given it to Babel so the latter could offer the opinion of a renowned author. At the end of the book was Kulikov's signature and a note requesting the 'opinion of the great and masterful author of *Red Cavalry*'.

'Are you sure?' I shouted into Gurian's ear.

'Absolutely,' he said, closing his eyes.

I kissed the old man on the forehead and left. I walked a long time through the streets, crossed the tunnel, and watched day break over Leme beach, lying in the sand. I thought about many things, about the precious stones. What to do with them? Sell them to finance my film? What film? Did I still want to make a film? I would throw them in the sea – I thought of Ruth, my father, Liliana, my life. I thought of Ivan: did he know the manuscript wasn't Babel's and did he dupe Plessner?

I decided to go to Gurian's apartment and get Kulikov's manuscript, wrap it, and mail it to Plessner in Berlin. He must have been very unhappy thinking that he had lost the Babel manuscript. But first I had an important thing to do.

Bathers began arriving with their beach umbrellas. The sun got hot. I rose, brushed off the sand that had stuck to my sweat-soaked shirt.

I called Liliana from a public phone.

'You nut, where did you get to?' I sensed she was happy and relieved to hear my voice.

'I'll be there soon and tell you all about it. I have to pay a call first.'

I caught a cab on Avenida Atlântica and told the driver to take me to Tijuca.

I still remembered the building and the apartment number.

I rang the bell.

Mildred opened the door.

'Remember me?' I asked.

'Yes. You disappeared. Come in, come in.'

'Is Negromonte in?'

'He's taking a bath.'

'What about Carnival?'

'We're making the costume. It'll be beautiful. Take a look.'

# THE LOST MANUSCRIPT

With a gesture she indicated Marijó, who was at the table embroidering a huge cape.

I gave her the box with the precious stones.

'Thank you very much,' said Mildred, taking the box and dumping the stones into a large container full of beads, sequins, bugles and colored stones. 'Don't you want to come in for coffee?'

'I can't. Tell Negromonte that I sent him a big hug.'

I left. When I got to the corner I stopped and clung to an iron post as if it were a tree full of flowers.

Everything was fantasy, a dream, a world of vast emotions and imperfect thoughts.